Twelve Harbours

Vinh Quyen Tang

The cover art and illustrations for 'Twelve Harbours' were created by Professor Võ Văn Trương as a generous contribution.

Nghĩa Lan Nhân

Recognition

(from the Vietnamese edition 'Bên Kia Bến Đỗ,' translated into English as 'Twelve Harbours')

First and foremost, I would like to express my heartfelt gratitude to two friends I once worked with on community publications. They have generously offered their help with 'Bên Kia Bến Đỗ'. Mr. Dương Quý Thưởng skillfully designed and arranged each page of this book to make it both visually appealing and reader-friendly. My dear "brother" Trịnh Vũ Điệp, a senior Scoutmaster, whose participation in community activities gave me the impression that he embodies the 10th Law of Scouting: "A Scout is pure in thought, word, and deed." He took the time to read the e-book version, carefully wrote a few lines of encouragement, and ... offered protection to a budding venture! He wrote: "Readers in their seventies or eighties will see a part of their own lives reflected in 'Bên Kia Bến Đỗ'. Surely they'll feel a rush of nostalgia as memories of fleeing war resurface, and a bittersweet gratitude as they recall friends of that era, some still here, some long gone... Let these emotions flow freely like water down a stream. Don't analyze or criticize them too much, just enjoy them, alright?"

Next, I'd like to express my gratitude to Mr. Trương, my "wanderer" friend. How else to explain how a Taberd alumnus and a Pétrus Ký graduate, having left high school over half a century ago, could meet again by chance within the pages of 'Bên Kia Bến Đỗ', here in a foreign land so far from home. Dr. Trương, former Vice-Rector of Concordia University in Montréal, Canada, is someone deeply committed to numerous charitable endeavors. From supporting efforts to preserve and promote traditional stage arts, to advocating for young people in difficult circumstances to continue their education, he has always shown great dedication. It is truly an honor to have him contribute his talent as a gifted artist, generously creating the cover artwork and meaningful illustrations for the book. This kindness from him and his wife, Mỹ-Liên, is something my wife and I will forever hold close to our hearts.

Lastly, but no less importantly, I'd like to acknowledge the contributions of Mr. Trần Lương Ngọc for his corrections of typos and spelling errors, which I believe have significantly enhanced the book's quality, if it had any to begin with. My sincere thanks to Mr. Ngọc for his kind support and encouraging words, as well as to Mr. Thưởng and other members of the community for their valuable assistance.

Though I was fortunate to have such wonderful help in presenting a more polished version of the book, as an amateur writer, it's inevitable that some mistakes and oversights remain. I hope readers can be forgiving of these imperfections. Thank you very much.

Tăng Quyền Vinh

Table of Contents

Preface

Let us sift through the ashes of history to uncover the pearls quietly glowing beneath layers of time's dust… Well, that may be the kind of lofty phrase one might use to open a tale like this. But to truly connect with 'Twelve Harbors', let us instead step into the Plum Tree Hamlet, gather a basketful of sour starfruit, and prepare for a grand memorial feast at the house of Mr. Tư (or Mr. Four; please see the note at the end of the Preface).

Together, we'll slice each starfruit in half and scrub the tarnished brass burner sets that rest year-round atop the family altar, removing their deep green-black patina, a long-forgotten ritual in today's world! Afterward, we'll carry them out to the yard to dry under the sun. Once dried, we'll polish them with crumpled newspaper until the golden brass gleams like a mirror, reflecting our own faces. And in that reflection, the faces of those from days long past seem to return as well, bringing with them anecdotes laughable yet pitiful, stories of bitterness and sorrow, and even moments of humiliation. Yet, woven throughout these tales are enduring examples of unyielding strength, integrity, and virtue.

These are the stories of ordinary, seemingly insignificant individuals who carried on their shoulders sacred and noble responsibilities. They were the ones who upheld the threads of society from one generation to the next.

They are often remembered with a shake of the head, a sigh, or a resigned acceptance of the saying:

"A woman's fate lies in twelve harbours; clear waters if fortunate, muddy if not."

So, is there a 13th harbour, you ask? And what do 'muddy' and 'clear' truly signify? While you may not find a definitive answer in 'Twelve Harbours,' you might discover cherished, familiar images and the forgotten lives that drifted along with the tides of the nation's fate - from the French colonial era, through the so-called Japanese occupation, and ultimately, the period of the country's division.

I look forward to meeting you again at Reed Field Wharf, nestled on the left bank of the tranquil An Thông Hạ Canal, which has flowed gently past the Plum Tree Hamlet since time immemorial.

Preface Footnotes

1. In this book, you'll find selected passages translated from the Vietnamese edition of 'Bên Kia Bến Đỗ'. Where appropriate, additional context has been included to help non-Vietnamese-speaking readers understand and appreciate the material more fully.

2. Some characters are addressed by a number—such as Mr. or Mrs. Four, Five, or Six. This reflects a Vietnamese tradition of referring to people by their birth order within the family, plus one. For instance, the first child is called Mr. or Mrs. Two, followed by Three, Four, and so on. Interestingly, there is no Mr. or Mrs. One!

3. The translation and supplemental writing in this book were completed by the author with significant assistance from ChatGPT.

Chapter 1: Floating Down the River

At the beginning of the 20th century, Vietnam remained a French colony. Across the country's three regions, from the North to the South, from bustling urban centers to quiet rural villages, and among people from all walks of life, from humble laborers to esteemed intellectuals, patriotic figures emerged to join the anti-French resistance. Their efforts took on many forms, ranging from peaceful reformist movements to direct and unyielding confrontations with foreign oppressors.

Some scholars drew inspiration from Japan's Meiji Restoration as a blueprint for social reform to rescue Vietnam. Their faith in Japan's strength was further reinforced with the outbreak of the Russo-Japanese War in 1904. News of Japan's victories echoed across Vietnam, arriving from distant battlefields. Headlines like "The Japanese Navy Sinks the Russian Fleet at Port Arthur," "The Japanese Army Advances to Occupy Mukden," and "Japan on the Path to Seizing Manchuria" captivated the public and fueled nationalistic aspirations.

Initially, the notion of 'Japan challenging Russia' seemed as improbable as *a grasshopper daring to topple a cart*. Yet, Japan rapidly dismantled Russia's formidable military forces, securing victory after victory both at sea and on land. This series of triumphs culminated in Japan's "astonishing annihilation of the entire Russian fleet" in a breathtaking naval battle in the Tsushima Strait, a clash so extraordinary it reverberated across the globe.

For a number of national liberation movements, seeking allied forces to free Vietnam from French colonial rule, the spectacular achievements of a small Asian country confronting a vast European power were like fuel added to the fire of confidence in the strength of the "yellow race." In practice, these victories served as a powerful wind propelling the sails of the 'Đông Du Movement' (Eastern Journey Movement), which advocated sending Vietnamese youth to Japan to learn the miraculous methods of modernization demonstrated by the Japanese people.

Ironically, forty years later, the geopolitical landscape changed swiftly. When World War II erupted, Japan's strength became a calamity for Asia. Japanese boots replaced the French, trampling Vietnam and spreading devastation throughout every corner of the country. Disorder ran rampant. The people suffered under a double yoke, beset by internal and external enemies, their families torn asunder. All that remained were shattered lives drifting to the four winds.

In the heart of the city of Saigon the atmosphere grew increasingly tense and oppressive. By the morning of March 9, 1945, the area around the French Governor-General's Palace was eerily deserted. Gone were the elegant carriages escorting dignitaries in their pristine white suits, leaving only two French policemen in their faithful white pith helmets standing guard.

By 2 o'clock in the afternoon of the same day, Jeeps carrying Japanese soldiers began to arrive, followed by a convoy of black-painted vehicles adorned with the red 'Rising Sun' flag, heading straight for the Governor-General's Palace. This unfolded before bewildered French soldiers lingering at the gate, awaiting news. The Japanese delegation claimed the necessity to discuss France's role in Vietnam, demanding a meeting with Governor-General Jean Decoux and compelling the colonial French authorities to provide rice to feed Japanese troops in Indochina. France, in a weakened position, reluctantly agreed. However, shortly after, Japanese Ambassador Matsumoto delivered a personal ultimatum, demanding that France cede all command of the military, police, and other armed forces to Japan.

Governor-General Jean Decoux harbored no further doubts. The entire afternoon's negotiation was a mere pretense, as outside, Japanese troops were plotting a coup to overthrow French colonial rule that very night. After the coup erupted simultaneously across the country, the Governor-General's Palace was swiftly sealed off, and all French officials were detained. Overnight, Japan supplanted France, occupying key provinces from north to south. Within a few short days, all of Indochina fell under Japanese dominion.

A fortnight before the Japanese forces toppled the colonial French regime, beneath the scorching Saigon sun, Officer Tư, a tall, affable figure often seen with a brown pipe between his smiling lips, stood quietly observing. The normally bustling streets of Saigon, now eerily deserted, served as a backdrop to Japanese soldiers conducting their intense daily drills. Their resolute expressions and unwavering grip on rifles adorned with bayonets conveyed a palpable determination, seemingly unaffected by the presence of the current French authorities in Vietnam.

In that moment, Officer Tư foresaw the nation teetering on the edge of a transformative change in occupying power. "Sooner or later, this police station will fall into Japanese hands," he murmured to himself, referring to the Second District station in Saigon where he reluctantly worked. A few days later, he took action - gathering Mrs. Tư and their daughters, Nhàn and Thanh, and bringing them to the bus terminal. Their destination was his hometown in the Cai Lậy countryside, where he hoped to shield them from the approaching chaos.

Six months later, in his ancestral hometown nestled deep within the Mekong Delta, on a tranquil evening in a quiet field, the setting sun cast long shadows on the swaying bamboo. A handful of golden rays seemed to conspire with his daughter Thanh, extending a fleeting moment of daydreaming for a young city girl who had fled the war-ravaged streets to find solace in her family's rural homeland.

Beside the fragrant vegetable patch near the ridge of white mangrove trees, Thanh perched on a plank at the riverbank's edge, engrossed in the task of washing dishes. Her eyes remained fixed on the water in the basin before her. A flood of memories inundated her heart, centered around Tâm, the man who inhabited her dreams. With her long, slender arm swaying gracefully in front of her knees, she rocked the final cup of water in the basin, repeatedly scooping and pouring, as if endeavoring to rejuvenate her recollections and fill her mind to overflowing.

From the horizon, the gentle breeze carried the fragrance of alluvial soil across the expansive rice fields. Drifting down the Nine Dragons River, once a guiding force for generations of pioneers cultivating and settling in the heartland of the South, were clusters of water hyacinths. A few lingering purple flowers, remnants of the dawn, swayed and bobbed, tracing an uncertain path on the journey that lay ahead.

"Thanh, why have you been outside for so long? Hurry in and help your sister with her bath," Mrs. Tư's voice called out from inside the house, pulling Thanh back to reality. She was Thanh's stepmother, a fact known to few outsiders, yet she embraced her role with wholehearted love and care for her stepchildren as if they were her own. Six years ago, tragedy struck when Thanh's birth mother met her untimely end in an accident that left an enduring scar on everyone's hearts.

In what initially appeared as a trivial incident, a minor cut on her thumb while scaling a fish for a family meal resulted in unforeseen consequences. Despite the superficial nature of the wound, her hand swelled the following day, and despite attempting various traditional remedies, none could alleviate her condition. Within two weeks, she succumbed to the illness, leaving three orphaned children in her wake. Thanh, the youngest, and Bình, the eldest son who had already joined the resistance against the French, had already left home. Thanh's elder sister, Nhàn, two years her senior, unfortunately contracted polio in childhood, making mobility difficult. Consequently, Thanh assumed the responsibility of assisting her stepmother in caring for Nhàn.

Before stepping inside the house, Thanh hesitated, lingering by the row of tamaru trees. She took a moment to quietly absorb the surroundings, realizing that these serene moments would soon be replaced by the bustling city life awaiting her in the coming days. As her gaze extended into the distance, past the lush green grove of water coconut palms lining the riverbank, the sight of the tall white mangrove atop a mound, bathed in the golden hues of the setting sun, invoked memories of Tâm.

In the days preceding her evacuation from the city, Thanh would approach the window each night, stealing glances through the thin curtain to locate the bright yellow glow in the hushed night. It emanated from the lone street lamp at the end of the police's compound next to the Xây-nho police station. Her heart would race with anticipation, yearning to catch a glimpse of a silhouette named Tâm, seated immobile beneath the light, eyes fixed on the book in hand.

Little did Thanh know that, at that time, Tâm wasn't engrossed in his usual studies but was dedicated to learning Japanese. In the wake of the world-changing events of World War II, while in Europe, Germany was displacing the French and establishing puppet governments sympathetic to its cause, in Asia, Japan was extending its occupation to various territories, including many parts of Vietnam. With the imminent shift in rulership from French to Japanese in Vietnam, many seized the opportunity to learn Japanese, harboring dreams of a better life, aspiring to become interpreters or secretaries for the Japanese forces, much like the previous generations who had worked under French rule.

In any colonial regime, possessing knowledge of the language spoken by the ruling power and demonstrating a willingness to cooperate with foreign authorities often brought advantages. However, Tâm appeared to be on a distinct mission aligned with a revolutionary faction, setting him apart from those who sought personal gains.

The image of Tâm sitting serenely, engrossed in a book by the roadside, remained a steadfast refuge for Thanh. Despite the tumultuous world swirling around them, Tâm's calm demeanor served as a reassuring anchor. It bestowed upon Thanh a rare tranquility, akin to a miraculous elixir that cast a serene spell over her each night. The nocturnal darkness concealed the harrowing truths of the day - mysteries that Thanh, at her tender age, hadn't comprehended fully but intuited through the eyes of adults, the whispered conversations, and the veiled remarks of her parents and neighbors. These concealed truths encompassed secret societies, revolutions, assassinations, torture, elimination, and all forms of agony and gruesome demise, camouflaged beneath the veneer of sanctity or demonic deception.

"Thanh, why haven't you come home yet?" Mrs. Tư's voice urged Thanh to take Nhàn to the river for a bath, a daily duty for Thanh since the two sisters found refuge in the countryside. Thanh quickly closed the pages of memories, hurried home along the quiet, flowing river.

Mrs. Tư brought out a chair and sat near the loom on her front porch, enjoying the afternoon breeze. From the open gate framed by two thick rows of bamboo, Mrs. Sáu's slightly stooped silhouette gradually came into view.

A well-known resident of Rạch Dừa village, Mrs. Sáu had earned a reputation as a skilled matchmaker. Finding her wasn't difficult. Anyone looking could head to the lively Rạch Dừa market, which opened daily along the Twin River even before the rooster crowed. Although it was a rural market, it bustled with activity as villagers from the surrounding hamlets came to buy and sell their daily goods. While most were there for shopping, Mrs. Sáu had a different purpose. She made regular trips to the market to pick up bits of conversation, her ears always tuned to news of families who had recently been blessed with newborn sons or daughters.

Upon identifying mothers with single sons or daughters, Mrs. Sáu would warmly approach them, showering them with attention and staying close as they moved from the fabric section in the upper market down to the fish stalls by the riverbank.

This routine paid off the very day Mrs. Tư and her family relocated to the neighboring village of Phú Quý. News of their arrival quickly reached Mrs. Sáu, who promptly began building a rapport with Mrs. Tư outside the market.

Today provided Mrs. Sáu the opportunity to "see the joints and bones" of Mrs. Tư's daughter, a matchmaker's phrase for assessing whether a girl might be a suitable bride for another family's son and, more importantly, whether the future mother-in-law would find her acceptable.

As Mrs. Sáu entered the courtyard, she offered a polite bow, her mouth visibly full with a chew of tobacco that bulged from one corner. Addressing Mrs. Tư with the warm familiarity of an old acquaintance, she said,

"Mrs. Tư, how are you? It's been a while since I last saw you at the market."

"Thank you, Mrs. Sáu. I'm fine. What brings you here today?"

"Oh, I won't keep it a secret from you, Mrs. Tư. I stopped by Mr. and Mrs. Hộ's place in the upper village and thought I'd bring you and the girls some fresh star apple fruit from my garden. A few years ago, on the advice of our neighbors, my husband planted a star apple tree in front of our house. To our surprise, it's already given fruit for two seasons. It doesn't produce a lot, but let me tell you, every fruit is well worth it, so sweet! Yesterday my husband picked a few ripe ones, and I brought them along for you and the girls to enjoy."

Without finishing her sentence, Mrs. Sáu asked if she could head straight to the back of the house to get a plate for arranging the fruits on the table. In truth, this was merely a pretext to search for Thanh and to have a look inside the house, sizing up the household's level of wealth or poverty. She paid special attention to the kitchen, drawing on her experience that a tidy, well-organized kitchen was a sign of a competent homemaker. "A good mother raises a good child," she often said.

Before Mrs. Tư could get up to stop her, she gave up and remarked, "You're really too kind! Bringing the fruits here was trouble enough, and now…"

Mrs. Tư had intended to continue with "…and now you're even setting the table for us," but Mrs. Sáu's voice rang out from the back: "I wonder if Miss Thanh is home, Mrs. Tư?"

"The two girls should be back any minute. I'm sorry, there's no one here right now to offer you water."

"Oh please, Mrs. Tư. I'm not a guest, am I? Don't trouble yourself about that."

Mrs. Tư watched as Mrs. Sáu carefully arranged the fruits on a plate, then asked, "Is there something you need from Thanh, Mrs. Sáu?"

"Well, I do have a little something to discuss, Mrs. Tư."

"Let me go inside and grab another chair for you. We can sit out here where it's cooler."

"Oh no, I can do it," said Mrs. Sáu, quickly heading inside to fetch a chair for herself. But before she could sit down, Mrs. Tư repeated her question, "So, what exactly brings you to see Thanh, Mrs. Sáu?"

"Well," Mrs. Sáu began, launching into a continuous stream of chatter, "I have a bit of news to share with you, Mrs. Tư."

As Mrs. Sáu went on, Mrs. Tư started to suspect that she might be assessing her daughter. She knew Mrs. Sáu's reputation as a skilled matchmaker, but with only two days left before their family moved back to Saigon, she hadn't expected Mrs. Sáu to visit. Mrs. Tư hesitated, unsure how to respond, when suddenly the sound of footsteps caught her attention. Thanh and Nhàn were just arriving at the porch. Mrs. Tư quickly called them over:

"Oh, you're back. Come here and say hello to Mrs. Sáu."

Thanh helped Nhàn hang a wet towel and two sets of clothing on the bamboo rack near the chili bushes beside the house before stepping out to greet Mrs. Sáu.

"Welcome, Mrs. Sáu," Thanh greeted with a polite nod.

Mrs. Sáu tilted her head and laughed heartily, revealing a trace of betel nut at the corner of her mouth. "Oh my... very impressive indeed. City girls are truly different; even their speech is more refined than others." She eyed Thanh with interest, adding, "Poor Miss Thanh, a city girl having to endure the hardships of rural life, with '*hands and feet covered in mud*' from morning till night."

Pausing as if struck by a sudden thought, Mrs. Sáu asked, "Oh, but how old are you this year?"

"She's seventeen," Mrs. Tư interjected.

"Ah, so she's born in the Year of the Horse..."

Mrs. Sáu suddenly furrowed her brow, recalling Mrs. Hộ's warning about avoiding Horse-year daughters-in-law, especially after the turmoil caused by her third daughter-in-law, born in that very year. After a moment's hesitation, Mrs. Sáu decided to shelve the thought. Her brows relaxed, then quickly arched into sharp, hawk-like curves, as though she had just spotted her prey.

Grinning widely, Mrs. Sáu asked, "Were you born at night?"

Thanh, intrigued, replied, "How do you know that, Mrs. Sáu?"

With a knowing smile, Mrs. Sáu explained, "Oh, I can tell. With your fair skin, long hair, beautiful face, and refined manner, you couldn't have been born at any other time. You see, a person born in the Year of the Horse who comes into the world during the day often faces hardships. They're destined to pull the carriage for others, so to speak. But a Horse born before the hour of the Rooster, as I suspect you were, belongs to… the Celestial Horse. That's a whole different story."

The two young sisters burst into laughter, prompting Mrs. Sáu to continue, "Seriously, Miss Thanh, girls born in the Year of the Horse often face many twists and turns in their love lives. Many will have two or three husbands before they settle down. For those lucky enough to keep just one husband, they often end up working tirelessly their whole lives to support his family. And those unlucky enough to be nicknamed 'Mrs. Horse' from childhood struggle to find a husband at all. But you, being a true 'Celestial Horse', will have it all: wealth, prosperity, and servants bowing at your feet."

Thanh remained composed and replied, "Well, I find enough joy just living with my parents, Mrs. Sáu."

Mrs. Tư, noticing Mrs. Sáu's conversation veering toward matchmaking, observed Nhàn standing quietly beside Thanh. While Nhàn seemed happy for her younger sister, a trace of sadness and worry flickered in her eyes. As the elder sibling, she couldn't help feeling a private sense of concern as her younger sister became the focus of marriage talk.

Seizing the opportunity to speak privately with Mrs. Sáu, Mrs. Tư sent the girls to the back to prepare bundles of fabric for the next day's market. "Alright, this is no place for children. Thanh, why don't you take your sister to the back and pack the fabric into the basket so that I can deliver it to the store at the market tomorrow."

Left alone with Mrs. Tư, Mrs. Sáu got straight to the point. "No need for me to beat around the bush, Mrs. Tư. Mrs. Hộ in An Phú Village asked me to find a daughter-in-law for her."

Mrs. Tư raised an eyebrow. "I heard Mrs. Hộ is looking for a wife for her youngest son who just finished studying in the city. With the Hộ family's wealth and their vast lands, I'm sure they have plenty of good matches to choose from."

"True, but so far she hasn't found anyone she's completely satisfied with. You see, ever since her eldest son returned from studying in France with a foreign wife, she's been thoroughly discouraged. Now, for her youngest son, she wants a local girl with a French education, someone who can keep him grounded here, instead of him following his brother's lead and heading off to France to bring back another foreign bride. But you know, in these villages, most girls can't even read or write in their own language, let alone French. That's why I think it's fate, Mrs. Tư, that your family moved here at just the right time. I believe it's no coincidence. This is meant to be."

Mrs. Tư asked curiously, "How old is Mrs. Hộ's youngest son?"

"He was born in the Year of the Cat…"

Before Mrs. Sáu could finish her sentence, she suddenly caught herself. "Oh no, the Tiger-Monkey-Rooster-Dog clash…"

Mrs. Tư, seemingly pondering the same concern, interrupted, "Hmm, not exactly compatible. Last year, a fortune teller in Saigon told me Thanh's zodiac sign clashes with the Cat."

"Don't worry about that, Mrs. Tư," Mrs. Sáu said reassuringly. "It's not as serious as it sounds. I've been matchmaking for decades, and I can tell you this kind of mismatch is no big deal. I've arranged marriages between couples with far more challenging compatibilities. Trust me, it won't be an issue at all."

Mrs. Sáu shifted her tobacco lump from left to right, then back again, before pausing as if she had just recalled something important. "Mrs. Tư, let me tell you this: while their signs might not align perfectly, the good news is that they don't have an 'aversion' to each other. Even if there were an 'aversion,' a simple offering at the temple can turn it into harmony. In reality, you don't even need an offering. Couples might quarrel during the day, but they usually reconcile by nightfall. The key is to avoid keeping silent and harboring resentment. That's when problems start."

Grateful for Mrs. Sáu's kind gesture of bringing over four star apples, Mrs. Tư had patiently listened to her tales. Yet with countless pressing household matters on her mind and only two nights left before she had to return to Saigon with Thanh and Nhàn, a sense of unease steadily grew within her.

Mrs. Tư, realizing it was time to address the impending matchmaking conversation, spoke firmly:

"Thank you, Mrs. Sáu, for considering my daughter. However, my husband is adamant that the day after tomorrow, we must take the kids back. Perhaps we can revisit this offer another time."

Mrs. Sáu, sensing the urgency, quickly replied:

"Oh, Mrs. Tư, I understand you need to return to the city. That's why I came over as soon as I could to bring you and Miss Thanh this good news. The Hộ family is wealthy, with large fields and gardens. Since they only have one younger son left to find a bride, they're very keen on having Miss Thanh join their family. If she marries into that household, she won't have to lift a finger. Her life will be so comfortable, so happy."

As the evening shadows grew longer, Mrs. Tư interrupted:

"Mrs. Sáu, please understand. Without my husband here, I can't decide my daughter's future on my own. And with just two days left, there isn't enough time to settle something so significant."

Mrs. Sáu reassured her:

"No worries, Mrs. Tư. I understand. Just give me a nod now, and tomorrow, they'll bring all the ceremonial gifts to your doorstep. Then, when you see Mr. Tư, you can discuss it with him. There's no hurry."

With little choice, Mrs. Tư reluctantly nodded her agreement. In that instant, the traditionally preordained destiny of a Vietnamese woman seemed to be sealed before Mrs. Sáu could finish the betel quid in her mouth. Thanh wept throughout the night, and, just like that, by the following morning, she was declared the fiancée of the youngest son from the Hộ family of An Phú village.

As the morning light broke, Thanh, fortified by her breakfast, reclaimed her determination. Dismissing the looming specter of an arranged marriage, she confidently strode out of her home, bidding farewell to her cloth-weaving companions. Along the narrow embankment beside a shallow ditch, she walked briskly, a purposeful gait unwarranted by any immediate urgency. Abruptly, teasing chants echoed from the rice fields being seeded:

"Ho... oh...,

Oh, the rosy-cheeked maiden,

Why won't you take a husband farmer?"

Điền, an incurable romantic, had persistently tried to propose to Thanh through his mother, yet his efforts had been in vain. Today, in this unexpected encounter, overwhelmed by his emotions, he borrowed the rhythmic chants to convey his pent-up feelings.

At the age of 15, Thanh had a family portrait taken at La Lumière photo studio on Galliéni Street. After the photo's development, the shop owner sought her father's permission to enlarge Thanh's portrait for display in the shop's front window. The beauty of her youth, now enhanced by the patina of maturity acquired through months of exposure to the natural elements of the countryside, showcased the resolute features on her oval face. These were the intrinsic qualities that her friends had recognized since childhood. Though seldom seen smiling, her eyes always emitted a friendly and approachable demeanor.

Raising her bamboo leaf hat, Thanh scanned the surroundings to find Điền. Her eyes suddenly sparkled, not like the romantic moon vying for attention amidst the stars in the night sky, but akin to the morning light warming the dawn. It subtly expressed empathy for Điền, transcending the playful chants from the rice field.

Mận, a girl who was sowing seeds in the adjacent field, had harbored deep feelings for Điền for a long time, yet all she received from him was indifference. Today, she seized the opportunity to engage in playful banter with him:

"Ho... oh...,

Listen here, my dreamy brother,

Don't chase after those fancy precious flowers.

Our village is full of wild ones in the fields,

Why not pluck them and bring them home for a little... display?"

In a teasing tone, she implied that Điền's affection for his love was so intense that he might as well place her on the ancestral altar to pay respects. Điền blushed, lowering his head with a shy smile. Ngạn, a boy standing beside him, didn't let the chance for a quick retort slip away and confidently cleared his throat before chanting in response:

"Ho... oh...,

You stay right there and wait,

When we're free, we'll come over.

Clip those wildflowers down,

Bring them home... to cook with brine!"

The group of boys erupted into laughter, drowning out the feeble curses, "Devilish creature", from the girls. Thanh secretly rejoiced as their banter provided an escape for her. Reluctantly, she continued walking along the dyke, under the shadow of dense tamanu trees, next to the water-filled ditch. Her heart stirred with fondness for the fields, gardens, and the people closely connected to them.

At the end of the day, as the night enveloped the surroundings in darkness, Mrs. Tư and her two daughters gathered around the woven rattan trunk strategically positioned in the center of the wooden bed plank beside the flickering oil lamp. They were engrossed in the task of packing up the last remnants of their belongings, diligently preparing for the imminent journey to reunite with Officer Tư.

Upon carefully placing her final possession, a pristine white áo dài (the traditional Vietnamese long tunic) that had remained untouched for months, into the trunk, Mrs. Tư motioned for her daughters to come closer. In a hushed tone, she imparted a cautious message: "Remember, when we reunite with your father, tell him that…" She paused, then pointed at Nhàn and continued, "…this ordeal was brought about by the Japanese soldiers. Understood?"

"Yes, Mom, I understand," Thanh responded promptly. Meanwhile, Nhàn remained huddled, her knees tightly pressed together, veiling her face in the obscurity of the night.

Mrs. Tư continued with a hint of worry in her voice. "I fear that inadvertently, you two might disclose the truth. If your father were to discover that this was done by the son of Mr. Hai, it would deeply unsettle him." Mr. Hai is one of the few remaining friends of Officer Tư. Considering Officer Tư's association with the French in the city, many of his village acquaintances shunned and ostracized him. Only Mr. Hai and a few steadfast friends continued to communicate with him, offering occasional visits. That's why he held them in such high regard.

Mentioning Officer Tư, Mrs. Tư directed her gaze into the dark, contemplating her husband's current precarious situation. Thanh discreetly glanced at her sister, startled, and exclaimed, "Sister is biting her lips again!" Mrs. Tư promptly leaned forward, embracing Nhàn. Her gentle hands caressed Nhàn's cheeks, and her words of comfort didn't cease, "It's okay, my child... it's okay. Mom apologizes to you. Mom will never mention that again. It's just that mom worries about you two and fears that your father will be upset. I feel sorry for him..." Mrs. Tư choked up, hastily wiping away tears with the cloth hanging from her shoulder, then consoled her daughter, "What's done is done; try to let it go, my child."

Thanh immediately thought of Mrs. Tư's previous admonition when Nhàn bit her lip until it bled at the mention of the son of Mr. Hai. Thanh hurriedly went to prepare a glass of saltwater to help her sister rinse her mouth.

"I have to go to Uncle Hai to tell him about his son," Thanh said angrily.

Mrs. Tư gently shook her head to dissuade her, saying, "No, dear, you can't." After a thoughtful pause, she advised, "Think about it. How will Uncle Hai handle this when there's such a wicked son in the family? If this thing is exposed, he would lose face in the whole village and might have to leave his ancestral home." Mrs. Tư looked into the emptiness ahead, expressing her deep concern. "And when the news reaches your father, it will cause him immense distress."

Mrs. Tư sighed deeply, stroking Nhàn's hair for comfort, "Hold on, my child. Mom is a woman too, and Mom understands you." Hearing this, Nhàn's tears suddenly burst forth. She buried her head in her mother's shoulder, sobbing uncontrollably. Mrs. Tư held her tightly, consoling, "Hang in there, my dear... Mom knows how you feel."

At this point, Nhàn's tears flowed even more freely. She pressed her head against her mother's shoulder, crying softly. Mrs. Tư embraced her daughter, comforting, "Be strong, my child... try to endure." Her mother's arms tightened around her petite frame, conveying the sacred promise of a lifetime, "Mom will always be with you." Forever, like a quaint melody of a lullaby in the wind:

"The plank is nailed down

The bamboo bridge sways precariously, difficult to cross

Difficult to cross, but mom guides the way

... As you go to school, mom enters the school of life."

If school teaches the daughter the three obediences and four virtues, then life teaches the mother cultivated with patience and endurance. Mrs. Tư gazed into the undefined space and murmured softly, "Endure, my child." The advice to her daughter seemed like a reminder to herself, to be strong and resilient in the face of the unpredictable storm always waiting somewhere for a woman.

In the darkness, Thanh, her sister, and mother struggled to find sleep. Thanh felt her sister's worries, becoming restless with anxiety. She kept tossing and turning under the invisible pressures closing in on her. Silently, she prayed that all the storms in life would soon pass. Next to her, Mrs. Tư didn't cease to blame herself for not fulfilling her duty as a mother. She ran her fingers through Nhàn's hair, tenderly resolving the tangles as she had done countless times before since misfortune befell Nhàn: "It's Mom's fault. Seeing you two with pimples, Mom went to Aunt Tám's garden in the neighboring hamlet to pick some remedial herbs, leaving you alone at home that noon."

Mrs. Tư, anxious about her children's fate on the journey ahead, couldn't bring herself to close her eyes. She stared into the quiet emptiness of the house, her thoughts drifting to the moment she would see her husband again. Looking at her two children, she silently thought,

"When you grow up and step into the world, you'll understand and love your father more."

As for Officer Tư, after sending his wife and two daughters to his ancestral village, he remained alone in the police quarters at the Xây-nho station. His son, Bình, had joined the resistance at the age of 17, creating a difficult family situation. While the father worked for the French, the son fought against them. Those who knew him often wondered, "Mr. Tư has only one son to carry on the family line - why would he let him join the resistance?"

At work, Officer Tư used to be drafted to join the secret police force tasked with hunting down intellectuals or party members involved in anti-French activities. Therefore, at home, he couldn't help but notice the signs of his son's secret activities, whether through Bình's irregular comings and goings or when friends visited him. They no longer led each other to the back of the sugarcane field to pick and eat guavas, laughing and chatting loudly. Instead, they often huddled in a secluded corner by the house, heads together in deep conversation for hours before quietly parting ways.

Though he didn't encourage Bình to join the revolution, he never discouraged him from doing so, despite the relentless worry about his son's safety and the unpredictable consequences for himself and the rest of his family. Mr. Tư kept his personal anguish buried deep inside, unsure whom to confide in. More than anyone, he knew all too well the price his son and even the family would have to pay for his decision to embrace the revolution.

After twenty-five years of service as a police officer in the Second District of Saigon, Officer Tư bore witness to countless heart-wrenching sufferings of ordinary people around him. Each morning, as he pedaled to work, a weight settled upon his heart. The anguished moans and desperate pleas emanating from the interrogation room of the police station reverberated in his mind. He couldn't escape the accusatory stares of political prisoners nor the hollow, defeated gazes of innocent bystanders falsely accused of crimes.

How could he forget about Tuất, just twelve or thirteen years old, who every day led his blind mother selling pig ears cakes around the neighborhood? Until he was coerced into providing intelligence tips to the police, only to end up tortured to death to silence him because he knew too much.

Then there was Ba Sử, who worked as a pig butcher. That day, as usual, at half-past five in the morning after finishing work, he rode his bike home, only to be stopped on the way and arrested for murder. The evidence was the traces of pig blood smeared on his clothes and hands. Ba Sử's life as a pig butcher was exchanged for the favor sought by a lowly police agent from his chief, in hopes of gaining a promotion for having solved a murder and robbery case in his precinct. The cries of injustice from Ba Sử would perhaps ring in Officer Tư's ears for the rest of his life.

He knew it all, he saw it all - the injustices, the cruelty, the immoral acts happening around him every day. But for the sake of his livelihood, he had to feign ignorance, turn a blind eye, and pretend as if it were all a matter of indifference to the world. Yet, he couldn't ignore his conscience. It tormented him, leaving him feeling buried in helplessness. As time passed, he feared the day when the perpetrators of all these evil deeds might come to kill him simply because he refused to join forces with them. That haunting fear followed him relentlessly, even seeping into his daily naps and nights of sleep. He often reminded Mrs. Tư and the children that if they needed to wake him up from his daily siesta, the habitual afternoon nap, they should tap his forehead instead of his feet. This precaution was to prevent them from inadvertently triggering a panicked reaction, which might lead to them being "kicked to death" in his startled state.

To dispel his relentless haunting fears, Officer Tư often squints his eyes tightly shut, even in broad daylight, whispering prayers for the nightmares to pass, pleading for them not to disturb him further. His colleagues noticed this ritual and dubbed him "Tranquil Tư", assuming he was meditating. Their assumption wasn't entirely baseless.

In his neighborhood, another police supervisor, Mr. Sáu, happened to be his next-door neighbor, separated only by a row of Carmona shrubs. A stretch of green hibiscus hedge, dotted with bright red flowers, served as a common fence for both dwellings. Mr. Sáu's grandson enjoyed picking tiny red Carmona fruits to eat, so whenever Mr. Sáu spotted an unlucky snail slithering on its branches, he would angrily grab it and slam it onto the road in front of his house. If the snail didn't die from a broken shell, it would succumb to the intense heat on the black asphalt or get squashed by passing vehicles.

Mr. Sáu often complained to his colleagues that he had asked Officer Tư many times to deal with the annoying snails on Mr. Tư's side of the fence. Although Mr. Tư would apparently oblige, he discreetly released these creatures onto the grass beneath the hedge fence, inadvertently allowing them to return and compete with Mr. Sáu's grandson for those tiny tasty fruits.

Throughout the story, while Mr. Sáu may intend only to vent his frustration with his neighbor, for anyone else, it becomes evident how ill-fitted the kind-hearted Officer Tư is for the cruel world around him.

Officer Tư's indifferent demeanor towards his daily duties at the police station, along with his passive approach in assisting the French troops in apprehending individuals suspected of anti-French activities, inevitably caught the attention of his French superior. Acknowledging Mr. Tư's merit for having served over two years in the expeditionary force to protect the "motherland" France during the Great War, the French boss did not reprimand him. Instead, he simply transferred Officer Tư to tasks that he deemed more suitable for him, such as market patrol or administering the ammunition storage in the warehouse.

After his wife and two daughters left for his ancestral hometown to take refuge from the war, he stayed behind at the police compound in Saigon's Second District. As time went on, the loneliness weighed on him more heavily.

Each day he set off on his old, creaking bicycle and returned by evening, then turned to drink to ease his sorrows. Staring blankly at the yellowed wall in an otherwise empty dwelling, he fiddled with his cup of rice wine as though trying to hold on to his last remaining soulmate. Many times he would sit, pipe clenched in his mouth, lost in thought for hours on end, reflecting on the wandering life that fate had laid out for him, uncertain where it might carry him next.

Drifting in and out with each curl of tobacco smoke in that hazy space, the image of a distant morning, when he was seventeen and weeding a field deep in the heart of the Mekong Delta, came to life once more before his eyes.

As the Mekong River nears the end of its arduous three-thousand-mile journey from the Tibetan Plateau, it bestows a precious gift upon southern Vietnam: fertile alluvial soil. Grateful for this bounty, the people of this abundant land have long referred to the river as the 'Nine Dragons,' honoring its nine major branches that fan out within the southern part of their country. Enriched by this nutrient-rich soil, vast swathes of land become one of the nation's rice bowls, sustaining its people and economy.

Yet, within this bounty lies a double-edged sword. The same richness that nourishes crops also fosters unwelcome intruders, noxious weeds and stubborn grasses, demanding eradication before cultivation can begin.

In his family, this formidable task falls upon the young shoulders of Tu, a mere seventeen years of age. From the crack of dawn until the oppressive tropical sun reaches its zenith, he toils on his family's farm, tending to the land with unwavering determination.

One day, amidst the elongated shadow cast by the solitary cork tree standing sentinel by the irrigation ditch, Tu's tranquil routine was shattered. His younger sibling, in a state of palpable panic, dashed along the narrow dirt embankment, beseeching him to return home urgently, citing the presence of French soldiers awaiting his brother's arrival, a cryptic summons that left Tu grappling with uncertainty and apprehension.

Upon arriving home, young Tu was startled to find a gathering of French and Vietnamese soldiers outside the courtyard. In his confusion, he overheard his father's solemn words, "They've come to conscript young men into the army." Tu understood the gravity of the situation immediately. His family had been deliberating on this matter, especially after rumors spread about the looming draft. With his eldest brother needed at home to help with farming and his youngest brother being only twelve, Tu knew his duty. Silently, he slipped away from the crowd, hastily gathering his belongings to depart.

His mother, teary-eyed and rushed, hastily gathered provisions: two pairs of black shorts, two shirts - one black, one white - and the family's sole bottle of medicated oil, which she handed to him to ward off the chilly winds of a distant land. Glancing over, she noticed a pair of wooden clogs under the bed, which he had never had the chance to wear, so she packed them for him. Two ripe oranges for offerings to their ancestors on the family altar were also taken down, wrapped alongside four gourami fish being dried under the sun on a flat bamboo basket placed on the roof of the house. Finally, she hurriedly brought over the newly-cooked rice in a pot. She scooped two handfuls of rice for him to take along for his anticipated journey to fight off Germany and protect France, a foreign country somewhere in the world; she didn't know exactly where, except for hearing once that it would take two to three months to sail there.

After two months of training at the Apricot Tree Camp on the outskirts of Saigon, he was escorted directly to the pier near the Thủ Ngữ flagpole, where he boarded a steamship bound for France to fight in defense of the "motherland" - a term ironically taught to colonial French school children to refer to the country that had invaded their land. According to the accounts of some knowledgeable comrades, he learned that Germany had invaded France after declaring war on it in 1914. Despite receiving support from the British alliance and several other allies, the situation was growing increasingly critical, prompting the French army to seek reinforcements from colonies like Vietnam.

The inaugural, unexpected journey across the vast oceans left an indelible imprint on the spirit of a youthful sailor, nurtured within the enclosures of his village's bamboo boundaries. Tư often recalled the suffocating moments in the cramped ship's hold, filled with the pungent smell of engine oil, which he endured for two long months. In his heart, he only awaited the day the ship docked at the next seaport, where joy meant not only setting foot on solid land, breathing fresh air, but also witnessing unfamiliar faces, strange scenes, and hearing foreign voices and music, as if from another world. There were many interesting things and unexpected events to be discovered, like the time at the Magadascar port when he was surprised to see many tourists standing on a ship's deck tossing coins into the sea. It turned out they were watching the indigenous people from small boats below dive down like fish chasing after the coins scattered.

Actually, even while living cramped under the ship's hold, he still held onto some unforgettable memories, even many moons later. Once, after the ship docked at the Cameroun port, his team had to sleep next to several rotten-smelling buffalo hide sacks. Among his fellow soldiers, one was curious and sliced open a sack with a pocket knife, "to see what's inside." It turned out to be filled with dates. So, they gathered for an impromptu date feast, providing some relief from the overwhelming smell of buffalo hide.

Upon the ship's eventual arrival at the Port of Marseille, nestled in the bosom of 'Motherland France', the origins of the subsequent journey remained shrouded in mystery. His lips were sealed tight about his adventures, sparing only morsels of tales from his travels. One such anecdote lingered: the tragic incident where three of his compatriots perished after consuming wild mushrooms in Southern France - a fate narrowly avoided by Tu, tethered to duty at the time. Another hint of his whereabouts surfaced in the form of a pair of goggles he brought home after the war - relics from a distant past, possibly tracing his steps through the desolate sands of Northern Africa during the conflict.

After the Great War, later known as the First World War, ended in 1918, Officer Tu was more fortunate than most of his compatriots in that he could return unscathed to see his country again. Sadly though, he was shunned by many members of his own family and friends because he had fought for the French and, after coming home, chose to stay in the city and work as a policeman for the French authorities.

He found himself torn between two worlds: one he longed for from afar, yet found distant upon his return. The buffaloes he had once herded, the muddy fields where he had joyfully waded to catch fish, and the old ancestral house he had cherished after hours of backbreaking farm work under a scorching sun. All were still there, yet somehow they felt dull and stagnant now.

On the other hand, there was the world he had tried to forget, yet which lingered in his mind. It wasn't any single thing he could name. Rather, it was the allure of streetlamps, flashlights, vehicles, car engines, and, to him, sophisticated people in uniform. This was a realm utterly unlike the impenetrable darkness that cloaked the countryside each evening after sundown, where daylight travel meant rowing a sampan along a creek.

In the end, what ultimately pushed him toward city life was something as ordinary as a hair bun, a style worn by his father, uncles, and most Vietnamese men in the countryside. French colonials had ridiculed it as a "chignon," and city dwellers dismissed it as a "garlic bulb." The thought of wearing it for the rest of his life filled him with dread.

Having caught a glimpse of a larger world, he could no longer imagine confining himself behind the village's bamboo fences. Despite the risks, he chose to stay in Saigon. Security concerns loomed over him, especially the fear of how the anti-French resistance forces might treat him if he returned to the remote countryside under their partial control.

With few options left, he reluctantly took a position as a police officer in Saigon's Second District. He considered himself fortunate for this opportunity, largely due to his French reading and writing skills, taught to him by a kind-hearted comrade during their two years of service in the French army. From then on, he rarely returned to his hometown, and his family ties steadily weakened. After his parents passed away in quick succession, his eldest brother all but disowned him. On the rare occasions he visited, his brother avoided him, leaving Officer Tư burdened with guilt and unease.

Chapter 2: Tempest by the Grave

Officer Tư had recently been reassigned to the Reed Field police station on the outskirts of the Saigon city. Though remote and isolated, it occupied a strategically important position for the French authorities. The Reed Field station, located just outside the Plum Tree Hamlet and slightly more than ten kilometers southwest of the city centre, had been established to prevent anti-French resistance forces from the western provinces from infiltrating the city.

Once he became familiar with the routes, routines, and duties of his new post and had reached a tentative sense of stability in his work, Officer Tư sent word for his wife to bring their two daughters back so the family could be together again.

His family was unaware of the turmoil he endured after sending them to the safety of his remote ancestral home in the countryside. Misfortune struck him on the very first day following the Japanese coup against the French. When Officer Tư reported to the Second District police station to present himself to the Japanese authorities, he was interrogated for an hour before being locked in a cell. The reason? Several weapons and rounds of ammunition from the armory under his watch had gone missing.

Unbeknownst to him, just hours before the coup, the assistant to the police chief and two French sub-lieutenants in charge of the depot had secretly taken some of the arms and fled to Cambodia to join the resistance against the Japanese.

At the time, Officer Tư believed the French had negotiated terms with the Japanese that allowed colonial government employees to continue their duties under Japanese supervision. But calamity struck so swiftly that he found himself subjected to two relentless days of interrogation. In the end, the Japanese handed him over to the Việt Minh resistance forces as part of a prisoner exchange.

As he was being escorted to the prisoner assembly point, the Japanese soldiers led him past the Ông Lãnh Bridge market. There, two female street vendors hurried after him. One pressed a guava into his hand, while the other offered him two 'bánh cam' (Vietnamese sesame balls) she had been selling by the market. It was a simple yet heartfelt gesture of gratitude. Since his reassignment to the guard post at that market, many vendors had come to admire him for his fairness and integrity in handling his duties.

While the previous officers had routinely demanded bribes from vendors in exchange for their market spots, Officer Tư never took so much as a single cent. Instead, he voluntarily arranged covered spaces under the market's eaves for the street vendors, ensuring they could do business protected from the elements.

The story of "Hai the butcher" is still fondly recounted by local residents. When Hai fell ill and had to step away from his stall for a few days, the previous officer seized the opportunity to give Hai's space to another vendor who offered a higher bribe. Upon learning this, Officer Tư intervened and made sure Hai got his stall back.

In gratitude, Hai wrapped up several kilograms of choice cuts to offer Officer Tư, but the gesture was swiftly rejected. With a stern yet memorable warning, Officer Tư said:

"Take it home for your wife and children. I'll let it slide this time. But if you try anything like this again, I'll have you jailed for bribing a law enforcement officer."

When he found himself at the mercy of the Japanese forces, he believed his life had reached its end. Yet the proverb he often repeated to his children, *"Do good, and you shall meet good"*, proved true for him as well. The prisoner transport truck intended to deliver him to the resistance forces broke down halfway, presenting him with an unexpected opportunity to escape. Fortunately, he fled to a small cluster of thatched-roof houses owned by basket-carrying street vendors, who graciously sheltered him for several months.

Their kindness and protection allowed Officer Tư to survive and live to see the day when he could reunite with his wife and children. Yet misfortune followed closely behind. After the Japanese defeat, Officer Tư returned to his former post to report in, only to find himself under suspicion by the French authorities. They speculated that his relatively smooth escape could only mean he was aligned with the Việt Minh resistance forces. As a result, Officer Tư was reassigned to a newly established police station in a remote frontier region southwest of Saigon—known as the Reed Field Police Station.

At Reed Field, Officer Tư would welcome his family into a small barracks community behind the police station. They would settle into a single-story townhouse unit designated for Vietnamese soldiers and their families. This housing, known as the "Backyard Townhouse," was named so because it literally hid behind a row of two-story houses facing the river, reserved for French soldiers and French officials stationed there.

That afternoon, as the Backyard Townhouse lay drenched by a torrential downpour, a brief reprieve arrived. The heavens took pity, breaking through the dark clouds and illuminating the earth below with shimmering rays of sunlight. This radiant moment came just in time to greet Thanh, her mother, and her sister as they reunited with Officer Tư.

The next morning, when Thanh woke up still feeling disoriented, she opened her eyes to see a yellow-plastered wall at the edge of the bed, instead of the damp-scented thatched wall she had grown accustomed to over the past few months. Suddenly, faintly from outside, she heard a vendor's cry, "Sticky rice… Sticky rice here," prompting her to step out onto the front veranda to investigate.

The sun had already risen above the corner of the street, flooding the lawn with morning light and blazing against the brick wall that separated the row of houses where they lived from the French quarters in front. Gradually, the bustling scene of a new day unfolded before Thanh's eyes.

Students, dressed neatly in black trousers and white shirts, cheerfully carried their school satchels as they skipped along to class. Most of the men, in their prime, wore either civilian clothes or police uniforms. Some headed to the market for morning coffee, while others made their way to the station to begin their day's work. Women of all ages, some soldiers' wives, others household helpers, carried baskets off to the market or sat having breakfast beside street vendors' stalls set out on the lawn.

On the cement veranda in front of the houses, two elderly women sat minding their grandchildren; nearby, an old man addicted to opium leaned against the foot of a wall, drifting listlessly in his own private reverie.

On the surface, the Backyard Townhouse resembled any small neighborhood, with familiar faces seen everywhere, mundane tales exchanged over cups of tea or rice wine at the street's end, and fairy tales whispered by grandmothers each night to lull their grandchildren to sleep. The men here, what were they, if not loving husbands, caring fathers, and kind neighbors who looked out for one another?

But unlike other small hamlets, here there were scenes of people torturing or even killing each other, sometimes just to climb the ranks and gain power. And unlike those peaceful villages, here stood a prison hidden behind the police station. Its damp, moss-coated walls, with only two small, iron-barred windows, hinted at the darkness within.

Even the innocent-looking bathhouse nearby, intended for soldiers to wash up after raids through muddy suburban swamplands, was steeped in mystery. From a distance, it looked no different from a simple warehouse, its walls painted a dull yellow like other colonial-era structures. Inside, it was empty and eerily cold. Upon entering, one saw only a row of showerheads lining the opposite wall. On hot, humid days, a few soldiers' wives might bring their children here to play in the running water. Occasionally, they would be suddenly chased away, and the mothers would hastily gather their children and hurry outside.

In a hidden corner of the bathhouse stood a waist-high cement basin, always brimming with water. As the mothers reached the doorway, they would often see two plain-clothed policemen dragging a handcuffed prisoner inside. Without a word, the mothers clutched their children tightly, bowed their heads, and rushed home. In their hearts, they knew what was about to happen. Even the children, though innocent, could sense their mothers' anxiety. A prisoner, usually a political prisoner, was about to be subjected to water torture.

Who could say how long the mothers of this country would have to keep shielding their children, ensuring that their innocent games of "cops and robbers" never turned into deadly, recurring tragedies, with brothers turning against brothers on the harsh stage of their nation's history?

Thanh had just returned to Saigon when her three closest friends came to visit the following day. Mỹ Lệ, Dung, and Loan, whom you can call Mee Lei, Yung, and Loanne, along with Thanh, had once been famously known as the "Quartet of Colette" from their childhood days at the Colette Primary School. They gathered around the dining table in Thanh's kitchen, chatting and laughing joyfully to compensate for the days of separation. After four years of schooling at Colette and experiencing the sweet and bitter moments of youth, they became inseparable friends, bonded like family despite their different circumstances and backgrounds.

The conversation among the 'four sisters' soon shifted to the topic that always came up during their reunions: love. The first target of their teasing and curious gazes this time was Dung. With her round face, honey-colored skin, and sparkling almond-shaped eyes, she had a natural beauty that needed no makeup, yet her expression seemed touched by a lingering melancholy from the distant past. Thanh, seated beside her, glanced her way and asked with interest,

"What about you and 'brother' Án?"

"You know, parents decide where their children should sit," Dung replied quietly.

Mỹ Lệ, the eldest of the group, teased her younger 'sister':

"Sure, but if the parents wanted to put you somewhere else, would you still agree?"

Then, squinting one eye at Thanh, Mỹ Lệ added with a grin, "She's head over heels for him. Just playing it cool."

Loan stepped in to defend Dung, turning to Mỹ Lệ and saying:

"Quit picking on Dung. What about you and Sứ?"

With her hair elevated like two waves caressing a boat, Mỹ Lệ responded with a dismissive smirk, a habitual expression borrowed from the colonial French, suggesting *"On s'en fout"* (We don't care). Despite her seemingly indifferent attitude towards life, it's her clear and bright eyes, often widening to reveal genuine interest in friends, that betray her disguise. In reality, those eyes reflect an underlying resilience ready to cast aside any lingering concerns about matters she deems as trivial, such as romantic affairs.

As if remembering something, Thanh curiously asked Mỹ Lệ:

"Oh right, before I left the city, I had heard you two wanted to get married. What happened to that?"

Loan jumped in to reproach,

"Not just for you Thanh, even for us. We were here with her, but she still keeps us in the dark."

Mỹ Lệ hesitated before whispering that her boyfriend Sứ had joined the Việt Minh, an organization that led a struggle against French rule. While Sứ's friends joined the anti-French resistance groups in the countryside, Sứ was ordered to set up a stall selling sunglasses near Saigon Market as a 'sleeping cell,' serving as a messaging center for the organization.

Pondering for a moment, Mỹ Lệ recounted for the first time to her friends:

"My father found out about what he did, and he almost died worrying... The marriage plans are as good as impossible."

The group sympathized with Mỹ Lệ's dilemma, gathered to console her, but again she brushed it off with a French shrug - C'est la vie (That's life). Suddenly, she smirked mysteriously:

"Who says you can't be married without a wedding ceremony."

The three sisters were stunned by Mỹ Lệ's bold suggestion, even though she may be half-joking. With Mỹ Lệ's determination, known to all, nothing seemed impossible once she set her mind to it. Loan expressed her admiration and sympathy to Mỹ Lệ, rather than giving advice or trying to stop her, although in Loan's mind, it was an unimaginable thing for her to contemplate. Thanh felt the need to steer the conversation away to avoid putting Mỹ Lệ in an awkward situation and turned to tease Loan:

"You are good at talking about others, but what about your relationship with Hùng?"

Hùng, Mỹ Lệ's brother, was once Loan's 'hero' until a day when her parents forbade her from meeting him, deeming him unworthy of their daughter. Loan, the daughter of a Provincial Chief, an esteemed government position reserved by the French authorities for a Vietnamese, exuded an air of aristocracy despite her youth. Though her friends dubbed her a 'princess,' her straightforward nature drew criticism for not aligning with traditional notions of nobility.

The wound in Loan's heart from her first love lingered, a fact known well to Mỹ Lệ, who maintained her friendship with Loan. To prevent any unintentional remarks that might make Loan uncomfortable, Mỹ Lệ turned to Thanh jokingly and asked,

"And what about you? Have you encountered any White Princes or Black Princes (referring to the two legendary wealthy landowner sons of the time) during your months in the countryside?"

Thanh sealed her lips, pretending to harbor a secret that couldn't be revealed, but eventually, she couldn't keep it to herself any longer:

"I have been committed."

Everyone rushed to express their thoughts; some blamed Thanh, while others threatened to 'break up' with her for breaking their oath of not keeping secrets from each other. Thanh calmly responded,

"Relax, relax. That was just a thing of the past. There was a 'beau prince' who proposed through a matchmaker, and my mom was forced by circumstances, so... yeah. But as soon as I got back here, I settled things with my dad. He's having someone return all the gifts to them."

The whole group breathed a sigh of relief, but Mỹ Lệ pressed on to make sure:

"So, you're still 'célibataire' (single)?"

"Oui, madame... Yes, ma'am. Are you satisfied?"

Time passed quickly when people have fun. Before parting ways, Thanh asked, "Who wants to visit my mom's tomb with me tomorrow?"

"What month is it now? I thought the Tomb-Sweeping Day passed a while ago," Dung asked.

"Yeah, but I missed visiting my mom's grave last year..."

Thanh trailed off, expressing her longing for her late mother.

The following day, Thanh rose well before dawn to prepare the offerings for the memorial at her mother's gravesite. She meticulously filled each compartment of the *"gamelle,"* a tin lunch box consisting of four stacking pails, to carry it to the cemetery. In the bottom pail, she placed rice and spread a layer of shredded fish floss on top, prepared from a snakehead fish by her own hands since yesterday. This dish was her mother's favorite during her lifetime, and since Thanh knew how to cook, she never forgot to make it as an offering on Tomb-Sweeping Days.

The third compartment held four plums and a cluster of chili salt for dipping. In front of Thanh's old house, there was a Vietnamese plum tree with bell-shaped fruits that, during rare leisure times, her mother would pick to share with her. Thanh fondly remembered how her mother would cut each plum in half before giving it to her, ensuring she wouldn't inadvertently eat any with worms inside. As for her mother, she would simply bite into the fruit after dipping it in chili salt. These were rare moments that made Thanh feel truly happy being with her mother.

The two top compartments of the *"gamelle"* were temporarily left empty, reserved for slices of roasted pork and sauces that

Thanh planned to buy on her way at the market near her friend's home. Thanh carefully placed the *"gamelle"* in her handbag along with a bundle of incense sticks, two candles, and a box of matches.

Thanh walked from her house to the bridge at the end of the street to catch a ride to the Xóm Củi market. From there, she walked for another 15 minutes across the Chà Và bridge to the front of the Cholon Post Office, where she caught a bus to meet Dung and Mỹ Lệ, who were waiting for her at Mỹ Lệ's house. The three 'sisters' then set off together.

Earlier, Thanh had also stopped by the Ông Lãnh's Bridge market to buy 500 grams of roast pork and two loaves of bread, which were part of the offering for her mother but also served as lunch for them afterward. Thanh intentionally brought an ample supply of 'provisions' because she also intended to share the food with Uncle Năm, a cemetery caretaker, in appreciation for his and his family's care of the tomb of her mother.

Outside the gate of the cemetery, Uncle Năm was sitting on a plank in front of his house, whittling a new fishing rod. Upon hearing footsteps outside, he looked up and instantly recognized Thanh. He quickly set aside his tools, ran to the gate, and greeted her:

"Is this Miss Thanh? Long time no see. How have you been, Miss Thanh?"

Since Thanh had been accompanying her father to attend her mother's memorial every year, she had become a familiar face to Uncle Năm. Thanh was also happy to meet him. She replied:

"I'm well, thank you, Uncle Năm. You, Aunty Năm, and Brother Rê are also well?"

"Thanks to heaven, our family is fine. The only thing is... in this wartime, not many people come here for ceremonial things. Except when they have to come here to bury their deceased relatives, you hardly see anyone around here. It's usually deserted."

"Last year I was evacuated to my father's hometown, so I couldn't come," Thanh explained.

"Oh, Miss Thanh, don't worry. Every year, my son and I take care of cleaning Mrs. Tư's grave, whether you and Mr. Tư come or not."

Thanh expressed her gratitude to Uncle Năm and followed him to pay a visit to her mother's resting place. The cemetery was dotted with dirt mounds, both large and small, each representing the final resting place of ordinary people in this part of the city. Few ventured here regularly to tend to the graves of their departed loved ones, especially during challenging times.

Uncle Năm took the lead, skillfully wielding his machete to clear a path through the overgrown grass. As they approached, the evidence of recent care for Thanh's mother's grave became apparent. The surrounding areas were dominated by tall weeds, but her mother's tomb stood out with fewer obtrusive plants, and the inscription on the tombstone retained its vibrant red hue, evidence of a recent coat of paint.

Driven by a sense of routine, Uncle Năm reached over the tomb to remove a few lingering vines, then stooped down to meticulously clear every tuft of grass beneath his feet. Thanh surveyed the well-tended grave of her mother, a sense of satisfaction settling within her. She expressed her gratitude once again to Uncle Năm for his thoughtful care.

As Dung and Mỹ Lệ arranged the offerings on the stone tablet at the base of the tombstone, Thanh stood beside them, her gaze fixed on her mother's name engraved on the tombstone. After a brief moment of reflection, she turned to Uncle Năm and spoke,

"Uncle Năm, may I borrow the can of red paint and a brush to apply another coat on the letters on the tombstone? I know you've already taken care of it, but since it might be a few more months before I return, I want to refresh the paint for my mother while I'm here."

"Of course, Miss Thanh," replied Uncle Năm as he left to retrieve the paint supplies.

Meanwhile, the group was disturbed by teasing shouts emanating from a nearby French outpost. Two Senegalese soldiers, African mercenaries hired by the French, were watering a vegetable garden behind a barbed wire fence. They pointed fingers, laughed, and shouted in the direction of Thanh and her companions. Unsettled by the situation, Thanh urged her friends,

"Let's light the incense and candles and then leave, guys."

Dung, clutching a bundle of incense sticks, swiftly planted them into the sand-filled can positioned in front of the grave. Mỹ Lệ couldn't help but mockingly chuckle,

"Look at her. The incense isn't even lit, and no one has prayed yet, but she's already stuck them in."

Remaining composed, Mỹ Lệ struck a match, igniting two candles. She carefully dripped wax onto the stone tablet, securing the candles in place. In a calm but authoritative tone, she issued the order,

"Let's expedite the ceremony and leave. It's not safe to linger here."

Keeping a watchful eye on the reactions of the two African soldiers, Dung suddenly whispered,

"They're coming this way."

Fortuitously, as Uncle Năm approached his house, he caught wind of the commotion from the French outpost. Exercising caution, he summoned his son to accompany him, and they hastened towards Thanh and her friends for protection.

Uncle Năm was merely taking precautions, having developed an acquaintance with the soldiers at the outpost over the past few months. Since the Japanese army overthrew the French authorities and assumed control of Vietnam, the French soldiers had been disarmed. While some French soldiers in the South fled into the jungle in search of a route to neighboring Cambodia, most remained in place - either guiding the Japanese forces around unfamiliar territories or identifying resistance elements to them.

The outpost, once manned by nearly 20 personnel, mostly Vietnamese soldiers, had seen a significant departure. Only a handful of scar-faced African soldiers and a French lieutenant named Paul, who had joined them from an undisclosed location, remained. They sporadically visited the village, ostensibly requesting fruits but, in reality, probing for information about the activities of the Vietnamese resistance to relay to the Japanese army.

As the three sisters raced halfway to Uncle Năm's house, a scar-faced soldier managed to catch up, just as Uncle Năm and his son arrived. Swiftly, they blocked the soldier's path with their machetes. Given the frequent coconut-sharing history between the soldier and Uncle Năm's family, they engaged in casual conversation with the sisters. The soldier, expressing a desire for a friendly chat, remarked that it had been a while since he last encountered a beautiful city girl. Sensing the tension, Mỹ Lệ, quick-witted, exchanged pleasantries with him in French.

Amidst their conversation, Paul arrived. He had been bathing when he heard a soldier's report and hurried to prevent his men from disturbing the civilians. Apologizing for his lack of time to don a shirt, he stood before them in khaki shorts, revealing a chest covered in hair. His face, concealed by a bushy red beard, left only two sparkling blue eyes filled with curiosity visible.

After Paul signaled for the scar-faced soldiers to return to the outpost, he apologized, saying, "I'm sorry that they have disturbed you all." Thanh reassured him, "It's okay. Maybe they just wanted to make friends when they saw strangers."

Paul inquired further, "Is today a special day? Are you here to visit your loved one's grave?"

"Yes, I'm visiting my mother's grave with my two friends here," Thanh responded. Paul extended his hand to shake Thanh's and introduced himself, "I'm Paul. And you?"

After the three sisters introduced themselves, Paul continued, "Where are you all from?" Quick-witted as always, Mỹ Lệ replied, "We live in the Xây-nho police housing area, and Thanh lives in the Reed Field police quarter." Mỹ Lệ's intention was to subtly convey that their families worked for the French government, in case Paul had any ulterior motives. However, he raised an eyebrow while looking at Mỹ Lệ.

Following a brief silence, Paul suggested talking privately with Mỹ Lệ and asked everyone else to proceed to Uncle Năm's house first. Thanh hesitated, reluctant to leave her friend alone, but then heard Paul ask Mỹ Lệ, "Are you Mr. Sáu's daughter?" Surprised, Thanh assumed they already knew each other, prompting her to pull Dung with her.

Mỹ Lệ asked,

"Yes, how do you know?"

"I used to work at the Xây-nho police station for a short time. Do you remember me?"

Mỹ Lệ suspected she had encountered Paul before but thought it might be because he resembled Jacques, the Chief Police's son, who had been pursuing her for a while.

"I'm sorry, I don't remember meeting you anywhere."

"Try to recall, on the night the Japanese military took power, was there a stranger hiding in your house?"

Mỹ Lệ finally remembered:

"Ah, you drank with my father that evening and stayed overnight at my house. You slept on the plank bed behind the kitchen."

"Yes, thanks to your father for hiding me for one night."

Paul spoke with a sly tone before continuing:

"And only until noon the next day, the Japanese soldiers came and arrested me. Do you know how they found out my whereabouts so quickly?"

"Sorry, it was unfortunate for you, but I don't know how they knew."

"It was your father who informed the Japanese authority that morning."

"I really didn't know about that. In the afternoon, my father was also detained by the Japanese. If he did that, it was only to protect the family, and I'm sure you understand the suffering of my family. We are all victims of the circumstances."

Paul raised his voice:

"I can understand that, but I just asked him to let me stay for two days so I could contact a friend to find my way to Cambodia."

"I sincerely apologize."

"What's the point of apologizing now? I was arrested and tortured for two days, and locked up in solitary confinement for a month. I should have known not to trust the deceitful Annamites."

Upon hearing Paul use such a derogatory term for the Vietnamese, Mỹ Lệ slapped him hard across the face and shouted loudly,

"You cannot insult my people. Whatever happened, it's only between you and my family."

Enraged and with a red face, he glared at Mỹ Lệ and yelled,

"Fine. I know you Annamites are very proud. Let me teach you a lesson, show you who's in charge in this wretched land."

He grabbed Mỹ Lệ by the throat until she almost passed out and proceeded to assault her.

Chapter 3: The Surrogate Mother

Seven months after Mrs. Tư brought her two daughters to reunite with Officer Tư, the inevitable occurred: Nhàn's pregnancy had reached full term. Officer Tư was deeply anxious as the outside world remained in turmoil, with chaos everywhere due to the power vacuum that emerged after Japan's surrender.

Despite the Japanese Emperor's declaration of unconditional surrender following the U.S. dropping two atomic bombs that devastated the major cities of Hiroshima and Nagasaki, not all Japanese forces withdrew from Vietnam. Some resorted to harakiri, a traditional act of self-disembowelment, driven by the samurai spirit. Others, fueled by intense nationalism and skepticism towards news of Japan's defeat, chose to stay in Vietnam. Furthermore, they adopted the Greater East Asia Co-Prosperity Sphere ideology, advocating 'Asia for Asians,' and retreated into the mountainous regions of Vietnam to support the Vietnamese resistance against the French.

These scattered forces, while not numerous, emerged concurrently with various armed factions, competing for influence to fill the power vacuum left by the French and Japanese military. Disorder permeated the region, stemming not only from conflicts between opposing forces but also from lethal internal disputes within certain martial factions. The situation grew increasingly complex, and the future direction of the country remained uncertain.

Meanwhile, the "*Motherland*" of France found itself depleted due to the aftermath of World War II. The French colonial apparatus in Indochina virtually collapsed after being under Japanese control. Consequently, the Allies tasked England with the responsibility of stabilizing the situation in Indochina, given the British military's extensive experience in colonial governance across Asia, from India to Malaya, and from Singapore to Indonesia. As a result, another piece on the geopolitical chessboard in Vietnam was introduced: England.

Today, Officer Tư bicycled over to Teacher Hai's house to invite him for a visit to the Xít Tê café. While the invitation was for coffee, Officer Tư's real motive was to pick up some "tuyau" (tips or insider information) and catch up on street news—he wasn't particularly interested in the coffee itself. In these turbulent times, power could shift at any moment. It was already unsettling for an average citizen, and even more so for a civil servant like him.

The Xít Tê café, a riverside bar with a rich history in this quiet hamlet, served as a gathering spot for district police officers and civil servants. There, they'd engage in idle conversation, swap local gossip, and hear the latest rumors from the streets.

The café originally began as a teahouse run by Mr. Sáu, who was affectionately nicknamed "Sáu Tea" by his patrons. When the French established a station nearby, Sáu Tea added coffee to the menu, and the place steadily gained popularity, even drawing in French soldiers. Over time, his name was Gallicized to "Six Thé." As the café's offerings expanded to include beer and small snacks, including dried shrimp, pickled shallots, and century eggs, its Vietnamese patrons jokingly "Vietnamized" the owner's name into "Xít Tê." The playful nickname stuck, and to this day, the café remains known as Xít Tê.

Although Officer Tư and Teacher Hai hadn't known each other for very long, the two men seemed genuinely close. In the neighborhood, few people truly knew Teacher Hai personally, owing to his dignified and reserved manner, but everyone had heard of him. He often sat on a folding cot in the front veranda of his home, reading books and newspapers or occasionally reciting poetry aloud when inspiration struck. His voice carried so well that even passersby on the street, several houses away, could hear him.

When it came to his friendship with Officer Tư, Teacher Hai often quoted a couplet from Nguyễn Đình Chiểu's epic poem "Lục Vân Tiên":

"Trong đời mấy bực cố-tri,

Mấy trang đồng đạo, mấy người đồng tâm?"

("*How many true friends remain in life?*

How many share our path and our hearts?")

These lines seemed to capture a sentiment common to both men. Each had a son who had joined the resistance against the French, even though they themselves were working as civil servants under French rule.

Sitting around a large table at the coffee shop, Officer Tư, his friends, and colleagues appeared quieter than usual. He broke the silence, voicing his concerns, "I wonder if the English plan to replace the French permanently and what their intentions are here."

Sergeant Cừ, a feared figure in Plum Tree hamlet, sighed reluctantly and added, "I haven't finished learning French yet. Where can I find my English to work for those English bosses? Or, worst of all, what if they bring in their own people to replace us?"

Teacher Hai, a respected figure known for his broad knowledge, attempted to console the two French workers with a half-joking tone, saying, "Relax, gentlemen. There's nothing to worry about. In this urgent situation, they won't replace you. Where would they find people to help them suppress these 'rebel forces' during the crisis?"

However, Sergeant Cừ remained uneasy and asked Teacher Hai, "I heard that General Soái in the army of the Hòa Hảo's Buddhist sect is siding with the French. Is that true, Teacher?"

"Well, it's said that he has a joint agreement with Colonel Cluzet," replied Teacher Hai.

Curious, Cừ inquired about the plans of the army from the Cao Đài Buddhist sect. Teacher Hai admitted, "I can only guess. I don't know the details of their affairs."

Teacher Hai shook his head in frustration, reflecting on how the political maneuvers of the "rebel forces" had brought discord to the religious sects, tarnishing the reputation of the two major religions born in the South. These venerable homegrown religions, deeply rooted in local culture, should be cherished, if not embraced.

Officer Tư excused himself earlier than usual and rode his bike home, burdened by personal worries. His eldest daughter, Nhàn, was due to give birth soon, he was told. Since the previous evening, his wife had reminded him to be ready to head into the neighborhood and bring the midwife, Mrs. Mười, to assist with the delivery.

Starting at noon the rain poured steadily, showing no sign of letting up. Inside Officer Tư's house, tucked away within the police compound, Mrs. Mười, the midwife, waited anxiously for labor to begin. Despite her vigilance, there were no indications yet. Mrs. Tư, gauging Nhàn's expressions, occasionally raised her voice in alarm, "It must be coming, Mrs. Mười." Drawing on her experience, Mrs. Mười knew it was still early, and a few more hours of waiting were inevitable. Seeking permission, she excused herself to attend to personal matters.

Before departing, Mrs. Mười reassured everyone that Nhàn's childbirth was in its early stages and posed a challenge due to being her first delivery - her body not accustomed to the process.

"By next time," Mrs. Mười added optimistically, "she would push it out in no time."

Shortly after the midwife left, Mrs. Tư panicked, exclaiming, "Her water has broken, my goodness!" Officer Tư, noticing the time on the pendulum wall clock, realized it was already deep into the night. Although the rain had stopped, venturing out at that hour was risky, especially outside the police compound walls in such tumultuous times. Still, with his daughter's life on the line, he didn't hesitate. Grabbing the flashlight prepared on the bedside table and instinctively tucking his revolver into his belt, he hurried out to fetch the midwife.

Tragically, by the time he returned, it was too late. The midwife could save only one life. Nhàn could not be saved, and she passed away as the ill-fated daughter of Mr. and Mrs. Tư. In memory of Nhàn's unwavering devotion to her parents, despite a life marked by illness, Officer Tư named the baby girl Thảo from the moment she entered the world.

Thus, only seven months after returning to the city with her mother and disabled sister, Thanh was confronted with another devastating loss that reshaped her life. With a profound sense of duty, Thanh took on the responsibility of raising her niece Thảo, serving as a surrogate mother in her late sister's stead.

Two days after losing his elder daughter, Officer Tư faced another wave of trouble. He was called in by the French secret police for questioning after a spiteful informant reported seeing him alone in a restricted area at midnight. The authorities were suspicious about how he had managed to return unharmed from a neighborhood controlled by the anti-French resistance forces.

Although he was not physically tortured, the mounting fear and veiled threats took their toll. Nights became sleepless, and his appetite vanished. He wasn't exactly afraid of dying, but his mind repeatedly replayed the torture scenes he had witnessed and heard more than once - victims' screams and pleas that now lingered in his memory, leaving him feeling ill without even realizing it.

From that point on, every night before going to bed, he placed a machete beneath the wooden platform where he slept. It wasn't much, but it gave him a small sense of security, a means to defend himself should he ever need it. Yet, no blade could shield him from the unease of living in a country mired in endless unrest under French colonial rule.

Chapter 4: Adrift in the Current of Life

More than three years after the tragedies that had upended Mỹ Lệ's life, her father passed away after a serious illness. With help from a relative, she secured a position as a "planton" (office courier) at the Indochina Locomotive Company. Her dedication, friendly demeanor, and knack for problem-solving earned her a promotion within six months, and she became a clerk selling train tickets at Saigon's bustling central station.

This brief period of stability provided Mỹ Lệ with a rare sanctuary amid the surrounding turmoil. The British had withdrawn from Vietnam after only six months, leaving the colonial French authorities to fend for themselves. Struggling to maintain control, the French authorities behaved like *'a child abandoned at the market, struggling to find its own way.'* They reverted to familiar tactics, sowing discord among armed factions that opposed French rule, manipulating alliances to weaken their enemies, and supporting criminal syndicates that operated casinos, opium dens, and other illicit businesses. These shady enterprises provided much-needed funding for their military efforts.

Among the infamous gang leaders was Năm Chảng, a 'Big Brother' who led a group of gangsters in his territory around Saigon Market. Năm Chảng's towering figure, measuring more than seven feet in height, was sufficient to inspire awe among his underlings. With a neck as massive as a bull's neck, carrying above a pair of stern, glaring eyes that could easily intimidate an unfortunate opponent. However, this did not mean he lacked intelligence; he was a cunning and resourceful individual.

The origin of his imposing nickname, "Năm Chảng" (Huge Năm), was telling. Born as Hổ (Tiger) in the Year of the Tiger, the fourth child in a struggling peasant family, his legend began at the age of seventeen.

It all started with a wild buffalo that repeatedly stormed into the village, wreaking havoc during harvest time. Villagers prayed fervently to hidden spirits and Buddhas, hoping the buffalo would leave, but their pleas went unanswered. Out of a mixture of respect and superstition, hoping not to provoke the buffalo's spirit, they nicknamed it "Ông Chảng," or "Mr. Huge." Despite their deference, "Mr. Huge" returned time and again to forage in the village fields.

In the midst of villagers' helplessness, not knowing what to do, young Hồ secretly devised a plan to kill "Mr. Huge." He ventured into the forest, chopped off a ton of rattan sticks, and brought them back to the village, rolling them into bundles the size of a basket. When "Mr. Huge" returned to the village, Hồ confronted it with four bundles of rattan. Each time "Mr. Huge" lunged forward, Hồ threw a bundle of rattan at it. The buffalo jabbed its horns at the bundle of rattan each time in response. Eventually, the bundles of rattan got entangled around both of the buffalo's horns, rendering its most dangerous weapon ineffective. Hồ cautiously approached and struck its neck with a machete until the buffalo collapsed. This miraculous feat later earned him the nickname "Năm Chảng" in the underworld, and the tale followed him into the realm of gangsters, garnering respect from his followers.

In Saigon, though the summer sun blazed mercilessly, it was also the season of the flamboyant Royal Poinciana, fondly known as "student flowers," that adorned schoolyards and lined the bustling streets. The fiery red blooms in front of Saigon Market enlivened an already vibrant scene, while commuters passing through the Saigon-Mỹ Tho train station couldn't help but feel a little more cheerful at the sight.

Amid the steady flow of people, Năm Chảng spotted Mỹ Lệ. Seated at a table in front of the Kim Điệp ice cream shop across from the train station on Lê Lai Street, he sipped his beer and caught sight of her. Her pink dress fluttered as she pedaled quickly past, her long, pale legs briefly visible beneath the hem. It was love at first sight. Captivated, he immediately instructed his two subordinates to find out everything they could about her.

It took no time at all for Năm Chảng's men to learn where Mỹ Lệ worked, and Năm Chảng himself wasted no time confronting her at the ticket counter. When he saw her up close, he was taken aback by her striking features: a long, well-proportioned face and a complexion as fair as a pomelo flower in bloom. He asked for a ticket to Mỹ Tho. Mỹ Lệ, composed and undeterred, simply looked at him and carried on with her duties. For Năm Chảng, this lack of fear, especially from a woman, was a disappointment. He was used to seeing people, especially women, react to him with unease or outright terror.

Mỹ Lệ asked for the fare, and one of Năm Chảng's subordinates stepped up to the counter to pay. She accepted the money, punched the ticket, and handed it to Năm Chảng. As he stared at her, Mỹ Lệ raised an eyebrow and asked, "Do you need anything else, sir?"

Năm Chảng smirked, intrigued by her calm and seemingly indifferent demeanor. Deciding to change his approach, he retorted, "I'm here to buy a ticket, of course, not to flirt with you, right?"

Her laughter was immediate and genuine. With her innocent face and friendly demeanor, Mỹ Lệ appeared approachable, almost inviting. Năm Chảng, catching a sudden interest, grinned smugly and continued his banter.

"I want to buy a ticket to Mỹ Tho," he said.

"I just sold you one," she replied.

"Well, now I want another. Can I?"

Mỹ Lệ sighed lightly, glanced down at the counter, and repeated the process. Năm Chảng watched her every move with a knowing smile, pleased with what he saw. In his eyes, she was a prize he was determined to win.

Holding the two train tickets, he waved at Mỹ Lệ from a short distance. "See you in a few days." Then, he took a few steps away, handing the tickets to one of his henchmen to resell and pocket some extra cash.

The following day, Năm Chảng discovered that Mỹ Lệ lived with her elderly mother and a three-year-old Eurasian son. He decided to use a familiar tactic, one that had proven successful on at least two previous occasions. He instructed his men to deliver daily gifts to Mỹ Lệ's mother: two kilograms of pork ribs, a snakehead fish, a chicken, enough to provide the family with indulgent meals. After a week of such offerings, he presented himself with a ceremonial tray adorned with betel nuts and three jewelry boxes. The boxes contained a jade bracelet, a gold necklace, and a three-carat diamond ring, together forming a grand marriage proposal.

In the past, Năm Chảng's lavish proposals had never failed. This time, however, Mỹ Lệ set a condition. She demanded that he personally help her exact vengeance on the French lieutenant who had assaulted her. Having tracked his movements, she knew that Paul, now discharged, was working as a Peugeot car salesman on Norodom Boulevard, just across from the Saigon Zoo. While Năm Chảng had never allowed anyone to dictate terms to him, the overpowering force of love compelled him to break his own rule.

Less than a week later, as the car crossed the Y-shaped bridge, Đực, Năm Chảng's loyal henchman, sat in the front seat. He pulled a revolver from his hip holster and handed it to Mỹ Lệ. "Sister Năm, this is from Brother Năm," he said, using the familial term, though Mỹ Lệ was not yet married to the gang leader. Mỹ Lệ stared at the revolver, her eyebrows arching in surprise. Though she had insisted that Năm Chảng let her personally handle the "wicked Frenchman," she had never imagined being handed a lethal weapon. The sight of the gun in Đực's hand sent a jolt through her. Đực quickly tried to reassure her. "It's easy, sister. When you meet him, I'll load the bullets for you. Just aim for his head, squeeze the trigger once, and he'll be dead before he can gasp. Go on, hold it now and get used to it."

Mỹ Lệ hesitated but eventually took the revolver. Its unexpected weight startled her. She gripped the weapon tightly, but a chill ran down her spine, and her hands began to sweat. The long-buried fears from her childhood, the ones she thought she had forgotten, came rushing back like a waking nightmare. In her mind, she heard the blood-curdling screams of tortured prisoners echoing from the second-floor windows of the Xây-nho police headquarters. These screams had pierced the walls more than once, reaching six-year-old Mỹ Lệ as she played innocently in the garden below.

Her last trip to the playground with her babysitter had been on a day when the sudden crackle of gunfire beyond that cold, unyielding wall shattered the stillness. The babysitter had scrambled to cover Mỹ Lệ's ears, but her small hands couldn't fully block out the harsh reality. The horrors of the world seeped into Mỹ Lệ's subconscious, eroding her innocence. Now, the weight of the revolver in her hand brought all those memories back, raw and unrelenting.

Mỹ Lệ stared out of the car window, delving into her own forbidden memories. The furrowed brow on her father's face, the apprehensive gaze of her mother, the hushed conversations, and the masked anxiety or pretended normalcy during meals following news of someone's demise, whether a close acquaintance or a distant figure. The question of 'who killed and why' was never openly addressed; instead, it lingered as unspoken inquiries in the minds of children. Each passing day, adults silently comprehended, while children persisted in their contemplations.

The image of a battered figure suddenly rushed into Mỹ Lệ's sight. It was pulled up, lying supine on the grass, its swollen body beneath the black fabric, a purplish face, two swollen eyes shut, providing a feast for the flies buzzing around. In the innocent mind of the child, all those horrifying things originated from the object she held in her hand. It was the perpetrator of torture, murder, live burials, and throwing people into the river to drown. She detested it and wanted to throw the gun away.

"He's here, sister," Đực's voice snapped her back to reality. The car came to a halt outside the perimeter walls of the Ba Son shipyard, a French shipbuilding and repair facility nestled near the Saigon commercial port at Bạch Đằng Wharf – also a historic cradle of the anti-French revolution for the Vietnamese workforce. Guiding Mỹ Lệ through the rows of stilt houses where the workers resided, Đực led her to the desolate warehouse at the rear. Once inside, a barren space unfolded, marked only by a handful of concrete columns supporting the roof. At the farthest column, deep within, Paul was bound, his head hanging limp against his chest, eyes shut; his whole body seemed devoid of life.

His once tall, imposing frame now appeared like a stretched animal hide, marred with countless purple bruises and bloody whip marks across his exposed chest, exactly the state Năm Chảng had wanted. When they had captured Paul, Năm Chảng, keen to appease "his lady," had ordered his men: "Beat him mercilessly, but let him live." As Mỹ Lệ entered and saw Paul's condition, her instinctive compassion made her hesitate. But the sharp sting of her past humiliation surged back, and with a trembling hand, she aimed the gun at him, shouting in French: "Why? Why?"

Paul slowly raised his head. As he lifted his eyelids, he was surprised to recognize Mỹ Lệ and hastily stammered:

"I deeply regret it, I sincerely apologize."

As Mỹ Lệ looked at him, she was stunned to see a face that was too familiar. The high, slender nose and the long, curving eyelashes always seemed to bring a smile to the sparkling eyes behind them. She could not have been mistaken. It was the face she had cherished, loved, and pampered for the past three years. It was her son, Sáng. "Father and son look so alike," she whispered to herself, even though Paul's eyes now looked tired and despondent after a day of torture. The fiery hatred in Mỹ Lệ's heart was suddenly extinguished without reason. How could she bring herself to kill a face that had been the meaning of her life for the past few years... until today, and would be forever in the remaining days.

Mỹ Lệ gazed at the gun in her hand, a sense of confusion washing over her. Hesitatingly, she spoke:

"You've ruined my life, do you realize that?"

"I know, I know. I've wronged you so much. Whatever you choose to do, I just hope you can eventually find it in your heart to forgive me."

"It's too late. My father died because of you!" Mỹ Lệ shouted vehemently.

Her father felt profound sadness upon discovering that Paul, laying blame on him, had directed all his anger towards his only daughter. Faced with unrelenting upheavals in the country and his personal life, he found himself powerless. To escape his sorrows, he turned to alcohol, and eventually, succumbed to an illness that claimed his life.

Paul whispered:

"I truly regret hearing the sad news about your father and the great loss to your family. I wish I could do something to alleviate your pain and your family's."

"We don't need anything from you..."

Before finishing her sentence, Mỹ Lệ burst into tears, dropping the gun, turning her head away from Paul's gaze, and covering her face as she sobbed. Paul mumbled, his words stumbling:

"I'm sorry... I'm so sorry. If anything I said has hurt you, please forgive me."

Mỹ Lệ's heart cried out, 'Do you know we had a child together?' but the words didn't come out; they choked in Mỹ Lệ's throat. She quickly turned away, heading toward the rays of sunlight streaming through the rusted iron door.

Đực stood outside, smoking and waiting. Surprised by the absence of gunshots, Đực asked, "Hey, why haven't I heard anything, sis?" Mỹ Lệ didn't respond; her gaze fixed beyond the shade of the old jackfruit tree canopy in front of the warehouse door. Her face was uplifted, bathing in the vast, vibrant blue sky and the radiant pink sunlight above. Đực hastily ran inside to observe, and disappointment marked his return with a gun in hand: "Sis, shall I finish it off for you?"

"No," Mỹ Lệ suddenly shouted. Đực, startled, "Why, sis? If I release him, maybe Brother Năm will kill me. He spent a lot to catch him." The more Đực spoke, the more he felt anxious about being held accountable by his boss for messing up the assignment. Without saying a word, he rushed back into the warehouse to complete the job on Paul. Mỹ Lệ panicked and ran after him, shouting, "Don't... don't... don't do that."

A black Traction, the kind often linked with the French secret police, sped into the Ba Son shipyard, screeching as it braked hard on the asphalt. It swung onto the shoulder, sending up a cloud of dust, before coming to an abrupt stop next to Đực's vehicle. The driver inside, who had been half-dozing, jolted awake in alarm. Sensing danger, Đực grabbed Mỹ Lệ and pulled her into the warehouse. He quickly shut the door, his hand gripping a gun, ready for the worst. It wasn't until he heard Năm Chảng's familiar voice outside that Đực let out a sigh of relief, fumbling to unlock the door and swing it open.

Năm Chảng entered, followed closely by a Frenchman in a faded white suit. The man's face was drawn and tense. In halting Vietnamese, he demanded, "Where's Paul? Where's Paul?" Đực guided them farther inside. The moment the Frenchman spotted Paul, he rushed forward and embraced him, murmuring softly, "Thank God, you're still alive."

This man was none other than Captain Gauthier, head of the Intelligence Services, known more infamously as the 'Deuxième Bureau.' To the public, the bureau's name stirred fear; to those fighting against French rule, it provoked deep resentment. After leaving the army, Paul had worked covertly for the bureau, his true role masked by a Peugeot dealership that served as his cover.

Năm Chảng signaled to his men to untie Paul. Captain Gauthier guided him out to the car. Mỹ Lệ watched the scene unfold as if she were watching a film on a screen - no anger, no sadness, just a profound sense of release. It was as if a weight had lifted. Everything that needed to happen had happened. Following Năm Chảng, she climbed into the car. On the way home, Mỹ Lệ thought of her son, aching to hold him close and tell him, "Mom just saw your father." She bit her lip, fighting back tears that threatened to spill, and whispered to herself, "He's still too young to understand."

With the tumultuous days behind her, on a serene Sunday morning, Mỹ Lệ felt a sudden urge to bring her child to visit Thanh. Thanh was engrossed in reviewing the payroll ledger of workers at the bureau when Lý, the maid, hurriedly entered the room to announce, "Miss, Aunt Mỹ Lệ has come to visit."

Recently, a wealthy friend of Thanh's father had persuaded him to invest in a business venture. They embarked on the project of demolishing the walls of an abandoned rice warehouse to sell the debris to construction companies. The 'two old men,' as they humorously referred to themselves, had entrusted the entire management of labor to Thanh, making her quite occupied in recent times.

Despite her hectic schedule, Thanh always found joy in meeting Mỹ Lệ. Among their close circle of friends, Mỹ Lệ was perhaps the closest. This connection wasn't only because of the incident during the Tomb-Sweeping trip that left Thanh feeling guilty, but also because Mỹ Lệ, with her elder sister personality, consistently stood ready to protect her friends as if they were her own siblings. This admirable quality both impressed and endeared Mỹ Lệ to Thanh.

Mỹ Lệ and Thanh enjoyed playing with each other's children for a while before Thanh asked Lý to take Sáng and Thảo outside to play in the garden. This allowed the two 'sisters' to spend some quality time together. Today, Mỹ Lệ intended to confide in Thanh about the tumultuous meeting with Paul. Initially, she felt that the encounter had freed her from the weight of vengeance she had harbored, but it apparently left a burden on her heart instead. However, as she glanced at the pile of papers on Thanh's work desk, Mỹ Lệ realized that it was not the right time to share her feelings with a friend. She casually made a few jokes and gracefully withdrew.

Before parting ways, though, Mỹ Lệ asked for a bottle of iodine solution to keep at her house, using the excuse that her son had too many scratches and bruises lately. Thanh called a taxi to take Mỹ Lệ and Sáng home. Mỹ Lệ waved goodbye, saying "Adieu" with a half-smile. Thanh reached into the car to ruffle Sáng's hair and urged Thảo to say goodbye to Sáng.

As the taxi rolled away slowly, Thanh waved goodbye. Looking at Mỹ Lệ's weary face, she felt uneasy. After taking a few steps into the house, Thanh suddenly wondered why Mỹ Lệ had said "Adieu" in bidding farewell today. It sounded as if it were for an eternal separation. Thanh pondered, "Why didn't she say 'Au revoir,' the usual farewell like always?"

After dinner, as was their daily custom, Thanh and her 'daughter' would sit outside on the stone-inlay concrete bench in front of their house, relishing the evening breeze. Lý, their maid, joined them, taking a seat on the cement chest covering the water meter. Following the routine, Thanh enveloped Thảo in a warm hug, inquiring, "Whose mother is this?" Thảo responded, "This mother is my mother." Thanh posed another question, "Whose child is this?" Thảo confidently replied, "This child is your child." This daily exchange seemed to serve as a ritual, a reaffirmation of Thanh's involuntary role as a mother, a pledge to live in a manner that would assure her beloved sister in heaven, who had entrusted Thảo to her care.

Later, Thanh asked Thảo whether she enjoyed playing with Sáng earlier in the morning. Thảo responded straightforwardly, "No." Lý chimed in, saying, "Perhaps he's not accustomed to our surroundings. He wasn't as active as boys his age usually are." Thanh, recalling Mỹ Lệ's contrasting claim that Sáng had become quite mischievous and prone to accidents, found herself perplexed. The more she dwelled on it, the more confusion set in: "Why did Mỹ Lệ ask me for the bottle of disinfectant?" In a moment of realization, Thanh exclaimed, "Oh no," and promptly urged Lý to summon a nearby taxi driver. As Thanh waited in front of the house for the taxi, a jumble of emotions churned inside her.

Speculations continued to accumulate in Thanh's mind as she retreated into her thoughts on the backseat of the cab. The taxi eventually halted at the entrance of the alley, where the darkening sky hinted at the lateness of the hour. Thanh, determined, hurriedly traversed the distance to Mỹ Lệ's house and knocked on the door. Aunt Six, Mỹ Lệ's mother, opened it, and upon entering, Thanh immediately inquired about Mỹ Lệ.

"Both mother and child went to bed early today, and I don't know why," Aunt Six replied.

Growing more anxious, Thanh rushed into the inner room while calling Mỹ Lệ's name. Mỹ Lệ, in the midst of putting her child to sleep, responded with concern, "I'm here. What's the matter?"

Seating herself beside the bed, Thanh questioned her friend, "What are you doing?"

"I'm putting my child to sleep. I noticed he was a bit haggard today, so I decided to let him sleep a little earlier," Mỹ Lệ explained.

"Tell me the truth, why did you bring back the bottle of Teinture d'iode?" Thanh asked.

Mỹ Lệ hesitated and countered, "How did you know I was only using Sáng as an excuse to obtain the disinfectant?"

"I knew it. Come on, Mỹ Lệ. If there's anything you need, you could have just told me," Thanh replied.

"What are you saying?" Mỹ Lệ puzzled.

"Just imagine, if something happened to you, how would Sáng and Aunt Six cope?" Thanh explained.

"What? Do you think I want to take the disinfectant to kill myself?" Mỹ Lệ rushed to hug Thanh tightly, tears of happiness streaming down her face. Mỹ Lệ tried to express gratitude through an admiring smile, "I'm sorry, Thanh, for making you worry and have to rush here to save me at this time of the day. I appreciate you so much."

Mỹ Lệ held onto Thanh, gently stroking her back, and clarified, "The other day, my mom accidentally cut her hand, and we were running out of medicine at home. So, taking the opportunity to visit your place, I thought of getting a new supply."

"You're really mischievous. Why didn't you say that the medicine was for Aunt Six?" Thanh asked.

"To be honest, I was afraid it would make you sad, as it would remind you of your mom's tragic end," Mỹ Lệ said, alluding to Thanh's mother's death due to a minor cut in the finger. Mỹ Lệ tried to lighten the mood with a warm smile.

Now it was Thanh's turn to feel overwhelmed with emotion. She hugged Mỹ Lệ, reproaching her affectionately, "With all the troubles you have, you're still concerned about me, and afraid that I'll be upset. Really!"

Since the fateful day at the graveside of Thanh's mother until now, Thanh had always felt guilty for failing to protect her friend. Thanh hugged Mỹ Lệ tightly and whispered, "That day, I shouldn't have left you alone with that devil."

Mỹ Lệ quickly responded, "Are you still thinking about that? Forget it. That's in the past for me now."

"Really? I thought you carry a deep hatred for him," Thanh said.

"Listen to me, the reason I'd like to meet you this morning was just that. I wanted to tell you about that devil," Mỹ Lệ explained.

"Why didn't you say anything then?" Thanh asked.

"Partly because I saw you were busy. But you know me, I would rather keep things to myself. At home, I planned to tell you everything, but when I got there, I hesitated and didn't know what to say. Talking about myself seems awkward, so I stopped," Mỹ Lệ replied.

"Now, tell me the truth. Did you meet him?" Thanh asked.

Mỹ Lệ discreetly glanced into the front room to ensure her mother was asleep. Leaning in close to Thanh, she began recounting every detail of her encounter with Paul. Tears streamed down her face as she recalled the shocking moment when she recognized the familiar features of Sáng on his father's face. A pang of regret consumed her, blaming herself for denying her child the chance to meet his father.

Suddenly, a knock on the front door startled Aunt Six. "Who's there?" she mumbled, sitting up at the edge of the plank bed and searching for her wooden clogs. Dragging herself to the door, she announced, "There's a Frenchman at the door." Mỹ Lệ jolted, briefly considering the possibility that it might be Paul, but she dismissed the thought. Thanh, sensing her friend's confusion, hurried to the door. If Paul hadn't promptly introduced himself, Thanh wouldn't have recognized him; he no longer sported the scruffy beard from their last meeting at the gravesite. Thanh rushed back inside to inform Mỹ Lệ, who angrily responded, "Please go out there and chase him away for me."

Having shared their deepest thoughts and emotions, Thanh understood that Mỹ Lệ's tough exterior was a façade concealing profound pain. Sitting beside her friend, Thanh offered advice, "Look, you're back at it again. If something is bothering you, it's better to let it out. Keeping it inside will do you more harm than good."

Listening to her friend's reproachful yet loving admonishment, Mỹ Lệ reluctantly decided to meet Paul. She stood still, observing him humbly clad in a crisp white shirt. The innocent and pitiable look on Paul's face, reminiscent of Sáng caught in mischief, sought forgiveness from Mỹ Lệ, challenging her earlier determination. Reluctantly, she retreated to the table, sinking into her chair. Intentionally, Thanh invited Paul to sit next to Mỹ Lệ before discreetly withdrawing to the kitchen to prepare some tea. Aunt Six insisted on boiling the water herself, prompting Thanh to bid farewell, in the hope that Mỹ Lệ and Paul would find some privacy.

Mỹ Lệ quickly pleaded with Thanh to stay, "You're leaving me alone? Are you trying to kill me?" Her words, whether intentional or not, stirred Thanh's guilt for abandoning her friend the last time. Hesitating, Thanh pulled a chair to the edge of the table.

Paul felt momentarily awkward in the presence of the third party but considered it better than facing outright rejection from Mỹ Lệ. He looked at her and, in an almost whispered tone, hesitated before saying, "Thank you for meeting me. I know, no matter how many apologies I offer, it might be futile, but I still want to say it. Please forgive me."

Mỹ Lệ sat quietly, her eyes fixed on the table. Paul continued, "In fact, for the past two years after returning to Saigon, I've been trying to find you around the Xây-nho Police Station, but no one knew where your family had moved to. Unfortunately, I had to meet you again in these circumstances. In any case, thanks to Năm Chẳng, who not only helped me finally locate you but also shared with me what you went through."

Paul hesitated, stealing a brief glance towards Thanh. Thanh could discern a desire in him to express more of his feelings toward Mỹ Lệ, yet he seemed restrained in her presence. After a moment of silence, Paul noted that although Mỹ Lệ wasn't responding directly to him, her demeanor displayed less anger and distress than during their previous encounter. Encouraged by this subtle shift, he mustered the courage to unveil the purpose of his visit:

"May I request the opportunity to meet our son?"

Mỹ Lệ burst into tears. Tears streamed down, soaking the palms of her hands covering her face. The dreams of hearing Sáng call out "Dad" seemed futile for so long, but unexpectedly, they could become a reality right before her eyes. Thanh handed a handkerchief to Mỹ Lệ and gently rubbed her back to console her. Mỹ Lệ's unexpected reaction left Paul bewildered. He stood up, intending to comfort her, but remembering the slap from years ago made him hesitate. Thanh helped Mỹ Lệ stand up, speaking softly into her ear:

"Let them meet each other, my dear. Look, he's been holding a little box tightly in his hands all this time; probably a toy for the child. Have pity on him."

Seeing Mỹ Lệ not resisting, Thanh turned to invite Paul to join them inside the next room to meet Sáng. As soon as Paul had the glimpse of his sleeping child on the bed, he rushed to embrace him, kissing his forehead, nose, cheeks, and hair. Thanh quietly slipped away from behind the house, bidding farewell to Aunt Six. Suddenly, she felt a lightness, as if she had just shed a heavy burden that had been weighing on her for years. The woman's intuition signaled to Thanh that a wonderful happiness awaited her friend.

Thanh smiled dreamily, stepping towards the front of Mỹ Lệ's house, then turned back to say to Aunt Six:

"Please tell Mỹ Lệ later that my daughter is too mischievous nowadays; her grandmother is getting tired of looking after her. So, I have to go back and put her to bed. You just say it like that, and Mỹ Lệ will understand!"

Thanh smiled as she walked away, satisfied with her subtle way of "returning the favor" to Mỹ Lệ. After all, when Mỹ Lệ had spun a tale about her son's antics earlier, Thanh now had her own excuse to quietly step back. Leaving her friend alone with Paul in their private space, Thanh held onto the hope that genuine hearts would find their way to one another. Silently, she prayed that the long-awaited dawn would soon arrive, its light shining on her friend, her son, and even Paul, illuminating the path to happiness that awaited them all.

Chapter 5: The Plum Tree Hamlet

Thanh's family had relocated from the police compound to nearby Plum Tree Hamlet the previous year, settling into a private residence purchased from an acquaintance. According to Thanh, the move was primarily motivated by concern for Thảo's future. Determined to integrate into the hamlet's community life, Thanh sought stable employment to support her family and ensure Thảo could continue her education as far as her ambitions would take her. Depending solely on her father's civil servant salary had become risky, especially given the country's uncertain conditions and her father's declining health.

It was here, in Plum Tree Hamlet, that Thanh began a pivotal transformation in her life, taking on the full responsibility of raising 'little' Thảo as a surrogate mother. When Thảo was just a toddler, she was fortunate to receive the loving care of her grandmother, Mrs. Tư. But as Thảo reached school age, Thanh stepped in fully, seeing Thảo's future as her own. As Thanh became familiar with the residents of Plum Tree Hamlet, she gained recognition as a kind-hearted, compassionate woman who regularly helped those in need. The community also respected her as a devoted and loving disciplinarian, determined to ensure her "daughter" Thảo received not only a solid education but also a strong foundation in good manners.

Plum Tree Hamlet, located on the outskirts of Saigon near the Reed Field police station's boundary, is known for its distinctive history and its friendly, industrious community - one that, while uniquely its own, has nonetheless been shaped by the tides of its time.

The hamlet predates the establishment of Gia Định Citadel, the southernmost outpost of the country founded in 1808. It was originally situated along the banks of an unnamed canal that gained historical significance in 1819, the Year of the Cat. That year, Emperor Gia Long decreed that the Deputy Governor of Gia Định Province widen the canal to more than 30 meters, facilitating smoother boat traffic and establishing a crucial waterway linking Gia Định City with the Mekong Delta. At that time, the canal received its official name: "An Thông Hạ Canal."

It was quite a tale of how the Emperor came to be acquainted with, and perhaps even fond of, an unnamed canal in the unassuming Plum Tree Hamlet. It began during one of the most infamous civil wars in Vietnamese history—the Trịnh–Nguyễn Civil War. At that time, Lord Nguyễn repeatedly fled south to escape the advancing Tây Sơn forces. On one such occasion, as the Tây Sơn army pursued them all the way to Gia Định Citadel, Lord Nguyễn was forced to abandon the city. Fortunately, a farmer from Plum Tree Hamlet arrived by boat, navigating the royal entourage through the narrow creeks, helping them evade capture and guiding them safely toward a larger river.

Misfortune struck, however, after they passed Plum Tree Hamlet heading west. The already narrow canal became further obstructed by sand buildup, severely slowing their retreat. As a result, part of the rear guard was left behind and overtaken by the Tây Sơn forces, who killed nearly all of them. The remaining boats carrying Lord Nguyễn managed to escape to the Ruột Ngựa Canal, then entered the Rạch Cát River. From there, they turned south, passing through the Cần Đước area before reaching the Cần Giờ estuary and escaping into the open sea.

From there, the Lord and his followers continued south along the coastline, eventually finding an entrance through the Tiểu inlet to Mỹ Tho province, where they sought temporary refuge. Their journey of displacement continued throughout the Mekong Delta region, with the Lord at times retreating as far as Cape Cà Mau, or even to the remote Thổ Châu Islands, to elude their relentless pursuers.

Thổ Châu Island, located in the Gulf of Siam, offered Lord Nguyễn an opportunity to meet the King of Siam and seek military aid. Additionally, Lord Nguyễn established contact with Portuguese and French missionaries, including Bishop Pigneau de Béhaine (Bá-Đa-Lộc), to whom he expressed the potential need for French support in restoring order to the country.

After ascending the throne, the King never forgot the small canal that had once saved his life. Beyond his deep gratitude to the farmer from Plum Tree hamlet who had guided his escape, he also recognized the canal's strategic importance. He subsequently issued a decree to expand it into a major commercial waterway, facilitating the transport of rice, fruit, and other goods from the fertile gardens of the Mekong Delta to Gia Định and, later, Saigon.

Given the prior relationship between Lord Nguyễn and Western powers, it is no surprise that later generations speculated whether the decision to expand the canal was influenced, in part, by pressure from the French, who had long recognized its strategic value. Indeed, forty years later, a popular saying emerged:

"The Western invaders march on Cần Giờ,

Don't waste your time pining and waiting, my dear."

The Franco-Spanish alliance had entered through the Cần Giờ estuary, using the An Thông Hạ Canal to connect with the Tàu Hủ Canal. They advanced through the Bến Nghé Creek, into the Saigon River, and surrounded Gia Định Citadel from all sides, leaving the imperial forces with no time to react.

To solidify their colonial regime, they built fortifications on high ground along this strategic waterway, including infamous outposts such as Fort Ô Ma and Fort Cây Mai, which remained in place until the mid-20th century.

Just 15 years after France imposed its protectorate over the Huế court, the French company 'La Société française des distilleries de l'Indochine' began construction on a grand distillery occupying four acres of wasteland on the right bank of the An Thông Hạ Canal. From that moment, the canal began to transform. its waters bustling with boats and its banks lined with tightly packed markets and shops.

On the left bank, directly across from the distillery, stood a row of two-story buildings painted yellow with green-shuttered windows. These buildings, reminiscent of the narrow townhouses along the Seine River, reflected the nostalgia of the French soldiers stationed far from home. Heading east along this row led to Reed Field Market, the hamlet's only marketplace, divided into two sections: Front Market and Back Market.

The Front Market was home to three meat stalls, along with numerous vendors selling textiles, bazaar goods, and school supplies like notebooks and pens. It also featured several cafés with views overlooking the river. The Back Market, in contrast, was primarily occupied by vendors dealing in seafood, poultry, and fresh produce. It was tucked behind three general stores that sold rice, coal, and kitchen supplies.

At the other end of the row of buildings was a three-way intersection, which could also be considered a four-way junction due to a pedestrian walkway that led directly to a towering iron bridge with wooden planks spanning the An Thông Hạ Canal. This bridge connected to the main gate of the distillery and was reserved for pedestrians, primarily workers commuting to and from the distillery each day. However, it was also frequently used by merchants from Plum Tree hamlet who traveled farther afield to purchase wholesale goods for resale. Locals referred to it as the "Distillery Bridge."

Near the foot of the bridge, in front of the distillery's two large iron gates, was a bustling depot for horse-drawn carriages, perpetually alive with the clatter of hooves and wheels, the comings and goings of people, merchants calling out to one another, and baskets and goods strewn everywhere.

Down by the canal, along a retaining wall lined with grayish laterite stones, was a horse bathing area where drivers would lead their horses to the river each evening for a wash. Occasionally, a stubborn horse would break free from its reins and run wildly, causing alarm among the adults but delighting the children, who would laugh and cheer with excitement.

During festive occasions, the scene stretching from the river to the riverbank became even livelier. Especially on "Quatorze Juillet" (July 14), France's National Day, there were boat races and swimming competitions on the water. Meanwhile, along the two paved roads flanking both sides of the canal, there were footraces, speed-walking contests, sack races (where participants hopped to the finish line with both legs inside a sack), and most exciting of all, a bicycle race from Reed Field Wharf to Sand Canal Wharf and back.

As for the water-based games, many people enjoyed the "duck-catching" event. The organizers would release a Siamese duck onto the river, and contestants would compete to swim out and catch it. Whoever succeeded won the prize.

Bần had lived on a fishing boat with his parents since the day he was born. He was as skilled at diving as a fish, having won the prize two years in a row. But by the third year, many were disappointed not to see him appear. When people asked around, they learned that a month earlier, he and his father had been navigating their boat along the Vàm Cỏ River when it got tangled in a patch of water hyacinth. His father ordered him to take a machete, dive in, and clear the way. After a few swings, Bần hurriedly climbed back on board, claiming that something horrifying in the water had bumped into him.

In a rush to deliver goods on time and earn money for his sick mother's medicine, his father grew impatient. He grabbed a pole, drove his son back into the river, and this time, Bần never resurfaced. All that remained was a spreading pool of bright red blood on the river's surface. Villagers say a crocodile likely seized him, holding him underwater until he drowned before dragging him ashore to be devoured.

When Thanh's family moved into Plum Tree hamlet, the row of two-story houses along the canal already had a life of its own, featuring a pawn shop, a tailor's shop, a photography studio, and two homes occupied by French soldiers with Vietnamese wives. There was also a laundry shop whose owners had a daughter about twenty years old, with shoulder-length hair and a gentle, modest appearance. She was always seen diligently working at a sewing machine near the front of the shop, mending and ironing freshly washed clothes, sewing on buttons as needed, and patching any tears. It seemed as if she lived in her own private world, indifferent to worldly affairs, concerned only with delivering perfectly cared-for garments to her customers.

Yet, whenever customers arrived, she greeted them warmly and cheerfully, conversing in Vietnamese or French if any French soldiers from the station came by. Of course, her friendly demeanor served a purpose. On several occasions, it helped her glean information about French military operations and raids, which she then passed on to the Vietnamese resistance forces.

Behind the row of houses stood a line of latrines, and each evening someone had to haul away the waste. This task had long been assigned to a brother-and-sister pair: Heo (Pig) and Chuột (Rat), the two children of Mrs. Trầu (Betel-Chewing Lady), who were known throughout the hamlet.

In the Plum Tree hamlet, even though not everyone knew her personally, everyone was familiar with Mrs. Bảy's family. Many residents, out of habit, referred to her as "Bà Trầu" (the Betel-Chewing Lady) because her mouth was always red from chewing betel. Whenever people saw her, whether she was bustling about washing rice by the side of her thatched hut or hurrying along to look for her two children working as hired hands for wealthier families in the area, any greeting to her would quickly be followed by her glancing around for a nearby clump of bushes, a patch of grass by the roadside, or the edge of a canal. She would then bend down as if searching for something on the ground, lean her neck forward, and spit out a wad of betel residue.

Most people who came to see her merely wanted to ask one of her children to help with odd jobs around their homes. Before responding, she would habitually grab the corner of her faded, deep-brown checkered towel, whether draped over her head to shield her from the sun or slung over her shoulder when in the shade, and use it to wipe away the streaks of bright-red lime juice that had run down the cuts and creases of her dark, hollow, weathered cheeks.

After her husband, Mr. Seven, was killed in the French attack on the Reed Field outpost on the outskirts of Saigon, she remained alone to raise their two small children, "Pig" and "Rat." These rather peculiar names, derived from their birth years, the Year of the Pig and the Year of the Rat, were chosen in the hope that lurking spirits in the underworld would be put off by these "ugly" names and leave her children unharmed. That was Mrs. Betel's explanation to anyone who either asked about the origin of her children's names or criticized her for giving them such "heartless" names.

As it turned out, Heaven did not disappoint Mrs. Seven. Both Pig and Rat stayed healthy and reached adulthood, even though they lived from day to day, never sure where their next meal would come from. If they fell ill, they would curl up on a wooden plank bed under a tattered blanket, praying that the next day would be better than the last, for they had no money to pay for doctors or medicine.

When Pig was eight years old, he began carrying out "liaison" tasks for his father's friends and comrades in the anti-French resistance. Occasionally, they would ask him to relay messages between people in the organization, such as delivering letters or passing along verbal notes. Initially, he didn't realize he was working for an anti-French resistance group because the messages were always something vague, like "Uncle Five, the ducks have eaten all the rice," or "My grandpa invites Uncle Four for a drink," even though his grandparents had passed away long before.

Still, he enjoyed meeting these uncles, because every time they returned from the Bàn Cờ district, they always remembered to bring him a bag of candy they called "Bàn Cờ candy". His favorite were the white candies with red stripes, sweet from the very first bite. He never thought to question why these men, who had traveled all the way from the countryside to the capital city of Saigon, always seemed to end up at the Bàn Cờ slums.

He had no idea that the Bàn Cờ district was actually a communications hub for the anti-French resistance; he was too young to grasp what was happening. Sometimes he even thought those pieces of candy were gifts from heaven. While his father was still alive, he worried that eating too many sweets would spoil his son's appetite for meals, so he often hid the bag of candy. Occasionally, wanting to reward his son, he would quietly take out a piece, hide it in his hand, and then lead the boy to bow at the family altar to pray for heaven's blessing. With great ceremony, he'd pretend to reach up and retrieve a "heaven-sent" candy. The boy accepted this "heavenly gift" eagerly, although deep down he sensed something was amiss.

By the time he turned fifteen, he no longer had any doubts. He answered the call of the homeland and slipped away to join the resistance with his 'uncles'. From then on, the 'Betel-Chewing Lady' lived with his sister, "Rat," in a tattered thatched hut by the river, doing odd jobs for people just to scrape by.

For the past few months, Rat had been assisting at the home of Ms. Thanh, well-regarded in Plum Tree Hamlet as a kind-hearted woman and the daughter of Officer Tư. Early that morning, Ms. Thanh sent Rat to pick up breakfast from Mrs. Five's bread cart.

Parked on a patch of grass along the Kinh Đôi canal, the cart was actually a modified bicycle with a wicker box attached behind the seat for storing French-style baguettes. Its wooden lid could flip up and rest on the front, forming a wide cutting board where Mrs. Five sliced the bread.

Rat pedaled over and pulled up alongside it, reaching out to grip the rattan rim around the box for balance. She was still a bit unsteady, her body swaying, yet she was already calling out:

"Mrs. Five, please give Ms. Thanh two piasters' worth of meat-filled baguettes," Rat called out.

Mrs. Five scolded her, "You lazy thing! Too lazy even to get off your bike, just hanging onto my cart like that. One of these days, it's going to collapse, and then I'll be left slurping porridge, you hear?"

Rat responded sheepishly, "I'm sorry, Mrs. Five."

Reaching into her basket and pulling out a fresh loaf, Mrs. Five asked offhandedly, "Oh my, is that how Ms. Thanh taught you to speak? You're so polite now."

Mrs. Five said this because she knew Rat often spoke brashly. She smiled, recalling a story she had recently heard from some of the other helpers at Ms. Thanh's house. Two days earlier, Rat had taken Ms. Thanh's clothes to be laundered, as usual. Suddenly, in front of a crowd, she shouted at the top of her lungs, "Why haven't I ever seen Ms. Thanh on her period?"

Her mother happened to be standing right there and gave her a swift smack on the head, scolding, "Don't you know you should be thanking Ms. Thanh instead of asking questions like that? Everyone in this hamlet knows she's kindhearted. She washes those 'soiled' clothes herself and never leaves them for us to do."

Thinking of Ms. Thanh, Mrs. Five remembered all the times she had helped her and her husband. Quietly, she murmured to herself, "Ms. Thanh is truly kindhearted; there aren't many like her in this world."

Returning to her task, intent on making a delicious portion of bread for Ms. Thanh, Mrs. Five placed her hand on the baguette and said to Rat,

"You're getting this for Ms. Thanh, right? I know she likes the end piece with less bread inside…"

After trimming the long baguette to size and slicing it open for the meat filling, Mrs. Five scooped out some of the soft interior. As she worked, she spoke aloud, almost as if to remind herself that she wasn't simply accommodating a regular customer's preference - this was for the person who had once saved her family's life.

"Two layers of salt and pepper," she murmured, "one on the bottom, one on the top, so it's evenly salted…"

With that, she sprinkled salt and pepper between the two halves before adding the meat. Then, flipping the chopsticks around, she muttered,

"I have to use the clean end of the chopsticks to pick up the meat for Ms. Thanh. If I use the same ones I use for sardines, she'll say the meat tastes fishy."

Ms. Thanh often praised Mrs. Five's bread, saying it perfectly suited her taste. In truth, however, there was another reason she kept to herself. Within the family, everyone knew she frequently praised Mrs. Five for her cleanliness and care in food preparation. Yet she avoided mentioning it to others, worried they might think she was criticizing other vendors for being unsanitary. On one cheerful occasion, she even joked that Mrs. Five had learned a thing or two about proper hygiene during her two years working for a French police chief's household.

It's hard to say exactly what Mrs. Five might have learned from the French, but everyone knew of her talent for adapting Western dishes into Vietnamese-style fare. Take her "steamed baguette," for instance, Thanh raved that it was "simply unbeatable." After parties at the French police chief's house, there would typically be a lot of leftover bread. The chief's wife dealt with it by allowing the household staff to take some home for their families. Grateful that Thanh had once introduced her to this job, Mrs. Five would sometimes bring all the leftover bread to Thanh's house and store it overnight.

Early the next morning, Mrs. Five would return to steam the bread in a bamboo steamer. Then they'd lay out a mat on the floor, gather around, and feast on these steamed baguettes spread with scallion oil, wrapped in lettuce, and dipped in garlic-chili fish sauce. When they wanted to be extra fancy, and had planned ahead, Thanh would buy shredded pork skin (bì) and some vermicelli to roll into the mix, turning it into a real treat. Ever since the French went back home, you rarely see this "colonial delicacy," except at Thanh's place.

Even now, on stormy days when business is slow, Mrs. Five sometimes asks Thanh to "help out" by taking any unsold bread off her hands. As a result, the following morning, Thanh's entire family happily returns to their old tradition: steamed baguettes for breakfast. While the French colonial era has long since passed, Mrs. Five's French-inspired bread dishes linger on as a simple yet lasting legacy of that time among ordinary people.

As for the husband of 'Mrs. Five the Bread Seller', he is, of course, Mr. Five, but he was also known by another nickname: 'Mr. Five the Earth Worker.' People called him that because they occasionally saw him diving into ponds or canals, digging up clay to fill in house foundations, or dredging mud to shore up eroded banks for well-to-do families in the area. All it took was someone paying twenty piasters or so, and Mr. Five would toil away at the earth all day for them.

Watching Mr. Five in the pond, filling the bank, was a pitiful sight. Even though he was near the shore, the water rose to his waist, forcing him to hold his breath, submerge his head, and dive down to the bottom to scoop up mud and clay to pack into the eroded area. His so-called "technique" involved a wooden frame shaped like an upside-down U, with a rope stretched tight between its ends. He used that rope like a blade to slice neat squares of mud under his feet, then dove down to hoist them onto the bank.

Before long, his eyes grew red from being underwater in the murky pond, churned up by the dredged mud. His breathing grew heavier and heavier. Mr. Five was no longer young, and it was hard to say how much longer he could continue working this way.

It was, however, rather unfair that Mr. Five was stuck with the name "Earth Worker," because if he'd relied solely on that job, where work came only once in a blue moon and at dirt-cheap pay, there'd be no way to earn enough to feed himself, let alone five mouths at home.

Mr. Five primarily worked as a "rice sack porter." Whenever a freight boat laden with rice arrived from the provinces and docked at Reed Field Wharf along the An Thông Hạ Canal, he and a group of fellow porters would gather onshore, waiting to be hired. Once hired, they would climb down into the boat, hoist hundred-kilogram sacks of rice onto their shoulders, carry them up to the dock, and stack them in the storage before the rice was distributed throughout the cities of Saigon and Cholon.

The problem was that even this main job was unpredictable, sometimes there was work, sometimes there wasn't. During harvest season, boats would come in daily, bringing load after load of rice. On those days, Mr. Five could earn enough to cover his family's groceries for several days. If luck was on his side, he might even stop by Mrs. Two's place afterward for a few cups of rice wine. There, he'd nibble on sour star gooseberries dipped in chili salt, chat with Mrs. Two, and share stories with his drinking buddies.

At the end of the day, the money Mr. Five earned depended on the number of rice sacks he carried. Whether it was much or little, each time he held the crumpled bills in his hand, his heart fluttered with the anticipation of reuniting with his wife and children waiting at home. Carefully, he wrapped the money in a worn piece of oiled paper, tucked it into the pocket of the black pajama shirt he carried, and headed down to the river to bathe.

Before wading in, he set his shirt on the grassy bank and weighed it down with a green stone to keep it from blowing away. Once in the water, he reveled in the simple joy of plunging his head under repeatedly, diving as long as his breath would hold, then surfacing and wiping the water from his face. Each exhale felt liberating, as if the day's fatigue had been swept away.

The water seemed to carry off life's burdens, and rising from it felt like a joyful return to the primal harmony of earth and sky - an embrace tied together by the love and laughter of his children.

Afterward, Mr. Five headed straight for the roasted meat stall to buy a small packet of roasted pork for his wife and kids. On the way home, he stopped at Mrs. Eight's stand for 50 grams of pork fat, a little treat for his "precious one," the tabby cat he relied on to keep the rats at bay.

Despite shouldering two jobs, Mr. Five still couldn't afford to put regular meals on his family's table. His 14-year-old son, Ổi, had to constantly scour the neighborhood's marshes and ponds in search of fish to supplement their food supply. On one occasion, Ổi joined Mr. Five in "working the land," reinforcing the foundation of Mr. Four's house, which had been severely eroded after several days of heavy rain. Once the water receded, standing under the neighbor's luffa gourd trellis and looking across the pond at the row of coconut trees behind Mr. Four's place, one could see clusters of exposed roots dangling in midair, with no soil to cling to.

While helping his father "work the land," Ổi's sharp eyes caught sight of a small patch, about the size of a basket's mouth, in the middle of the pond. The water rippled and bubbled there, and he immediately knew it was teeming with tiny fry. From his fishing experience, he understood that if there were baby fish darting around on the surface, the mother fish must be lurking below, guarding them. Ổi tucked that information away for later.

That afternoon, before going home, he still had to stop by Mrs. Two's place to split a stack of firewood piled in her front yard. She had just bought it from a firewood boat arriving from Cần Đước the previous noon. It was twilight by the time Ổi returned home. He headed straight for the rainwater jar behind the house, scooping several ladles over his head and body for a quick wash before going in for dinner. He wolfed down three bowls of rice in a row, partly because he was hungry, but mostly because he was excited about fishing the next day.

After dinner, he grabbed his fishing rod and went off to find bait. The bamboo rod he used for casting was tall, easily two or three times his height, and he also used it to help gather bait. Leaving the narrow alley, he headed directly to an abandoned rice warehouse at the end of the road. He often climbed over the back fence there to chop down wild banana plants growing behind the warehouse, which his mother would slice up for a family salad.

Approaching the base of the warehouse wall, Ỗi slowed his steps, scanning it carefully. He soon spotted three lizards clinging to the wall behind a dim yellow streetlamp, waiting to snatch unsuspecting insects. Fixing his sights on the largest one, Ỗi raised his fishing rod in preparation. With a slight flick of his wrist, he swept the rod across the wall, striking the lizard around its midsection and knocking it onto the grass below.

Dazed, the creature flailed its four legs wildly among the blades of grass, twisting and turning in a desperate attempt to flee. Before it could scramble away, Ỗi was already upon it, quickly enclosing the lizard in his hand. He then slipped it into an empty matchbox he had ready in his shirt pocket.

The next day, during his midday break, Ỗi hurried home to fetch his fishing rod and lingered a moment to prepare the bait. The lizard from the previous night was still very much alive, its body clasped firmly in Ỗi's hand, leaving only its tail wriggling now and then, and its oval head protruding like a blank white pumpkin seed.

Ỗi took the hook and pushed it straight into the lizard's mouth, pressing it deeper bit by bit until it reached the creature's belly, bending its body wherever the hook went and leaving only the tail twitching as fish bait. Eyeing this "tasty lure," he seemed pleased but couldn't help wondering if a lizard would be as effective as a frog for bait. Normally, he preferred using frogs as bait, but yesterday he had to head home early to split wood and didn't have time to visit the water-hyacinth pond in the neighboring hamlet to catch any.

Poor Ổi was gradually becoming accustomed to taking lives - albeit small ones, such as lizards or frogs - to help support his family. Meanwhile, another child the same age, stumbling upon a lizard egg tucked in a wall crack, might experience a heart-melting moment, marveling at that fragile, pale shell. Thảo, Officer Tư's granddaughter, had her own encounter that would leave a mark on her young psyche: one afternoon, on her way home from school, she spotted a dog-catcher's truck creeping along the road. Two workers, armed with long nooses, roamed the sidewalk, searching for strays. Terrified, Thảo raced home with a single thought: saving Ky, her beloved dog. To her relief, Ky was there as always, innocently wagging his tail in a happy greeting. Thảo's heart was pounding. She scooped him up and dashed inside, where they hid together beneath the wooden bed.

However one chooses to judge these contrasting childhood experiences, they undeniably shape the values and outlooks of the adults these children will become. What sort of world will emerge in twenty or thirty years, when "Uncle Ổi" and "Auntie Thảo" are grown, each bringing their unique formative experiences into the society of tomorrow?

That evening, from Officer Tư's kitchen, "Brother" Three, the cook, eagerly brought over a steaming bowl of tiny fries (cá lòng ròng) braised in pork fat, still wafting fragrant curls of steam. Officer Tư reached for a tender mango leaf, wrapped it around a few of the miniature fish coated in a richly hued caramel sauce and sprinkled with whole peppercorns, then popped the bundle into his mouth. It was an uncommon treat "graciously bestowed by the heavens," as he would say. Finally, he raised his small cup of rice liquor for a quick sip to wash it all down.

Mrs. Tư brought over a plate of fried gourami fish topped with chili fish sauce, setting it in the middle of the table beside a bowl of sour soup with bean sprouts and taro stem. Then she pulled out the small stool tucked under the table and sat next to Officer Tư. As part of her daily habit, both before and after every meal, she pressed her hands together, thumbs pinning a pair of chopsticks between them, and murmured a brief prayer of gratitude to the farmers who toiled so hard to bring rice to the people.

Just before taking her first bite, she cast a glance at the pot of braised tiny fish, then turned away with a disapproving mutter, "Eating this… it's so heartless." Half joking and half serious, Officer Tư responded, "It's that kid Ổi's fault. He caught the mother fish this afternoon, leaving the baby fish on their own. And even if we hadn't eaten them, in a day or two those baby fish would've been gobbled up by bigger fish anyway, no chance of surviving."

Officer Tư gazed into the distance and quietly added, "And as for that boy, what's he supposed to do? If he doesn't go fishing, should he stay home and eat dirt?"

As for Thảo, she had now turned eight and was attending the third grade with Teacher Mùi at Lý Thái Tổ Primary School, located near the Reed Field market. Continuing a family tradition started by Thanh, about a month before the school's opening day, Thanh would buy fabric to sew three new sets of clothes for Thảo's upcoming school year. Two weeks prior to the start of the term, Thanh would take Thảo to the bazaar outside the market to gather all the necessary school supplies, including notebooks, pencils, pens, ink, erasers, rulers, and more. This ensured that Thảo was fully prepared on the first day of school each year. Additionally, Thanh would purchase wrapping paper to cover the notebooks and labels to neatly write Thảo's name, class, school, and academic year.

Tonight, just three days before the school's opening day, Thanh meticulously arranged all the books, notebooks, and sheets of wrapping paper on the dining table at home. Thảo graciously assisted in covering the notebooks and books, while Thanh, seated at the adjacent table, dedicated herself to filling in the labels. With unwavering concentration on each calligraphic letter, she inscribed Thảo's name and the school's name with a calligraphic pen she always kept at home, accompanied by two ink bottles. The blue ink, usually reserved for writing wedding congratulatory notes, flowed smoothly as she crafted the labels for Thảo's notebooks.

Upon completing their respective tasks, the mother and daughter turned their attention to organizing Thảo's school bag. Thanh had a rule that prohibited toys from being kept in the bag, but Thảo had a fondness for playing with the fluffy, pristine white lining sheets inside injection medicine boxes. Aware that her mother prioritized education, Thảo requested permission to bring these lining sheets to school as blotting paper to prevent ink smudging in her notebooks. Thanh, seeing through her child's intentions, nevertheless readily offered an approving smile and quietly praised, 'She seems quite clever, and no less mischievous than I was at her age!'

Since the time Thanh felt comfortable letting Thảo go to school alone, without the need to accompany her every day as she did for almost two years before, she began to consider fulfilling her dream of finding a profession to support herself. In reality, she cared little for herself; her main concern was for her aging parents, and most importantly, for Thảo's future - how to ensure that her child would receive a good education and thrive.

Fortunately, there was an accelerated nursing course organized at Chợ Rẫy Hospital, and Thanh hurriedly enrolled. As of now, 'Nurse Thanh' has graduated and has been practicing administering injections for the local community for a few months.

During the time she was learning her profession, poor Thảo, every night after dinner, would often be brought out to play the role of a patient for Thanh's practical training. One night it might be a bandage on the hand, the next night on the forearm, and another night a bandage wrapped around the head. At least, after Thanh graduated and began practicing, Thảo also received a corresponding reward - keeping some soft, pristine white papers found inside a few French medicine boxes to play with.

As part of Thanh's newfound career, every day after dinner, she would ride her bike into the alleys behind her house to visit patients. Usually, when she went out, she brought Thảo along to avoid unwanted attention from young men. However, when going to the homes of patients for injections, she didn't bring her daughter along, fearing exposure to infectious cases.

Today, Thanh went to Uncle Tám's, the mason's, house. After years of hard work, Uncle Tám had managed to save up a bit to build a house with brick walls and a tin roof - an upscale dwelling in a place where most houses were made of mud walls and roofing covered by dried coconut leaves. However, since his tuberculosis worsened, he no longer had the breath to perform strenuous mason work, and the family had fallen into hardship. When his mother was still alive, she looked after the children at home, allowing his wife to sell food on the streets to earn a bit of extra money for rice. Tragically, his mother passed away a few months ago. Now, Aunt Tám, his wife, had taken up making paper bags for a local grocery store. Every afternoon until evening, Aunt Tám and her three children would sit on the ground in front of their house, folding and gluing paper bags. Each completed bag brought in just 2 cents.

Since early morning, Sóc, the 12-year-old eldest son of Aunt Tám, had been wearing a stack of empty cement bags on his head, carrying them to the riverbank to shake off dust. Typically, he had to stand under the scorching sun until noon, raising a cement bag high, letting it float in front of him, while using a stick to beat the bag until it was visually clear of dust. In the process, fine cement dust flew in all directions, scattering in the wind like misty smoke, and before long, white cement powder covered his hair, ears, face, and bare chest. The external dust could be washed away by jumping into the river, but what about the harm caused by the cement accumulating daily inside his two young lungs? It seemed like no one wanted to know, except for Thanh, who often shared her concerns with Thảo.

Thanh had just parked her bike in front of Uncle Tám's house when she heard Aunt Tám's voice.

"Dear Miss Thanh, how are you?" Aunt Tám greeted.

"Welcome, Miss Thanh," echoed the voices of Aunt Tám's children. They were sitting on the dirt, circling around piles of cut-up papers retrieved from cement bags.

Aunt Tám instructed her son, "Sóc, go pour some water to offer Miss Thanh."

"It's alright, Aunt Tám. I've had my meal before coming here," Thanh said, touching Sóc on the shoulder, signaling that he didn't have to stand up.

"How is Uncle Tám doing? Is he feeling better nowadays?" Thanh asked, her inquiry echoing more like a prayer than a casual question, knowing the fate of a patient entering the final stage of this debilitating disease.

"You know, I didn't dare to come and invite you lately. The money we earned is not enough to eat, let alone buy medicine for him. We can't keep bothering you for the medicine all the time; it's not right. My husband is also reluctant to trouble you, so he said, 'Let things be as they may,'" Aunt Tám explained.

"Well, sickness is nobody's fault. Uncle Tám shouldn't worry about troubling me. I'll do what I can. Today, I received some bottles of sample medicines from the pharmacist, so I brought them to administer to Uncle Tám," Thanh replied.

"My family and I are really grateful to you. Not only for the medicine but also for your kindness. We truly don't know how to repay you," Aunt Tám expressed her gratitude.

Thanh stepped around to where Aunt Tám's daughter, Mận, was sitting. Mận is the same age as Thảo but, due to family circumstances, couldn't go to school. She sat beside the cracked bowl of paste in the dim light of a flickering oil lamp nearby on the ground. Holding a piece of dried coconut shell, Mận dipped it into the bowl and then spread the paste onto the edge of each square sheet of paper. Her brother folded and sealed it to make a paper bag. Mận's slender arms repeated the skilled, monotonous motions, resembling the drawing of a dead-end alley in the darkness of the night.

Thanh sighed wearily as she entered the house, ready to administer the medicine to Uncle Tám. On her way back home, she struggled to pedal her bike, burdened by a sinking heart and a melancholic sadness. She felt powerless in the face of the tragedies surrounding her, sympathizing with those in need but lacking the ability to alleviate the heart-wrenching situations unfolding before her.

Even the free medicine samples she obtained from pharmacists, often sold by other nurses for extra income, were used by Thanh to provide free injections for her patients. In some cases, as with another patient, Mr. Năm, she even spent her own money to buy medicine. Mr. Năm's eyes had become severely infected, swollen, and red from inflammation. Fearing he might go blind if left untreated, Thanh purchased vials of antibiotics out of her own pocket and administered them regularly.

Thanh often questioned how much she could truly do for people like Mr. Năm and Uncle Tám, especially given the precarious state of her own family's situation. The worsening health of her father weighed heavily on her, as she constantly worried about the consequences should he face early retirement - or, worse, lose his job altogether. If that were to happen, the entire family's livelihood would rest solely on her shoulders.

Chapter 6: A Chance Encounter

Thanh's growing concern about her father's mental state seemed increasingly justified. Each passing day, he showed more signs of paranoid behavior, even though he managed to maintain a veneer of normalcy at work and with those around him.

That night, Officer Tư stayed up late entertaining a childhood friend from his ancestral village. He was sipping tea and chatting with Mr. Ba, a traditional herbalist from Cai Lậy's countryside, who had just arrived in Saigon that morning.

Flashlight beams flickered suddenly through the row of tall paperbark trees lining the house, followed by a distant command: "Owner, open up! We're soldiers; we're searching the house." As soon as Officer Tư heard the voice, he recognized it as Mrs. Gấu, a former colleague.

Mrs. Gấu had been the first female police officer in the district. "Gấu Người" ("Human Bear") was originally her late husband's nickname, given due to his dark complexion, large frame, and intimidating presence. He had also been a police officer until the resistance force, the Việt Minh, ambushed and killed him during a nighttime patrol in the ramshackle riverside neighborhood behind the station.

Moved by the plight he left behind, a widow with five young children, the French police chief appointed his wife to fill her husband's position. Another reason was that she could speak French, admittedly not much, but still more than the broken "pidgin" her husband had used. On several occasions, the chief heard her speak French and was generous with his praise.

After a year of training, she began daily patrols with Vietnamese and ethnic Cambodian police. Before long, she had earned the respect of her colleagues and inherited her husband's nickname, thus becoming Mrs. Gấu.

Tonight, Mrs. Gấu and her squad were on patrol, checking the homes along both sides of the main road leading to the station. Even though only "people of note" lived on this street, or at least families very familiar to the district police, they still occasionally faced nighttime inspections. Stopping at Officer Tư's gate, Mrs. Gấu pretended to call out loudly:

"Open up! Open up! Soldiers here, for house inspection!"

Officer Tư slowly opened the door and stepped out, looking around as if searching for someone, then asked, "Wait a minute, you said there were soldiers—where are they? I don't see anyone."

Mrs. Gấu cleared her throat, trying to sound authoritative. "They're right here, all around you. How can you not see us?"

Officer Tư locked his gaze on her and said,

"A soldier without a gun? How could that be a soldier?"

Not one to yield, Mrs. Gấu snapped back,

"No gun, you say? Well, how about a bayonet?"

The soldiers burst into hearty laughter. Before moving on to the next house, a young soldier proclaimed, "Looks like you've lost this round, Officer Tư!"

Officer Tư smiled and walked back inside. Glancing around and not seeing Mr. Ba anywhere, he poured himself a cup of tea and sat waiting. He remained puzzled until Mr. Ba reappeared through the back door, soaking wet. It turned out that as soon as he heard commotion out front, he slipped out the back and dove into the pond, hiding underwater.

Mr. Ba was a traditional herbalist, ostensibly in Saigon to gather medicinal ingredients, but in reality he had come to the Bàn Cờ slum to work as a liaison for the anti-French resistance, much like Pig's 'uncles'. If not there, he would head to the shantytown in Khánh Hội. Teachers and traditional healers from the countryside often stayed at Officer Tư's house whenever they came to Saigon on such missions. Although Officer Tư likely suspected his home was being used as a safe house for overnight stays during these liaison activities, he feigned ignorance. Such was the strength of their bond as people from the same hometown. And although he was always on edge whenever they visited, Officer Tư still welcomed them warmly, with genuine kindness.

If Officer Tư harbored any worries or anxiety, he concealed them so well that no one had noticed - until one morning. As Thanh sat down for breakfast, she sensed a change. There was a restlessness about him, his eyes frequently darting towards the dishwashing area in the backyard, a quiet tension etched in his distant gaze. Thanh felt her own unease grow as she picked up on her father's troubled mood. She wanted to ask, but the words wouldn't come. What would she even say? And what if he got upset? Even in their best times, their family wasn't accustomed to opening up about emotions.

When Thanh returned from the market, her father hurriedly intercepted her before she could carry the groceries to the kitchen. He pointed towards the large 250-gallon clay jar, which stored fresh water reserved for family cooking, and instructed Thanh, "Go tell the maid to dump all the water from that jar out."

"Why, Dad?" Thanh asked in confusion. "If we dump that water, what will we use for cooking our rice?"

"Tell the maid to fetch fresh water from the rainwater barrels in the back of the house," replied her father.

"Is this water contaminated or something, Dad?"

"Last night, I saw Mạnh sneak into our house and pour a basin of blood into that jar."

Mạnh, the police officer, replaced Officer Tư on patrol duty at the local market. However, after a brief period of Mạnh overseeing the market, he faced reprimand for extorting vendors. He falsely accused Officer Tư of informing the authorities about his misconduct.

"Why would Officer Mạnh do something like that, Dad?" Thanh inquired.

"Earlier, I had a run-in with him, and he holds a grudge, aiming to frame me with some fabricated trouble," her father explained.

Thanh quickly ran over, opened the lid of the water jar, and took a peek inside. Startled, she asked, "I still see clear water, Dad."

"I asked you to empty that jar; just do it," her father insisted.

Thanh reached for the aluminum can hanging nearby, intending to scoop up some water to double-check. This infuriated her father, and he shouted loudly, "Don't touch it. Stay away. If you guys don't do it, I'll do it."

Upon his sudden outburst, Thanh quickly raised her hand in surrender, saying, "Alright, Dad, let me call Lý to change the water."

Officer Tư, with a sense of hesitation, walked through the house's corridor, passing the row of paperbark trees by the edge of the fish pond. After a moment of contemplation, he hesitated before grabbing the bicycle parked by the side of the house and pedaling out of the gate in a state of dejection.

When he arrived at the "Xít Tê" café, an informal hangout spot for his friends and colleagues, Officer Tư pulled up a chair next to Teacher Hai. Almost at the same time, Sergeant Cừ walked in, dragging over a chair and grinning broadly. Teacher Hai casually remarked:

"Something must be going on today to make Sergeant Cừ look so pleased with himself."

Sergeant Cừ ordered a coffee with milk, leaned back, and burst into laughter.

"I just heard from the ethnic Cambodian soldier's wife about how Mrs. Five speaks 'pidgin' French, and it's so funny I almost died laughing."

He went on to explain how, back when Mrs. Five first started working in the household of a French police chief and his wife, she once ate something, nobody knew what, that gave her a terrible stomachache. The problem was that the indoor toilet was always locked because the homeowners didn't want the help using it. Whenever they needed someone to clean the toilet, the chief's wife would hand over the key. Poor Mrs. Five was in such dire straits that she didn't have time to run to the public toilets. Panicking, she rushed over to beg the chief's wife for the key:

"Madame, Madame, donnez-moi the 'lặc-lìa-lặc-lọi' so I can go 'tủm tủm xà xà!'"

Here, "donnez-moi" means "Please give me." The French word for "key" is "la clé", but in her moment of urgency, Mrs. Năm only vaguely recalled the sounds and ended up calling it "lặc lìa lặc lọi." And since she hadn't learned the French words for "go to the toilet," she improvised the onomatopoeic phrase "đi tủm tủm xà xà." She even spiced things up with animated gestures that made her intent unmistakable to any French onlooker. Truly a universal sign language in action.

Sergeant Cừ hadn't even finished laughing when a boy named Đực suddenly appeared and whispered something in his ear. Đực was only twelve years old, yet he spent his days hauling a large thermos around the neighborhood, selling ice cream.

Sergeant Cừ had convinced him to act as an informant, occasionally giving him a few coins in return.

This time, Đực brought news about Mr. Hai - Sergeant Cừ's biological father. After Sergeant Cừ's mother passed away, Mr. Hai lived alone in a small thatched hut he had built himself, sharing it with a young woman he considered his "second wife." She had been an orphan from an early age, making a living by getting 'bánh men' (yeast-based pastries) from a wholesaler and selling them door-to-door.

Upon hearing Đực's report about his father, Sergeant Cừ's face went cold as stone, and anger flared in his eyes. Though he remained physically present, his mind seemed elsewhere. Suddenly, he buried his face in his hands, weaving his fingers into the thick hair above his forehead before slicking it back toward his nape. He repeated this motion several times, then sprang to his feet and stormed off.

Observing Sergeant Cừ's behavior, Officer Tư grew uneasy. Although he hadn't known him long, he had noticed on more than one occasion that Sergeant Cừ displayed this same hair-smoothing gesture just before torturing a prisoner. Then Officer Tư recalled Sergeant Cừ's short, thick thumb - what he believed to be a killer's thumb. At that thought, a chill ran through Officer Tư, raising goosebumps across both arms despite the scorching sun outside.

Officer Tư's intuition proved correct, but this time Sergeant Cừ was even more brutal. After rushing to his father's dwelling, he grabbed a wooden boat oar and struck him on the head until he died. Then he took the hammock rope, tied it above his father's ankles, and dragged the corpse through the muddy fields in the pouring rain to a duck-guarding shack in the middle of the paddies. He stuffed the body into a water jar out front, then let it roll into the canal to hide the evidence.

Heaven does not tolerate wrongdoing. While out fishing, Ổi happened to seek shelter from the downpour in that same shack and witnessed everything Sergeant Cừ did. When Ổi got home and told his father, the man forbade him from mentioning a word of it to anyone. People often say "silence is golden," but in this case, it was to keep him alive. Sergeant Cừ had murdered his own father to win favor with the French boss, after repeatedly trying, and failing, to stop Mr. Hai from meeting his older brother, who was fighting with the Việt Minh resistance force against the French.

A few days later, when the water receded, someone spotted the water jar down in the canal and discovered Mr. Hai's body inside. Sergeant Cừ then falsely accused Ms. Tư, his father's lover. Sergeant Cừ even boasted that, to torture Ms. Tư, he didn't need to beat her at all. Each day, he simply stripped off all her clothing and forced her to stand pinned against the wall, while he passed judgment on one part of her body or another. In addition, he placed a nest of fire ants at her feet and poured sugar water onto her private areas. By the second day, she had no choice but to sign a confession.

The relentless cruelty surrounding Officer Tư exacerbated his anxiety and fear for his family's safety, particularly for his son who had joined the anti-French resistance. His mental state seemed to deteriorate further each day. One morning, as sparrows chirped energetically from the branches of the paperbark trees Officer Tư had planted when the family first settled here, Thanh stood by the water basin, preparing for her daily routine of brushing her teeth and washing her face. Though still groggy, she couldn't help but notice something unusual: her father standing silently nearby, his eyes fixed on the top of one of the slender, towering trees.

Wiping her face, Thanh inquired, "What are you doing, Dad?"

Mr. Tư remained silent, taking a step closer to Thanh, his eyes still locked on the tree's apex. He whispered his command, "Go see the handyman 'Bảy', and ask him to cut down all these trees."

Puzzled, Thanh furrowed her brows, concerned about her father's recent peculiar behavior. This row of trees was nurtured by him, with eager anticipation for the day it would cast shade along the corridor beside the house.

The front door of Thanh's house seldom saw use; family members and visitors alike walked straight from the corridor to the side door, sheltered by the paperbark trees. Officer Tư would daily set up a reclining chair on the walkway, engrossed in reading the newspaper or contemplating poetry. Passersby, if inclined, would be familiar with Cung Oán Ngâm Khúc or Chinh Phụ Ngâm, the Vietnamese classic poems he recited loudly each day. If not reading poetry, he would engage in a game of chess. The chessboard, always prepared for battle, rested on a small table between the two middle trees.

These trees had become integral to his daily world. So, why the sudden decision to cut them down? Moreover, every evening he eagerly awaited the return of the sparrow flock to their nests, relishing the lively chirping on the branches. While some in the house disliked the early morning bird chorus, Officer Tư found joy in waking up to their cheerful melody. The more Thanh pondered it, the more perplexed she became.

Officer Tư, upon returning from his coffee break, inquired, "Why haven't you cut down the trees yet?"

Attempting to subtly dissuade her father, Thanh responded, "I thought you enjoyed bringing the reclining chair under this row of paperbark trees to read the newspaper in the afternoon?"

"From now on, I'll sit in the hallway in front of the house. It's quieter there."

"What are you talking about? You never liked sitting right in front of our house, facing passers-by on the street. There's more privacy on the side of the house, and there's also a cool spot for you to play chess."

Officer Tu didn't reply; he bowed his head sadly. Ignoring Thanh, he let his gaze wander toward the top of a tree, his distant eyes conveying thoughts to a faraway place. Then, he silently entered the house. The next morning, as Thanh brushed her teeth, he approached and whispered, "Today, you must cut down this row of trees."

"I thought you had changed your mind."

"Last night, I saw them gathering again."

"Who are you talking about?"

"Those guys killed by the police. They gathered here, planning revenge."

"Where did you see them?"

"They're hiding on the top of these trees."

Feeling a sense of dread, Thanh asked, for the sake of asking,

"The tree branches are so tiny; how can they hide up there?"

A profound sadness overwhelmed Thanh; she had no more doubts. Her father's mental state had deteriorated drastically. There was no time to wait; she had to act now - finding immediate treatment for him. But... how to convince someone who could no longer distinguish between reality and illusion that they were living in a world that is not real? And how to handle the stigma associated with mental illness in society? Numerous unanswered questions besieged her. Exhausted, Thanh slumped into the chair beside the dining table.

Mrs. Tu returned from the market, and before she could put the basket down, little Thảo clung to her, asking if Grandma had bought rice cakes for her to eat. The scene was so familiar on other days, but today it stirred worries in Thanh. She wondered how the family's situation would turn out if her father were suddenly fired from his job. Being a civil servant, he normally could rely on a pension and 'Rappel' (retirement and pension benefits) to maintain a stable life in old age. But what if he were fired or forced to retire early? Thanh was troubled by negative thoughts when a maid, the one who cleaned and rolled up the mat on Mr. Tư's bed every morning, hurriedly approached and whispered in her ear: "Miss Thanh, why does Mr. Tư have a machete under his pillow?"

Thanh's face turned pale. The situation was becoming more critical than she had thought. Thanh began to worry about the safety of the household members. She quietly advised the maid: "From now on, every night before going to bed, remember to hide all the knives in the kitchen."

"Where should I hide them?"

"After washing the dishes each night, gather all the knives and place them in a basket, then hide them under your bed. Only take them out to use the next morning."

Thanh then approached her father for an investigation, "This morning, the maid found a machete on your bed. Did you whittle the fishing rod yesterday and forget it there, Dad?"

Officer Tư, lost in a distant gaze, murmured to himself, "Tonight, they'll come back, and I'll kill them all."

"Who, Dad?" Thanh hesitated to ask, but in her heart, she already knew the answer. They were just imaginary enemies in her father's troubled mind. Officer Tư turned away and walked off, as if he hadn't heard the question or didn't want to answer.

All night long, Thanh lay awake, trying to figure out how to help her father. Her family had only recently moved to Plum Tree Hamlet and hadn't formed many connections yet. She thought about her father's old friends and acquaintances, but since her family had moved to this remote place, they hardly had any opportunity to see them again. As for his colleagues at the Reed Field station, some were good and some were bad, and she wasn't sure whom she could trust. In the end, Thanh decided that, in order to keep this matter absolutely secret from the staff at the Reed Field station, she would have to seek help from Officer Tư's former friends at the Xây-nho station.

Thanh quickly thought of Mỹ Lệ. Even though she had relocated from the police compound after her father's passing, she continued to stay in touch with some old acquaintances. The following morning, Thanh braved a nearly six-kilometer bike ride under the scorching sun to reach her friend's house.

After Thanh shared the entire situation, Mỹ Lệ fell into silent contemplation, brainstorming ways to assist. Suddenly, she asked, "Do you still remember Uncle Năm Hoan and Uncle Tư Cổn?"

"Yes, I remember them. Those young uncles used to drink with our dads."

"Yeah, we call them 'uncle' because they're friends of our fathers. Actually, they're not much older than us. They started working early, just right after they finished Brevet (First Level Secondary School Certificate)."

"I know. They were just four grades above us... But, why did you bring them up?"

"I heard they got promoted quickly because they were trained and developed through the French system. Unlike our fathers who could go so far in their career, because they spoke only broken French."

"Where are they now?" Thanh eagerly asked.

"These two uncles now work at the Central Police Station. Uncle Năm Hoan seems to be the head of the personnel department, and as for Uncle Tư Cổn, I'm not sure; he seems to be involved with the 'secret police' unit. I wonder if they can be of any help."

"Thanks, at least they know my dad. Let me check them out."

Thanh parted ways with Mỹ Lệ without any specific plan. These two 'uncles' weren't close family friends whom she could ask for advice on her father's situation. However, to avoid letting people at the Reed Field police station know, fearing the impact on her father's job, Thanh thought she should at least meet Uncle Năm Hoan first. He worked in the personnel department, so he might be able to offer a solution, she thought. As for Uncle Tư Cổn, who worked in the 'secret police' unit, the mere thought of it sent shivers down Thanh's spine. The next day, Thanh rode her bike to the Central Police Station, intending to find Uncle Năm Hoan. However, he was away on a business trip. Thanh had no choice but to find her way to visit Uncle Tư Cổn. As the daughter of a police officer, she had no problem finding someone who could direct her to Tư Cổn's office.

Standing nervously outside the office door, Thanh initiated the conversation:

"Excuse me, Uncle Tư, I am the daughter of Mr. Tư formely from the Xây-nho police station."

Tư Cổn, after a moment of squinting, recognized Thanh. He used to notice 'little Thanh' since the day he came to her house to have occasional drinks with her father and eagerly seized the opportunity.

"Oh, you're Thanh, right? My, just call me 'brother.' It sounds better."

Tư Cổn wrapped his arm around Thanh's shoulder, guiding her to a guest chair, then pulled his chair to sit across from her. He chuckled, showing all of his teeth, and asked, 'Did you come to visit me?'

"Yes, I had the chance to return to the Xây-nho station to visit Mỹ Lệ, Uncle Sáu's daughter, and I heard from her that 'uncle' work here."

"Don't call me 'uncle,' call me 'brother,'" Tư Cổn insisted.

Since entering his office, Thanh had already endured Tư Cổn's unwarranted shoulder hug, and now she had to tolerate his inappropriate words. His demeanor and language offended her deeply, but she endeavored to remain composed while seeking assistance for her father. Yet, her instincts warned her that someone like him thrived on exploiting others rather than offering genuine help. Furthermore, noting his current job title as displayed on his desk, Deputy Chief of the Central Bureau of Intelligence, Thanh felt an even stronger urge to maintain a safe distance. 'Predators like him will seize any sign of weakness,' she thought, swiftly avoiding divulging the real reason for her visit.

"My father is approaching retirement age, so I wanted to inquire about pension matters from Uncle Năm Hoan. Unfortunately, he's on a business trip today, so I took the opportunity to visit you."

Tư Cổn slyly placed his hand on Thanh's thigh.

"That's great! Let me take you to Brodard for ice cream, and then we can chat more."

Thanh promptly stood up, taking a step toward the door, suppressing the indignation in her heart to respond calmly, "Thank you, but I have to go home. My father is waiting." Tư Cổn was taken aback by Thanh's determined attitude. Before he could resort to other tactics, Thanh had already reached the door. He looked after her with regret. Instinctively, he briefly considered using force, but the thought of Năm Hoan and the connection with Thanh's father made him refrain from any violent action. He could only sit there, regretting and watching his prey slip away.

On the way back home, Thanh reproached herself for not being as cautious as she should have been, lowering her head against the rain and pedaling her bike as fast as her small legs allowed. It was a visible attempt to channel her anger into battling the elements. Even the heavens seemed to agree, unleashing a downpour like a waterfall. Undeterred, Thanh persisted in challenging the forces of nature. Grinding her teeth under her palm-leaf conical hat, which shielded her from complete soaking, Thanh pedaled recklessly, flying through the wind, cutting through the rain. Approaching an intersection simultaneously with a white Peugeot, she was fortunate to encounter a slow-moving vehicle, avoiding a direct collision. However, the bike's rear was lightly brushed, causing Thanh to fall onto the wet pavement, with her limbs scraped.

Trường, a young owner of the car sitting in the back, hurried to help Thanh up, unexpectedly facing her fierce reaction. As Trường knelt behind Thanh, she shouted, "Get away!" and swung her arm, knocking him onto the road. His once bright white suit was now soaked with rainwater and mud. Surprisingly, Trường didn't get angry but was captivated by Thanh's radiant face, her eyes expressing more determination and sensitivity than anger or hatred.

Trường tried to express concern, but with a more cautious attitude:

"Please allow me to take you to the hospital."

Awkwardly standing up, feeling a sharp pain in her knee, Thanh collapsed into Trường's waiting arms. Trường guided Thanh to sit at the back of the car, instructing the driver to take her to Grall, a high-end hospital built for French citizens during the colonial years.

Trường's warm voice and caring demeanor made Thanh feel safer. "What about my bike?" Thanh reminded.

"Don't worry, the bike is in the trunk; the driver will take it for repairs later."

"Thank you," Thanh said, touching her knee apologetically, "I'm sorry for being impolite earlier." Hearing Thanh suddenly soften her tone and address him as 'anh' (older brother), Trường smiled and introduced himself:

"I'm Trường. May I know your name?"

"Yes, my name is Thanh."

A moment of silence enveloped them, each person lost in their own thoughts. Thanh began to feel uneasy sharing a ride with a stranger. A comparison between Trường and 'Uncle Tư Cồn' suddenly occurred to her. One side had made Thanh cautious from the very moment of their greeting, while the other had the potential to dismantle Thanh's defensive instincts.

Trường broke the silence, expressing his regret, "I'm sorry, Thanh. The driver tried his best but couldn't avoid it, leaving you in this situation."

"No, it's my fault for rushing headlong without paying attention to the road."

"As long as you're safe, that's what matters. Do you feel better now?"

Thanh rubbed her injured knee, tried to stretch her leg, then nodded and said, "The knee doesn't hurt anymore. Maybe you can just fix the bike, and I can ride it home."

Trường advised Thanh to let the nurse take care of the scratches on her hands and arms to avoid infection. Although Thanh was haunted by the risk of Tetanus infection (causing lockjaw) that apparently led to the death of her biological mother, her greater concern was that if something happened to her, there would be no one to take care of her elderly parents and the daughter of her late sister.

Thanh hesitated but eventually agreed to accompany Trường to the hospital. She whispered anxiously:

"I hope the doctor will examine me quickly; my father is waiting at home."

Trường reassured her, "I'll take you back. Where do you live?"

"Near Reed Field Police Station, but I wouldn't want to trouble you."

"Oh, that far? And you pedaled your bike all the way here? Don't worry; I'll take you home. I'd like to visit your part of town anyway."

"It's a suburban area, half rural, half urban. There's not much to see."

"Actually, I've been away from Vietnam for six years and just returned a few weeks ago. While away, I missed it a lot, and upon my return, I felt restless, wanting to revisit the familiar places. As for new places like Reed Field District, I haven't had the chance to visit it before; I would really like to explore it now."

"Apparently, you went abroad for studying, so are you an engineer or a doctor?"

"Yes, I did study in France, but why do you assume my profession could be as such?"

"Well, I've heard that wealthy people send their children to study in France hoping they will become engineers or doctors. Of course, there are also those who, after being away from home, become carefree, abandon their studies, and bring back a foreign wife."

"Why didn't you consider me part of the third category then?"

Thanh looked embarrassed, glancing through the glass window. The raindrops had become sparse. Trường intended not to delve further into his personal life, as he was unsure about the future, but found Thanh's comments intriguing. Hesitatingly, he said:

"In addition, there is a fourth category you didn't mention."

Thanh responded, "I just casually made a general remark; I don't know anything about those categories."

"Back in France, I befriended an older fellow who had graduated as an engineer. After returning home, I visited him, and... you know what he is doing now."

"Probably working for the government or teaching, right?"

Trường nodded again, appreciating Thanh's response.

"You know, you always have interesting observations, or at least thoughts that make people ponder."

"If you think I sound rustic, just say it; I don't know much about your world."

"But, I genuinely think so. Your observations indicate that in our society, people study to either pursue positions in government or become educators. And that's just what it was throughout our history. People would try to pass a national exam to be a mandarin; if that didn't work out, they'd return home to be a teacher, still commanding some respect from society. Today is no different. Students studying abroad return home with a degree, regardless of their field of specialty, just to aim for positions like deputy director or department head in the government. Otherwise, they follow the teaching path to become 'professors', which is also held in high esteem. It's a cycle of one generation teaching the next, without ever applying what they know for any practical applications that could help develop the country."

"So, is your friend in a government position or teaching?"

"No, he manages the family's coal and rice depot. Unfortunately, he often endures public mockery, being called the 'Engineer who sells coal.'"

"It seems like a waste of education, doesn't it?"

"Indeed, he couldn't apply his technical learning effectively. However, he might be contributing to society in a vital way, fostering the development of commerce and industry, aligned with the principles of the Duy Tân Reform Movement."

"National affairs can be overwhelming for me; I struggle to manage my own home. But you've sparked my curiosity; I'm interested in knowing the path you've chosen in serving the country."

"Currently, I don't fit into any of the categories you mentioned, and the future is uncertain." Trường hesitated, reluctant to divulge too much about his personal life, but he continued: "I studied engineering and have graduated, but I hesitate to call myself an engineer because I've never practiced the profession, except for a brief period as an intern at a French water pump manufacturer."

"You're too modest. I know of a friend of an uncle who falls into the third category, marrying a French wife and claiming to be an engineer. However, according to his colleagues, he only graduated as a technician."

Trường smiled, reflecting on the circumstances of the people and the country, a place where the light of modern science and technology had yet to reach every corner. He had graduated in Agricultural Engineering, but he refused to let his father pull strings to secure him a Director General position at the Ministry of Economy. He had chosen 'agriculture' out of an idealistic desire to serve his homeland, not to perpetuate a bureaucratic system.

From a young age, Trường had admired the revolutionary views of scholar Phan Châu Trinh, which were partly influenced by the role of Japanese merchants in building their own nation. Phan Châu Trinh was the proponent of the Duy Tân (modernization) movement, advocating the principle of "expanding people's knowledge, invigorating their spirit, and enhancing their livelihood." The last principle, as he understood it, meant that in the country's situation, there needed to be a focus on developing business to ensure that people's basic needs - enough food and appropriate clothing - were met.

"We've reached our destination, and the rain has finally ceased," Thanh's voice interrupted Trường's reflections.

The car came to a stop under a canopy of tamarind trees. Trường attentively guided Thanh to the medical examination room, observing each careful step she took on the damp asphalt. Above them, fresh green tamarind leaves, still glistening with raindrops, gracefully allowed a few sunbeams to playfully dance on Thanh's shoulders and the hair of the two wanderers.

After leaving the hospital, Trường suggested taking Thanh home, but she declined, wishing to avoid arousing more suspicion from her father about the reasons for being away from home all day. Besides, she was also reluctant to have Trường meet her father in his current state of mind.

While cycling home, an unbidden smile graced Thanh's face. Memories of her engaging conversations with Trường flooded her mind, vividly portraying his free-spirited charm as a refined gentleman. She replayed the touching yet slightly awkward moments when she felt his caring attention. Their brief, unexpected encounter amid the pouring rain felt like a magical event, leaving the sky aglow with warmth in Thanh's heart.

As she pedaled along, attempting to elongate the joyous moments with each revolution of the bike wheels, groundless worries began to insidiously seep into her soul. These unfounded concerns cast threatening clouds on the horizon, representing an accumulation of persistent unrest that had shadowed Thanh throughout her formative years.

Upon arriving home, Thanh was met with her father's distant and mysterious gaze, again casting a shadow over the flickering rays of spring in her heart, replaced by the swirling dark clouds of reality. That night, in the encompassing darkness, Thanh lay awake, contemplating whether to return to the 'Central' Police Station the next day to seek out Uncle Năm Hoan. Despite the fear instilled by her encounter with Tư Cồn earlier, Thanh's woman's intuition offered a sense of reassurance regarding Năm Hoan. Despite her optimistic thoughts, finding comfort and courage through self-convincing proved to be a struggle as she yearned for a peaceful night's sleep.

Fortunately, as Thanh had anticipated, Năm Hoan harbored fond memories of the good old days shared with Officer Tư and was willing to extend a helping hand. He personally drove the department's Jeep to Thanh's house, feigning an invitation for Officer Tư to join him for a drink. However, Năm Hoan had a different agenda; he headed straight to Chợ Quán Hospital and urgently advised Officer Tư to be admitted for treatment. After numerous persuasions, Officer Tư reluctantly agreed to undergo the "electric shock" treatment, involving the passage of a hundred volts through his temples.

From that point onward, Thanh dedicated herself to visiting and caring for her father daily. Aware that the "electric shock" treatment induced a "feverish" feeling, Thanh concocted watercress and lettuce soup to "cool down the temperature." Understanding that this procedure could weaken patients, she diligently prepared dishes rich in meat and eggs to provide nourishment for her father. The journey to the hospital involved crossing three imposing iron bridges, a challenge even for young men on bikes. Undeterred, every noon, carrying a basket of rice and chicken, Thanh persisted in cycling up those daunting bridge slopes to deliver food to her father.

No external force compelled her to endure the painstaking effort of pedaling up those stiff slopes; she could have walked her bike to the top of the bridge instead. However, she chose to undertake the challenge as an expression of gratitude to the divine, the Buddha, and her ancestors. Thanh fervently hoped that their watchful eyes would protect her father and aid in his swift recovery from the harrowing ordeal.

Chapter 7: The Upheaval

The desperate attempt by war-weakened France to hold on to its colony in Indochina after the Second World War had proven futile. Their negotiated withdrawal from Vietnam left behind a fractured nation, torn by deadly animosity between North and South, and marked by the unprecedented mass migration of people from one region to another. Officer Tư and his family, like so many of their compatriots in the South, were left to endure the turmoil that followed in the wake of that historic upheaval.

It all began in May of 1954, when the French faced a devastating defeat at the Battle of Điện Biên Phủ. Even weeks later, Sergeant Cừ couldn't eat or sleep soundly, his mind consumed with anxiety. He kept wondering what would happen to him if France chose to withdraw its troops from Vietnam.

That morning, looking utterly dejected, he bicycled to the Xít Tê café to glean whatever street news he could about the ongoing negotiations, among three or four factions he wasn't quite sure. Several major powers were meeting at the Geneva Conference in Switzerland, seeking a resolution to end the Indochina War.

The moment he spotted Teacher Hai, without even offering a greeting, he asked,

"Any new developments, Teacher?"

"I've heard it's still in the negotiation phase," the teacher replied.

"Do you think the French will pull out of Vietnam?"

"If they wanted to wash their hands of us entirely, they wouldn't be proposing a division of the country to salvage the South. In principle, the South would belong to the State of Vietnam, independent under the leadership of Chief of State Bảo Đại, but in reality, there'd still be elements of the French Union framework involved."

"Does King Bảo Đại agree to that?"

"What king would want to see his own country split in half? But you have to feel for him. Given the current circumstances, it's like the major powers decide where to put him, and that's where he has to sit."

"How do they plan to divide it, Teacher?"

"Rumor has it they're still negotiating, with all sides haggling back and forth."

"So, the dividing line between the two regions hasn't been decided yet?"

"Not yet, from what I hear, but each side seems to have presented its own position."

"Do you think the French will make concessions?"

"Whether they want to or not, they'll have to. France has been essentially bankrupt since World War II and hasn't been able to recover. Even though they've received post-war development aid from the United States, they've spent most of it trying to shore up their colonial power in places like Africa and Indochina. So now, it's as if France has no significant cards left to play in these negotiations."

"Well, I wonder where all this is headed," he mused.

"As of today, I've heard rumors that the French are suggesting the 18th parallel as the dividing line between North and South Vietnam. Meanwhile, the Chinese propose moving it slightly south to the 16th parallel, possibly to claim the imperial capital, Huế. Those Sons of Heaven - you know how they are. And the

117

Việt Minh? It seems they're quietly pushing to extend the boundary even further south, to the 13th or 14th parallel, probably to take control of Đà Nẵng and Hội An as well."

Two days later, everything was finalized. On July 21, 1954, the Geneva Armistice Agreement was officially announced in Geneva, Switzerland. This marked the formal end of French colonial rule in Indochina. The agreement established the 17th parallel as a temporary demarcation line, dividing Vietnam into two regions for a two-year period, after which a general election was planned to reunify the country.

However, in reality, this division became long-term, leading to the establishment of two opposing governments: the Democratic Republic of Vietnam in the North and the Republic of Vietnam in the South. Nominally, the difference between the two regimes lay only in the word "Democratic," but in essence, they represented a vast ideological divide: Communism in the North and Capitalism in the South.

The Geneva Agreement also stipulated a 10-month period, starting from the day Vietnam was temporarily divided, during which both governments could safely transfer their troops from various regions to their respective territories. During this time, citizens were also free to move between the two regions.

This provision led to an unprecedented mass migration in Vietnamese history. Millions of people moved from the North to the South, while tens of thousands of soldiers and civilians who had fought against the French under the Việt Minh in the South now "regrouped" to the North.

By this time, Officer Tư had recovered from his illness. Upon hearing the news of the ceasefire, he, like so many others in families across the South, was filled with eager anticipation for the return of loved ones who had left home to join the Việt Minh resistance against the French. Unfortunately, not everyone would see their hopes fulfilled. Most of the young men and women who had departed with fiery determination to win independence for their homeland had either sacrificed their lives in the pursuit of their sacred mission or, if fortunate enough to survive, were now heading north as part of the regrouping process to continue pursuing their ideals.

What had begun as joy and hope for Officer Tư's family - anticipating a reunion with his son Bình - gradually gave way to unease and mounting anxiety. Weeks passed without any word from Bình, Officer Tư's only son. The once-lively household grew quieter; laughter and conversation dwindled. In his sorrow, Officer Tư turned to alcohol for comfort.

Thanh watched her father brooding over his cup of rice liquor, his eyes often distant, staring at nothing or at the bottom of the empty cup. She worried that, if this continued, her father's old illness might resurface.

"I can't just sit at home and wait forever," Thanh thought, resolving to visit the regrouping sites herself to look for her brother. After asking around, she learned of several locations where Southern militia members aligned with the Việt Minh were gathering to await Russian and Polish ships that would transport them to the North. She chose to begin her search at Xuyên Mộc in Bà Rịa, as it was closer to Long Thành, where a relative had reported seeing Bình. Thanh made the journey alone, since Officer Tư was uneasy about venturing into former Việt Minh strongholds, even during the ceasefire.

For the past three days, while preparing for her journey, Thanh couldn't help but think of Tâm, her secret love. She wished she could see him again, though she didn't know why or what she would say if they met. The fleeting thoughts came and went, leaving her with a gentle flutter of lightness.

At the crack of dawn, Thanh boarded a shared taxi to Firewood Hamlet. From there, she walked for nearly half an hour, crossing the Chà Và Bridge until she reached the bus stop that would take her to the Eastern Bus Station. Once at the station, she managed to catch an early coach bound for Long Thành, where she planned to visit Aunt Tư, her mother's cousin. After disembarking from the bus onto the main road, Thanh climbed into a horse-drawn carriage bound for the market area, scanning her surroundings for a house that lingered in her childhood memories. It would be on the right side, painted yellow, with two Java rambutan trees out front, their branches laden with clusters of bright red fruit.

After spending the night, Thanh and Aunt Tư made their way to Xuyên Mộc in search of Bình. Upon arrival, the scene before them was oddly festive: the road stretching from the market to the dock teemed with activity. Groups of soldiers in olive-green uniforms gathered in small clusters, smoking and chatting, while families nearby wept and said their goodbyes to loved ones preparing to regroup before heading North.

Thanh and her aunt spent the entire morning showing two old photographs of Bình to every soldier they encountered, asking if anyone recognized him. Soldier after soldier shook his head, saying they didn't know him. As the hours passed, hunger and discouragement set in, and they were about to abandon their search when Aunt Tư suddenly spotted a familiar couple from her home town. They, too, had been searching for their son, and fortune had smiled on them: they had found him. The couple, now reunited with their son, sat under a coconut tree beside a pond, enjoying lunch with several soldiers in front of another relative's house.

Seeing the new visitors, the host instructed their eldest son to wade into the pond and gather more snails to boil, adding to the three snakehead fish already grilling over the fire. As the meal unfolded, and the rice wine circulated, the soldiers started recounting their experiences in the mountains and jungles, the treacherous terrains they'd crossed and the life-or-death moments they'd survived.

Thanh sensed that, after learning about Bình's case, the soldiers were gently trying to prepare her family for the worst. Their words, though considerate, carried the quiet implication that Bình might have met a tragic end.

Two days later, as Thanh rode the bus back to Saigon, she smiled at the memory of a soldier's extraordinary tale about a "giant python." After a grueling day trekking through the jungle, he and his comrades had stopped to rest on what they assumed was a massive fallen tree. Only later did they realize they had been sitting on the back of a colossal python.

The snake was so massive and ancient that it could no longer slither, its body covered in moss and vines from years of remaining still. But movement wasn't necessary. The soldier described how it would simply open its enormous mouth and suck in its prey with a storm-like force, effortlessly drawing the unfortunate victim into its stomach.

The soldier went on to say that they were fortunate another group arrived in time, recognized the notorious creature, and pulled them to safety. According to him, an even larger python, ten times the size, lurked in the neighboring jungle. Legend had it that this giant snake once swallowed an entire platoon and even managed to consume a French tank whole.

Since Thanh's return, Officer Tư had grown more withdrawn, spending his days in silent contemplation and responding to his wife's attempts at conversation with nothing more than indifferent murmurs.

Determined to continue her search for her brother, Thanh decided to set out again after a week at home. This time, her journey would take her to another regrouping site in Cà Mau, at the southern tip of the country.

Before her departure, Thanh received devastating news: Tâm, her childhood idol, had been ambushed and killed while attempting to return to Saigon just before the ceasefire took effect. The news hit her hard. Though her love for Tâm had always been unspoken, the loss weighed heavily on her heart. Seeking solace in the thought that Tâm had lived a life of bravery and idealism, she resolved to carry on.

On this second journey to search for her brother Bình, Thanh returned to her paternal hometown and sought help from Uncle Sáu, Officer Tư's younger cousin, as a guide. After arriving in Cà Mau and staying at another acquaintance's house, Thanh and Uncle Sáu set out early the next morning. Under the blazing sun, they trekked nearly two hours to reach the ferry station. From there, they boarded a cargo boat traveling along the Cà Mau River, eventually turning south onto the Ông Đốc River. Their journey carried them through the U Minh forest and down to the river's mouth, where a regrouping site lay near the estuary.

Thanh and her uncle took turns seeking information about Bình. Leveraging his local connections, Uncle Sáu located two officials in charge of the soldier registry for the area. Despite spending an entire evening searching, they found several individuals with the same name, but none of the records matched Bình's parental information or hometown. In the end, Thanh and her uncle were left without any definitive answers.

The next day, Thanh and her uncle reluctantly headed to the bus station to return to Cai Lậy. By chance, they struck up a conversation with some soldiers there, and one of them, named Cường, paused when he saw the old photograph Thanh carried. He mentioned that his unit had once included someone from the city who looked just like the man in the photo, though he had known him by another name, "Đức."

Thanh and her uncle discussed the possibility that Bình had changed his name to protect his family. It wasn't uncommon for those involved in the resistance to adopt aliases. Cường's recognition gave them a glimmer of hope that this might be the lead they had been searching for.

When they asked Cường for more information, he explained that he didn't know where "Đức" was now. The last time he saw him, "Đức" had mentioned he might be sent abroad to support revolutionary efforts in Latin America, perhaps even Cuba. Cường recalled "Đức" saying, "My superior thinks my knowledge of French will make learning Spanish easier."

The truth of this claim remained uncertain, but it became an accepted family story, told and retold to maintain Officer Tư's sense of hope and peace. Clinging to the comforting belief that his son was alive and serving the revolution alongside Fidel Castro, Officer Tư found solace and lived out his remaining days in tranquility.

Chapter 8: The Caring Hearts

As the Việt Minh forces in the South regrouped and moved north under the terms of the Geneva Agreement, thirty-six thousand French troops stationed across the North withdrew to the southern side of the 17th parallel. Against this backdrop, Prime Minister Ngô Đình Diệm, representing Emperor Bảo Đại, who was residing in France at the time, established a government in South Vietnam under extraordinarily challenging and complex circumstances.

The main obstacle lay in the fact that, although France had recognized Vietnam's independence, it still temporarily retained control over foreign affairs and national defense in the South. Meanwhile, various political and military factions vied to fill the power vacuum left by the French. Some aligned with France, others gravitated toward the United States, and a royalist faction sought to restore the absolute monarchy of the Nguyễn dynasty. This struggle for dominance sent ripples throughout the region, driving social upheaval even into the most isolated corners of society.

One significant challenge faced by Prime Minister Ngô Đình Diệm's government was a coup attempt orchestrated by Lieutenant General Nguyễn Văn Hinh, the Chief of Staff of the National Army. However, General Hinh's plans ultimately faltered due to a lack of sufficient backing from the French government, despite its covert attempts to establish a pro-French regime in the South.

By July 1954, after reclaiming administrative control from the French, Prime Minister Ngô Đình Diệm formally announced the formation of his government. Amid ongoing political turmoil and armed power struggles, the government soon faced an unprecedented challenge: a mass exodus of people from the

North to the South. With limited resources, it had to manage the reception and resettlement of nearly a million refugees, a migration that starkly highlighted the country's profound and tragic division.

The northern migrants who resettled in the South after their exodus were scattered throughout various regions. In Plum Tree Hamlet, a number of abandoned rice warehouses along the banks of the Reed Field Canal were converted into temporary shelters for the migrants. These warehouses had been left empty as the demand for year-round rice storage had declined, thanks to the increased frequency of transport trucks and buses delivering rice from the western provinces directly into Saigon.

One particular warehouse at the foot of the Distillery Bridge had been crowded with over five hundred migrants for several weeks. The only available convenience was a water fountain just outside the warehouse wall, where residents fetched water for cooking and washing dishes. For bathing, they had to rely on the water from the An Thông Hạ Canal, which flowed right in front of the warehouse.

Fortunately, not long afterward, thanks to the resourcefulness of the priests and the support of the government, the migrants were able to secure a relatively stable livelihood. Many resettled in newly formed Catholic villages, building modest churches with their own hands. Others found their place within long-established local communities.

Although the refugees and the locals shared a common heritage, their integration into Southern life wasn't entirely seamless. Misunderstandings arose, sometimes over something as trivial as differences in accent, and other times over more significant matters, such as religious practices or deeply rooted customs. Yet, throughout these challenges, the deep-seated national sentiment prevailed, helping to bridge divides during these trying times.

An early success story of refugee integration in Plum Tree Hamlet is that of Mr. and Mrs. Cai, who opened a noodle (phở) shop that the neighborhood fondly referred to as "Mrs. Cai's Phở." Despite their success, a minor issue emerged over time. The alley near the phở shop became known locally as "Mrs. Cai's Alley," a name that carried unintended and inappropriate connotations for Northerners - something the Southern residents had never anticipated.

While Southern simplicity can be endearing, it often translates into a casual approach to various aspects of life, including language. Both North and South are home to Vietnamese people, yet distinct geographical and historical influences have shaped notable regional differences. In Hanoi, with its long-standing traditions and polished cultural norms, it's difficult to imagine an alley earning such a nickname. To locals in the South, the Northerners' more polished and reserved way of speaking seemed unfamiliar and overly formal. On the other hand, Southerners prided themselves on their forthrightness, often declaring: "What you see is what you get!"

When it came to cuisine, thanks to Mr. and Mrs. Cai, the residents of Plum Tree Hamlet were introduced to the quintessential Vietnamese dish of phở. Morning, noon, and evening, the enticing aroma of phở would waft through the air, greeting anyone who walked by the shop. Near the cherry tree in front, they would see Mrs. Cai diligently preparing each bowl beside two steaming pots - one for the broth, the other for blanching noodles. Above her hung rows of fresh red beef slices, a mouthwatering sight for all passersby.

For those who couldn't afford to eat phở, the price of each bowl was still well known, thanks to a playful rhyme sung by local children: *"With five piasters in hand, we'll head to Mrs. Cai's."* The tune parodied a popular line from the song Tàu Đêm Năm Cũ by Trúc Phương, which goes:

"As the night fades, I arrive at the station to bid farewell to the soldier heading to the mountains. Holding hands firmly, I etch this moment into today's emotions..."

Thanks to the migrant community, many locals began to take note of the water spinach growing plentifully in the once-neglected ponds and swamps. The daily meals of Plum Tree Hamlet's residents became more diverse, enriched by northern-inspired dishes like tangy, crunchy water spinach salad. On special occasions, they might enjoy a plate of water spinach stir-fried with beef. More often, though, it was something simpler: a bowl of water spinach soup with a touch of lime, sometimes made more flavorful by the addition of a few dried shrimp when supplies permitted.

Northern housewives, on the other hand, initially found themselves overwhelmed by the abundance of food and produce at the Reed Field Market each morning. One soldier who had migrated south often recounted his amazement upon seeing the duck eggs sold behind the market. "My goodness," he said, "the eggs here are enormous! Each egg in the South is nearly twice the size of the ones in the North." Reflecting on the prices, he would click his tongue in astonishment and add, "They're unbelievably cheap. Back in the North, people would only buy one or two eggs at a time, but here in the South, they sell them by the dozen, and sometimes more! A dozen might mean 14 or even 16 eggs. What a treat!"

Over half of the initial refugees who had taken shelter in the warehouses eventually settled in a Catholic hamlet established by the priests along the left bank of the Kinh Đôi canal, directly across from Plum Tree Hamlet. This new community brought employment opportunities and revitalized what had once been a desolate area. Historically, the site had served as a key defensive outpost for the colonial government, intended to block resistance forces attempting to infiltrate Saigon from the western provinces. Even now, remnants of that period lingered: a moss-covered French outpost still stood, its fortress walls surrounded by dense, towering grasses, reeds, and bulrushes that nearly concealed the long-abandoned gun loopholes.

Through their relentless determination and industrious efforts, the migrants gradually transformed this once-neglected wilderness into a thriving residential area. They made use of whatever nature and history, whether by intention or chance, had left them. Rubble bricks from the dismantled walls of the French fortress were repurposed as building materials for foundations, homes, or schools. At the same time, local fishermen harvested fish and shrimp from the rivers and canals, using nets and traps to supply food for their families or to sell for income. Every day, in the morning and again at noon, groups of women dressed in black skirts and Northern-style kerchiefs tied around their heads could be seen walking to market, with baskets of fresh fish and shrimp swinging at their sides.

Wild reeds growing abundantly in the marshlands behind the Catholic hamlet were harvested, split, dried, and woven into mats to sell at the market. Initially, only plain mats were made, but later, patterned mats became available as well.

These northern migrants are often admired by locals for their hard work and determination. Occasionally, they even encounter Samaritans willing to lend a hand, as seen in the case of one mat seller. Instead of taking his mats to the market like others, he carried them on his shoulder and walked through the alleys of Plum Tree Hamlet, calling out to sell them. By chance, Thanh learned that this man was the father of Quyên, one of her "daughter's" classmates. From that moment on, she always bought her mats from him. Twice a year, she would even visit his house to order a fresh batch for her family's four wooden platform beds and two standard beds.

The first time Thanh visited Quyên's home, she was impressed by how diligent Quyên was - after school, she cared for her younger siblings and helped with the cooking. From that point on, Thanh made a habit of giving the family two bolts of fabric each year, enough to sew three sets of black pants and white shirts for Quyên to wear to school. Thoughtfully, Thanh chose the same fabric that Thảo wore, ensuring Quyên wouldn't feel self-conscious about her clothes.

While Thanh's amicable relationship with the northern migrants was not uncommon, it didn't mean that the integration of refugees into local life went entirely smoothly. Although Vietnamese people across the country are fortunate to share a common language and many similar customs, the nation's rugged geography and its historical development through various eras have inevitably led to misunderstandings, sometimes resulting in regional prejudices or, at the very least, unfounded suspicions between the North and the South. Consequently, as large numbers of Northerners migrated to the South, certain social frictions arose. Yet, as the saying goes, "the heart has its own reasons," and this sentiment was evident in the attitudes of the younger generation, who, undeterred by societal barriers, sought to connect with one another.

One such young man was Tuế, the son of Mr. and Mrs. Cai, who ran the phở shop. About thirty years old and still unmarried, he worked as a photographer for the Ministry of Information. Each morning, as he rolled his Mobylette out to the front gate, he would pause for a few minutes to observe the bustling morning scene, still somewhat unfamiliar to him. He found it fascinating. Amidst the lively chatter and shouts of children heading to school with their satchels, he enjoyed watching others stop here and there along the roadside, rummaging through bushes, grass, ditches, or at the base of streetlamp posts to catch crickets.

Along the way, a few civil servants pedaled their bicycles to work, while other men cycled in the opposite direction, heading to the market for coffee. Workers from the Distillery hurried along, lunch tins in hand, their heads bowed as they made their way to their shifts. Among the women strolling leisurely along the roadside with baskets in hand on their way to the market, Tuế couldn't help but glance around for a particular young woman he had once encountered by chance.

That day, as he hastily pushed his bike out of the house, she happened to be walking by in front of the shop, and his front wheel almost brushed her. He came to a sudden stop and quickly apologized. She responded in a serious tone, yet what struck him was the sense of empathy and harmony reflected in her expression, from her eyes to the corners of her mouth.

Never before had he felt such an immediate sense of familiarity and friendliness with someone he'd only just met. After many months of upheaval and uncertainty in his life as a refugee, the unexpected warmth in her demeanor seemed to reignite his hope for this new chapter. It quietly drew him in, leaving him to daydream in broad daylight, yearning for a connection with someone he still barely knew.

Ironically, reality often intruded into his dreams, stirring countless questions. Would his parents accept him marrying a Southern girl? More crucially, did the woman in his dreams share his faith? His hopes lifted momentarily when he recalled seeing Thanh wearing a cross pendant around her neck, until … he realized it held no deeper meaning.

During the blending of Northern and Southern cultures, Southern girls often found themselves captivated by Northern boys' way of speaking, which they described as "clever and charming," a sharp contrast to the straightforward, at times curt, manner of many Southern men. As they grew more drawn to their Northern counterparts, these girls noticed another common trait: many Northern boys were devout Catholics who regularly attended weekend church services. This observation gave rise to a trend among Southern girls - wearing necklaces adorned with cross pendants, hoping to catch the attention of a Northern suitor. Yet for Thanh, as for many other girls, the cross was nothing more than a stylish accessory, a trendy piece of jewelry rather than a symbol of shared faith.

These minor daily misunderstandings among migrants were not unique to Tuế; many others encountered similar situations often attributed to so-called "language barriers." In reality, these were merely slight differences in accents compared to local Southern residents. Nothing illustrated these so-called "language barriers" better than what transpired one afternoon at Mrs. Hai's shop.

In Plum Tree Hamlet, near the Xít Tê café, stood Mrs. Hai's humble store, nestled within a modest thatched house along the road leading to Reed Field Market. It was the sole inheritance her late husband left behind after succumbing to a terminal illness. The family's modest savings, earned during Mr. Hai's career as a machinist, had been entirely depleted by his medical treatments. After his passing, Mrs. Hai had to work tirelessly to scrape together enough money to open a small general store, hoping to support her two children. Her elder child was diligent and eager to learn, while the younger one, carefree and wayward, spent most of his days wandering and playing, becoming a constant source of worry for her.

Mrs. Hai's shop wasn't exactly a restaurant, nor was it a bar, even though eating and drinking took place there every day, twice a day. The first round came in the late morning, when the laborers finished unloading heavy sacks of rice, each weighing hundreds of kilograms, from the boats and stacking them in a nearby warehouse. Exhausted, they usually worked only until midday. After washing up in the river, a few would wander over to Mrs. Hai's shop to drink before heading home.

Later in the afternoon, Mrs. Hai prepared for the second group: workers from the distillery, who rode their bicycles over after their shifts ended. They'd pull up chairs around two low, round wooden tables shaded by the star gooseberry tree.

Poor Mrs. Hai. A widow trying to make ends meet, running a shop selling odds and ends like salt, sugar, and snacks to support her children, she still had to accommodate her daily crowd of drinkers, joining them for a few glasses to keep them company. By dinnertime, her face would be flushed red, her steps unsteady, her feet stumbling over one another.

One day, Uncle Three and Uncle Six, the rice sack porters, arrived a little later than usual because three rice boats had docked simultaneously. After earning a decent sum hauling sacks of rice, they decided to stop by the market to buy roast duck and roast pork, a rare treat for their families. As soon as they sat down at Mrs. Hai's shop, three friends who had arrived earlier insisted they each drink a penalty cup of rice liquor. At Mrs. Hai's, cheap rice liquor was the only alcoholic beverage available.

Uncle Seven, who had been waiting idly, watched Mrs. Hai as she poured her homemade vinegar from a large jar into smaller bottles for sale. Nodding in admiration, he raised his voice, slightly slurred, and declared to his drinking buddies:

"I bet none of you know what sound a hen makes."

Seeing everyone smile but not reply, Uncle Six said:

"Well, hens go 'cluck cluck,' don't they?"

"Nope, that's not it. Let me tell you this story," Uncle Seven interjected. "The other day, there were two hens. One went, 'Cluck, cluck, cluck. Cluck, cluck, cluck - what's that huge clump?' And you know what the other hen said in response?"

Mrs. Hai, as usual, was busy with her work but kept her ears tuned to the men's banter at the table.

"What, is that hen possessed or something, talking like a human?" she quipped.

"Possessed or not, I don't know," Uncle Seven continued, "but the other hen immediately replied, 'Cluck, cluck, cluck - it's a tobacco clump. It's a tobacco clump.'"

Mrs. Hai blushed, this time not from the liquor but because she realized Uncle Seven was teasing her. Busy with her work, she had tucked a large wad of betel quid, 'huge' as ever, into the corner of her mouth, saving it to chew later. The drinking buddies, feeling triumphant, toasted each other with cries of "Cheers, cheers!"

On most days, they were content to drink with just a few gooseberry fruits that Mrs. Hai picked from the tree in front of her shop, paired with a small dish of chili salt. But this time, in high spirits, Uncle Seven ordered some dried squid to nibble on as well.

By chance, a funeral procession happened to pass by on the road. One of the mourners, speaking in a Northern accent, cried out, *"The yellowed leaves stay on the branch; The green leaves fall instead; Oh heavens above!"* Uncle Seven, slightly inebriated, slurred his words as he imitated the accent: *"Why fret over that? As long as there are hens and roosters, there will be more chicks."*

It was unfortunate that people from the same country could be so out of sync with one another, seemingly lacking empathy despite sharing a common language. Uncle Seven wasn't heartless or malicious; he was simply somewhat ignorant and found the Northerners' more poetic way of speaking peculiar. Compounding this divide was the legacy of French colonial "divide and rule" policies, which had entrenched cultural differences between regions.

During the colonial era, the French administration divided Vietnam into three distinct regions, imposing separate governance systems: the South became a French colony, while the North and Central regions operated under French protectorates with differing administrative structures. In addition, there was a deliberate effort to dissolve Vietnam's national identity by merging it with Cambodia and Laos under the control of a French Governor-General of Indochina. This intent became apparent through the movement of Vietnamese people to Laos and Cambodia in search of work, where they established families and left behind generations of descendants.

Inevitably, these policies and migrations led to initial, inadvertent clashes between the people of the two regions. Yet, amid those regrettable misunderstandings, many instances of shared camaraderie and national solidarity among Vietnamese also emerged.

In response to the hardships faced by migrants from the North, numerous organizations, schools, and individuals initiated charitable efforts grounded in the principle of 'Lá lành đùm lá rách' ("*The good leaves protect the torn ones*"). Among them was Principal Hương of Lý Thái Tổ Elementary School, located near the Reed Field Wharf.

He parked his worn Mobylette just outside Thanh's gate, dug into a weathered leather pouch strapped to the back, pulled out a small black notebook, and walked into the yard.

Lý, the housekeeper, was watering some potted plants in front of the house when she spotted him. She quickly went inside to alert Thanh.

"Ms. Thanh, there's someone here to see you," Lý said.

"Who is it? A man or a woman?" Thanh asked, looking up from her work.

"It looks like Principal Hương from the school," Lý replied.

"Please invite him in, ask him to have a seat, and bring him some tea. I'll be there shortly," Thanh instructed.

After Lý left, Thanh quickly organized her papers and rushed out to welcome her visitor.

"Good afternoon, Principal. I'm sorry for the wait. How have you been?" she asked warmly.

"Thanks to Heaven, I'm still managing to run around and look after the children at school. Thank you for asking. And how are you and Mr. and Mrs. Tư?" the principal replied, his voice measured and courteous.

"We're all doing well, thank you. Please, have some tea. With the New Year approaching, I imagine you're busy with the 'Spring Giving Tree'?" Thanh inquired, referring to the annual fundraising event for underprivileged students.

The principal took a careful sip of tea, placed the cup back on the saucer, and hesitated briefly before speaking again. "You're right, Ms. Thanh. The Spring Giving Tree keeps us busy as usual. But... there's something else on my mind, something I was hoping to discuss with you, if you have a moment."

"Yes, of course. If there's anything you need, please let me know. My family is happy to do whatever we can to help the students," Thanh replied sincerely.

"That much we've come to expect from you," the principal said, a note of gratitude in his voice. "You and Mr. and Mrs. Tư have always been extraordinarily generous with your contributions to the school. Because of that, we make a point to acknowledge the noble deeds of your family whenever we can."

He fidgeted slightly, his fingers brushing the edge of his teacup, before continuing with a hesitant tone:

"And it's precisely because of that generosity that I feel uneasy about what I'm about to ask. As you've likely noticed over these past months, thousands of Northern migrants have been temporarily housed in the rice warehouses. Until now, Father

Thế has managed to move more than half of them onto the undeveloped land on the far side of the Kinh Đôi canal."

"Yes, I've seen a few of the women from there passing by recently, bringing fish and shrimp to sell at the market."

In reality, Thanh's kind heart often moved her to help people in need. Not only did she meet these new arrivals, but she also made an effort to understand their struggles so she could lend a hand. Recognizing her compassion, some of them would stop by her home on slower market days, asking her to buy up the leftover fish or shrimp they hadn't been able to sell. At times, if someone faced personal difficulties, such as needing money for a sick family member's medicine, she would give them a bit of extra money.

Just recently, Thanh encountered another of Thảo's classmates, a girl named Xuân, who had been forced to leave school in order to help her parents earn a living. Learning of the family's situation, Thanh visited Xuân's parents and offered to provide clothes, books, and writing supplies so that Xuân could return to school. However, the family still relied on the income Xuân brought in, which was needed for her father's medical care. Thanh suggested a solution: Xuân could work for her a few hours after school, doing simple household chores in exchange for a fair wage. Grateful for this arrangement, Xuân's parents agreed.

Although she called it "odd jobs," Thanh handled the arrangement delicately, mindful that Xuân was in the same class as her "daughter". She carefully chose tasks that wouldn't make Xuân feel uncomfortable, often assigning her to help copy ledgers.

The principal took another sip of tea before continuing. This year, he explained, the need for student assistance was greater than ever. Many of the newly arrived families from the North were still sheltering in the empty warehouses, and their children depended on support from the local community to have a chance at attending school.

Last year, Thanh and her family contributed five "Spring Giving Tree" packages. Three of them included enough notebooks and writing supplies to last an entire school year. The other two contained plain fabric for two sets of black shorts and white shirts, suitable as school uniforms.

Thanh smiled warmly and said,

"Oh, that's no problem at all, Principal. Of course we should help. Let's double it this year—please count on our family for ten gift packages."

"Wonderful, wonderful! Thank you so much, Ms. Thanh, and please also extend my gratitude to Mr. and Mrs. Tu," the principal exclaimed.

He expressed his heartfelt gratitude to Thanh and her parents before heading out. Climbing onto his aging Mobylette, he pedaled away with some effort, bound for his next benefactor. At over sixty, he still braved the scorching sun to secure support for "his kids" at school. It was a poignant reminder that the country needed only peace; caring hearts and helping hands were already in abundance, ready to build and contribute.

Chapter 9: The Forbidden Word

Peace is not easy to secure, especially when political and social turmoil, threatening the South's stability, had been simmering for a long time and was on the verge of boiling over from the start. The South Vietnamese government initially grappled with unrest caused by remnants of paramilitary groups. Among the insurgent factions persisting from the colonial French regime, the Bình Xuyên paramilitary force rose prominently. Exerting substantial influence over the Saigon-Cholon metropolitan area, they controlled ports, long-distance bus stations, numerous entertainment venues, and internationally renowned gambling establishments such as Kim Chung and Đai Thế Giới casinos.

The Bình Xuyên forces had previously formed alliances with both the French and, at different junctures, with the Việt Minh - a Vietnamese organization striving for independence from the French - depending on the shifting dynamics of the conflict to mutually exploit advantages.

Bình Xuyên later formed a coalition with units from the armed forces of the Cao Đài and Hòa Hảo religious sects, exerting pressure on the government to secure broader participation in the new cabinet of Prime Minister Ngô Đình Diệm. Following the government's rejection of this coalition's demands, Bình Xuyên forces initiated military actions, launching attacks on the National Defence Headquarters and the Governor General's Palace, later known as the Independence Palace - the central seat of power for the Republic of Vietnam government.

However, in a decisive three-day operation, the National Army's Paratroopers expelled the Bình Xuyên from the metropolitan area, seizing a key position near Chánh Hưng's pig slaughterhouse and pushing them to the city's outer edge. Saigon's southern flank was naturally defended by the Tẻ Canal, a waterway flowing over four kilometers westward from the Saigon River before merging with the Bến Nghé Canal to form the Đôi Canal, which continued its course southwest toward the Mekong Delta. The Bình Xuyên forces, scattered along both sides of these major canals, were spread from the Khánh Hội area in the east to the Rạch Cát area in the west.

While the majority of the Bình Xuyên forces were compelled to retreat to their concealed hideout in the forest of Rừng Sát, some scattered units remained covertly stationed on both sides of the major southern canals, biding their time for a new opportunity. Four months later, Prime Minister Ngô Đình Diệm assigned Colonel Dương Văn Minh of the Army of the Republic of Vietnam to launch Operation Hòang Diệu, sustaining the pursuit of the Bình Xuyên rebels.

The uncertain and unstable situation in South Vietnam weighed heavily. If the pro-American government succeeded in restoring order, it could destabilize the social standing of the old French-aligned factions, including Trường's family. Anticipating an uncertain future, Trường resolved to leave the country and move to neighboring Cambodia, where his paternal uncle, a long-time hotel owner in Phnom Penh, could provide a valuable connection.

Trường also maintained a friendly relationship with Cambodia's Prince Norodom Sihanouk, a connection that dated back to their shared time at the Collège Chasseloup-Laubat in Saigon. Trường believed the prince, as an honorary reserve officer in the French army who had trained at the esteemed Saumur Cavalry School in France, would likely steer Cambodia closer to France than to the United States.

While Trường was packing for his trip to Phnom Penh, the capital of Cambodia, a radio broadcast from the next room caught his attention. It relayed news of a conflict in Saigon: Bình Xuyên forces had retreated to the Bình An area near Plum Tree

Hamlet, and government troops were preparing to pursue them that very night.

Concerned for Thanh's safety, Trường quickly made his way to Plum Tree Hamlet to offer any assistance he could to Thanh's family. Starting from the First District, he drove along Trần Hưng Đạo Boulevard, but his progress was soon blocked. After passing the Central Police Station, the road ahead was impassable due to fierce clashes between government forces and the remnants of Bình Xuyên, who had stayed behind to defend the Đại Thế Giới casino in Cholon.

Determined to reach Thanh while avoiding the blocked combat zone, Trường parked his car by the roadside and took off on foot, heading south. Navigating through winding alleys, he was surprised to see that these smaller streets were buzzing with activity, a sharp contrast to the deserted boulevard and closed shops along the main roads. Hoping to find a path to the Tàu Hủ canal, which would connect him to the waterways near Thanh's area, Trường stopped to ask locals for directions.

Upon arriving at the canal, Trường discovered an unusual calm. Families that typically anchored their boats along the waterway had been relocated for several days to evade potential danger. Fortunately, his path intersected with a father and son who owned a fishing boat. Through adept negotiation, Trường secured passage on their smaller vessel, albeit at a substantial cost, allowing him to reach the Plum Tree Hamlet.

As the boat gently glided into the An Thông Hạ Canal, nearing the Distillery Bridge, Trường noticed groups of people hurriedly crossing over it, evacuating Plum Tree Hamlet in a continuous stream. Adults and children alike gathered on the grassy area outside the wall of the French distillery. Trường initially assumed they believed they were now safely distant from the war zone and had chosen to pause and seek refuge by the wall. Without the time to confirm, he quickened his pace toward Thanh's house.

Meanwhile Thanh's family, unsure where to find shelter, considered returning to the housing area at the Xây-nho police compound, hoping to encounter acquaintances who could offer a place to stay overnight. However, Trường brought grim news that all major roads had been blocked, making it nearly impossible to reach their intended destination.

Curious about the crowd seeking refuge outside the liquor factory's wall, Trường learned that they believed it to be safer, assuming the Bình Xuyên would avoid attacking a French-owned liquor facility. Rumors circulated that the Bình Xuyên enjoyed French backing, leveraging that influence in their contest against Prime Minister Ngô Đình Diệm's regime, particularly as they vied with the United States.

A realization dawned on Trường. Having previous connections with the Chief Accountant of the liquor factory through banking services, he proposed to Thanh's family that they follow him to seek temporary shelter in the chief accountant's apartment within the distillery compound, ensuring an even safer refuge.

The entire family unanimously agreed to seek refuge, with the exception of Officer Tư, who staunchly insisted on staying behind to guard the house. Using the rationale that he was accustomed to the sounds of bullets and bombs, Officer Tư remained determined to hold his ground. Thanh assumed the responsibility of leading her mother and little Thảo, following Trường towards safety.

He led the family across the Distillery Bridge, stopping in front of two iron gates that were usually guarded by a tall 'Chà Và' soldier, his face largely concealed by a thick beard beneath the black turban wrapped around his head. These Sikh soldiers of Indian origin, celebrated for their valor in the British colonial army, were frequently hired by French companies in Vietnam to serve as "gardiens" (gatekeepers) to protect French-owned properties. Anticipating potential unrest, the distillery had stationed four Sikh guards armed with rifles at the gate.

When Trường arrived at the factory gate, he asked to see Mr. Beausoleil. One of the Sikh guards stepped into the booth and made a phone call. Shortly after, Mr. Beausoleil came out to meet Trường at the entrance. His family lived in a charming row house within the factory compound, and he spoke to Trường in French. Mr. Beausoleil said they could stay the night, but there were only two spare beds, enough for Thanh's family. As a result, Trường accepted sleeping on a camp bed set up on the front porch.

After everyone else had gone to bed, Trường and Thanh lingered on the porch, quietly exchanging thoughts. The earlier rumble of cannon fire, which had continuously echoed from the distant horizon, had faded away. The fiery trails of bullets that had streaked through the sky were now gone, leaving only a blanket of twinkling stars in the calm night. In that stillness, Trường patiently waited for Thanh's response. He had already hinted at marriage twice before, only to be met with her quiet hesitation.

Despite cherishing their friendship, Thanh had never allowed herself to break free from the constraints of duty to her family, which she imposed upon herself. However, on this particular night, Trường seized the opportunity to seek clarity from her before departing Vietnam.

"The state of the country is still so chaotic, don't you think?" Trường inquired.

"Yes, when do you think things will get better?" Thanh responded.

"If I knew the answer, I wouldn't have decided to leave the country. The United States, being a superpower that survived World War II, might be able to help the government and eventually suppress rebels like the Bình Xuyên. But the question remains: What happens next? What will be the outcome of the upcoming general election between the North and the South? Who will emerge victorious, and who will face defeat? And, crucially, whether the losing side adheres to democratic principles and lays down their weapons after the election?"

"The situation is indeed too complicated, isn't it? I don't want us to find ourselves fleeing to the countryside once again to seek refuge from the war."

Trường, understanding the gravity of Thanh's concerns, offered a tactful solution, "Then let my parents come and ask your father for our marriage. After that, we can take your parents and little Thảo to live peacefully in Phnom Penh."

This proposal aimed at safeguarding Thanh's entire family, acknowledging the paramount importance she placed on her familial commitments. Despite Trường's assurance and capability to fulfill his promise, Thanh found herself unable to accept his offer. Memories of the farewell party at Trường's house flashed through her mind. On that occasion, whether intentional or not, Trường had disclosed two suitcases packed with stacks of hundred-piaster bills, along with mentioning his family's extensive investments in the import and export of farm equipment and agricultural products in Phnom Penh, Cambodia.

Suddenly, Trường startled Thanh with his earnest inquiry, "What do you think?"

Moved by the realization of Trường's sacrifices and his consistent efforts to aid her and her family during challenging times, even at the risk of his own life, Thanh expressed her deep emotions, "You know, it touched me so much, the thought that you've sacrificed a lot to help me and my family in difficult times, even when it could endanger your life, like this time. And I really haven't been able to do anything in return..."

Trường interrupted, "This is the biggest obstacle. You're too rational. What I hope for is for you to question yourself: Do you love me? I'm just waiting for that. I'm waiting for the answer from your heart. I never thought of myself as a loan shark demanding repayment."

"I'm sorry. I truly apologize. I misspoke. Although my words were sincere, they may have come out the wrong way," Thanh responded.

Trường, softening his stance, "Actually, the one who should apologize is me, for unreasonably snapping at you."

"No, the fault is mine. I apologize. I often pride myself on my straightforward nature, but in this matter, it seems like I keep avoiding, not daring to face your question. Until recently, I realized that the reason might be that... for me, love and marriage are just one and the same."

"What do you mean? You can't move towards marriage because you haven't loved me?" Trường questioned, deliberately twisting her words to elicit the forbidden word - Love.

Understanding the manipulation, Thanh thought, 'Why is that so difficult for me?' She intimately reached out to hold Trường's hand and said, "You should be a lawyer. Very good with your line of questioning!"

Trường, genuinely perplexed, "Well, I truly don't understand."

Avoiding Trường's expectant gaze, Thanh looked into the distance and whispered, as though to herself, "I can't say I love you when I think I can't move towards marriage. What would people say about a woman who only has a lover and no husband?"

"So that's what it is. Whether near or far, the reason is still because of the duty you feel toward your family that prevents you from thinking of marriage. So what about your own future?"

"My future is Thảo," Thanh replied without hesitation.

Trường nodded gently, "I understand. You willingly sacrifice the intermediate generation."

The apparent casual statement from Thanh, albeit unintentional, helped Trường realize the harsh reality. The love Thanh had for him, even as beautiful as embroidered flowers on silk, could not compare to the two words "bổn phận" (duty) engraved on stone tablets and etched into the hearts of Vietnamese women for generations. Trường raised his head, searching for a confidant beyond the Milky Way, yet found himself lost in the feeling of being adrift amid countless stars.

The next morning, the sky was clear with gentle clouds, bathed in the morning sunlight that gleamed brightly on the extensive cement ground, seemingly endless within the vast compound of the distillery. The crowd of refugees began to leave. The sound of gunfire had ceased. A new era began. Whether it was for good or for bad, who could predict where the winds of change would steer the Vietnam ship.

Chapter 10: The Wind of Change

In the final months of 1954, following the Geneva Accords, French forces withdrew to the south of the 17th Parallel, and by April 1956, they had completely exited Vietnam. During this period, South Vietnam underwent significant political upheavals, culminating in the 1955 referendum that deposed the country's last monarch. Turning the page on feudal history, a new era began with the birth of the Republic of Vietnam.

The newly formed government embarked on various social reforms, focusing on developing an educational system centered on the native language to replace French, which had been extensively used under colonial rule. Equal emphasis was placed on preserving and revitalizing the nation's cultural heritage and values.

Over the past few days, Mrs. Tư, the wife of Officer Tư, had often complained that, on her way to the market each morning, women from the "Campaign Against Illiteracy" would stop her and insist that she read newspaper headlines out loud for them. When she stumbled over the words, they encouraged her to attend their evening classes to learn how to read and write.

That night, after finishing dinner, she took a notebook and pencil from atop the rice jar and settled at the dining table under the yellowish lamp to practice. At the front of the house, Officer Tư sat at the guest table reading the newspaper, keeping up with the government's progress in rebuilding the country, including attempts to reform the education system left behind by the French.

He suddenly remembered that a few days ago, Thanh had whispered to him, "Watching Mom learn to read is hilarious.

She gets some words right, some not. For the words she doesn't know, she studies them for a bit, then just blurts out something." Curious about her progress, he walked behind his wife to see how far she'd come. He noticed the rows of words she was practicing: written again and again were four words: "con tôm, con trp." ("big shrimp, …??").

He asked,

"What are you writing?"

"I'm practicing the words 'con tôm' and 'con tép' ('big shrimp' and 'small shrimp') to get used to them," she replied.

"So, for the word 'con tép' (small shrimp}, why are you always writing '*trp*' instead of '*tép*?"

"Well, isn't it 'r pê ép' which makes 'tờ ép = tép'?"

"Oh dear," he said, exasperated. "It's 'e pê ép', not 'r pê ép'!"

"'E' or 'r,' what's the difference? You're always picking on me!" she grumbled.

After finishing her writing practice, she moved on to reading practice. Officer Tư, having returned to his chair to read the newspaper yet still curious about his wife's progress, listened attentively as she read aloud:

"Nước Việt Nam ta... Nước Việt Nam ta có hai mươi lăm chị đàn bà..." (Our Vietnam... Our Vietnam has twenty-five women...)

Puzzled, he edged closer to see what she was actually reading. It turned out that the text said, "Nước Việt Nam ta có hai mươi lăm triệu đồng bào" ("Our Vietnam has twenty-five million compatriots"). Internally, he nearly burst out laughing, but decided not to "correct" her again. He realized she still couldn't sound out words well and was merely echoing what she remembered the teacher saying. Unfortunately, her teacher happened to be from the North, pronouncing it as "hai mươi lăm *chiệu* đồng bào", leading to a classic "talking at cross purposes" moment.

As soon as the situation in the South stabilized, democratic mechanisms were quickly established, leading to the election of a Constituent Assembly. The first Constitution was drafted and promulgated. Parliamentary elections were held, and the people of Saigon eagerly participated. On a personal level, this period left Thanh with an unforgettable memory of democratic activity.

In the excitement of welcoming a new wave of change, Thanh eagerly followed her two friends, the daughters of Teacher Hòa, to Lý Thái Tổ Primary School, located behind Reed Field Market, to help count ballots after a day of voting. The vote counting lasted until well past midnight. Thanh pleaded with her two friends to escort her home to explain to Officer Tư the reason for her late return. Thanh had accurately predicted her father's reaction, he was standing in the front yard, holding a feather duster, waiting for her. Fortunately, thanks to the presence of her two friends, she avoided an unjust "introductory lesson" on democracy.

To advance social reform, two years after its establishment, the National Assembly passed the Family Protection Law, ensuring women's equal rights and officially abolishing polygamy. While society still had its share of men setting up "second households" here and there, the ones who faced the most trouble were perhaps civil servants who had "made a mistake" and now found themselves awkwardly unsure of how to resolve the situation. As a result, these men weren't particularly fond of the Women's Solidarity Movement, which advocated for gender equality.

Sergeant Cừ was sitting at the Xít Tê coffee shop with a few friends when Officer Tư rode up on his bicycle. Sergeant Cừ widened his eyes and looked Officer Tư up and down before smirking and remarking:

"Wow, Officer Tư, what's with the full suit today? And you're even rocking those 'two-tone duckbill shoes' too."

Mr. Sáu, sitting next to him, nodded knowingly.

"He's been off voting, what else?"

Sergeant Cừ commented nonchalantly:

"I wonder who Officer Tư voted for?"

Officer Tư took a sip of coffee, smiled mysteriously, cast a sideways glance at Sergeant Cừ, and declared:

"Thirty-five."

"Going to vote, but acting like you're playing the lottery, Officer Tư."

Teacher Hai chuckled, as if he'd just understood Officer Tư's remark. Stroking his chin and tilting his head toward the sky, he said:

"Hmm... it's like the lottery but not quite the lottery. People can interpret it however they like. That's quite a clever answer from Officer Tư."

Mr. Sáu frowned in confusion:

"I've heard of candidates with symbols like 'The Plow,' advocating for land reform and giving farmers their own fields, or 'The Book and Lamp,' calling for literacy and the enlightenment of the people, as well as 'The Lightbulb,' symbolizing national liberation and bringing the light of progress to our country. But I've never heard of a symbol like 'Thirty-five.'"

Teacher Hai nodded.

"You guys don't realize it. Officer Tư is very shrewd. Let me ask you: according to the numbers game (*số đề*), what does '35' stand for?"

Mr. Tư quickly replied,

"Well, '35' is the goat, but what does that have to do with the election?"

"Exactly, there is a connection, that's the point. Let me ask you another question: which candidate supports the Vietnamese Women's Solidarity Movement?"

Mr. Tư slammed the table and burst out laughing.

"Aha, so it's the lady candidate Nguyễn Thị Hồng, with the emblem showing three women in light-blue long dress. Their slogan is... hmm, what is it again?"

Teacher Hai supplied the answer,

"Mrs. Hồng is part of the Women's Solidarity Movement. The motto for their women is: 'Get to know one another, learn from one another, encourage one another, and elevate each other's knowledge.'"

Sergeant Cừ shook his head in admiration at Officer Tư.

"So it's '35,' the shaggy goat. Looks like you're voting for Mrs. Hồng, huh? Man, you really know how to woo the ladies."

He took another sip of coffee and declared, "Alright, I give up," before turning to the shop owner and saying, "Hey, Sáu, put today's coffee on my tab, would you?" The civil servants who frequented this café often ran a tab, enjoying their coffee now and paying at the end of the month when their salaries arrived. With that, Sergeant Cừ bid farewell to the group, promising to revisit the debate another time.

The winds of change had instilled a renewed sense of confidence in the southerners, including Officer Tư, who now felt reassured and inspired to hold a grand commemoration for "Ông" (a term of respect for a notable figure). Thanh's family maintained a tradition of observing two major ancestral death anniversaries each year: one shortly after Tết (Lunar New Year) for her paternal grandfather and another in June for her grandmother. Alongside these, they also held an equally elaborate ceremony in honor of "Ông."

Everyone in Plum Tree Hamlet knew of "Ông," a military officer who had accompanied Lord Nguyễn on his retreat to the south but tragically died in battle and was later deified. His deification decree was brought to a shrine erected on an islet in the middle of the Kinh Đôi canal. While few remembered his actual name, the fame of the shrine extended far and wide.

Twice a year, during Tết and the anniversary of "Ông," crowds flocked to Plum Tree Hamlet, taking ferries to the shrine to pay their respects. Even during the French colonial era, the authorities permitted the annual commemoration of "Ông" to take place on the police station grounds. Though this gesture may have served political or manipulative purposes, the event was grandly organized with full ceremonial traditions. The morning began with a procession of *Ông*'s deification decree, followed by midday offerings of meat and sticky rice at an altar temporarily set up in the district fire station. In the evening, a stage was erected for *hát bội* (classical Vietnamese opera) performances, featuring three full-length plays that lasted throughout the night.

In Officer Tư's household, everyone was bustling around, preparing for the private commemoration of "Ông." Ba Su had just finished spreading a patterned mat on the plank bed in the front room when Thanh called out:

"Ba Su, Mrs. Sáu is almost out of beer. Run to the Xít Tê shop and buy two bottles for her."

Ba Su lingered for a moment to finish setting up two more mats on the other platforms in the back room before heading out. Thanh called after him:

"Make sure to get two '33' bottles with the pineapple logo! Mrs. Sáu is picky; she won't drink just any kind of beer."

For the past few years, Thanh had made a habit of "inviting" Mrs. Sáu to take charge of preparing the boneless duck dish for family feasts. Mrs. Sáu's home was in Bình Tiên, three bridges away from Plum Tree Hamlet. Even walking briskly, it would take nearly an hour to get there, but her renowned culinary skills had reached Thanh's ears.

While cooking, Mrs. Sáu needed a drink or two to keep the energy flowing, or to entertain the kitchen spirits, as she often put it. This time, upon arriving at Thanh's house, she noticed an unfamiliar face and asked:

"Who's this Ba Su kid? I've never seen him before."

"That's my nephew from the countryside. My father brought him here a few months ago," Thanh explained. Mrs. Sáu was still curious:

"Is his name really 'Ba Su'? That sounds so strange."

The whole house burst into laughter. Mrs. Quản Tư clarified,

"His name is Phúc, Mrs. Sáu. The kids in the house tease him for being so meek and gave him that ridiculous nickname."

Mrs. Bảy, a neighbor who was chopping garlic and chili nearby, couldn't hold back her laughter and felt the need to chime in with the full story:

"Mrs. Sáu, you won't believe it. Here's how it all started…"

Mrs. Bảy, known for her ability to chop garlic and chilies without tearing up, was always assigned the "job" of mincing them for family gatherings and ceremonies. As she rhythmically chopped fiery red chilies on the cutting board, she tried to stifle her laughter while recounting the origins of the nickname "Ba Su" to Mrs. Sáu.

"When Ba Su first arrived, Officer Tư got him a position helping as an apprentice lathe worker at the distillery. After receiving his very first pay at the end of the week, he rushed straight to the market to buy two 'cóc' (ambarella) fruits to eat. A few days earlier, Mrs. Tư had noticed some delicious 'cóc' at the market and brought them home for the kids. Since Ba Su had never tasted this fruit before, he found it incredibly good and had been waiting for his chance to indulge.

'Wow, so now he's got some coins to spare, huh?'"

"Well, he could eat whatever he wanted, no one stopped him. But here's the thing. When he got home, he complained bitterly. He said to Mrs. Tư, 'Why are the ambarellas you bought so tasty, but the ones I bought today are so pungent?'"

"Strange! Why was that?" Mrs. Sáu asked.

Mrs. Bảy explained, "Mrs. Tư noticed he was still holding a paper bag in his hand and asked him to open it. Turns out, he had bought two chayote squashes. He'd taken a bite out of each, thinking they were ambarellas, and then tossed them aside."

Mrs. Sáu burst out laughing, "So the boy ate chayote - 'Su' in Vietnamese - thinking it was ambarella. No wonder the family calls him Ba Su after that!"

After taking a sip of her beer, Mrs. Sáu added, "And you send this kid to buy liquor for offerings to the kitchen spirits? I'm afraid the spirits will scold me for it!"

After a long day of feasting and celebrating, relatives from near and far gathered in the backyard as night fell, unwinding from the pressure of ensuring everything went just right - preparing delicious food, hosting guests properly, and more. Even then, the evening didn't go without food. This time, the leftover batter from the morning's 'bánh xèo' (a Vietnamese dish somewhat like a stuffed pancake) was mixed with coconut milk to make an impromptu batch of sweet snacks.

They ate, talked, and laughed the night away. The conversation wandered from one topic to the next, but as tradition dictated, whenever someone from the countryside came to visit, these cozy gatherings would inevitably include a round of riddles. Most were well-known folk riddles, repeated year after year, yet they never seemed to lose their charm.

If a riddle was about a shrimp, it would go as:

"*Head like a bamboo shoot, back like a dragon's curve, born white, dies red: what am I?*"

And if the riddle was about bamboo:

"*An old man long gone; his eyes wide open, his beard still on: what is it?*"

This year, with Ba Su being naturally quiet, the younger kids clung to him, some urging, some pleading for him to join in the fun. He kept refusing at first, but eventually, he gave in. And once he started talking, there was no stopping him. He let loose a 'rafale' (a rapid-fire burst of words, like a machine gun unloading bullets):

"*Tàng huê lượt nằm trên mặt nước.*

Táng thê lương kẻ nhớ người thương.

Cha mẹ nàng thác xuống âm dương.

Sanh con cháu xuất gia đầu Phật.

Là cái chi chi?" (*What is this?*)

Everyone was taken aback. Once they recovered from the initial shock, they burst into laughter, thoroughly amused by Ba Su, even if they couldn't quite make sense of what he had said. Apparently, the riddle's answer was "the lotus," though no one fully understood why.

With the riddle game over, the crowd turned their attention to Thanh's Uncle Bảy. Thanh glanced at him and asked,

"Uncle Bảy, when are you going to cut off that 'chignon' (French for a bun)?"

Uncle Bảy lowered his head without replying. Like many men in the countryside, he still wore his hair long, tied into a small bun at the nape of his neck. Ba Su, his son, whom Officer Tư had brought up to Saigon for a few months to learn a trade, spoke up:

"I haven't seen anyone here wearing a 'garlic bulb' bun, Dad."

Uncle Bảy cleared his throat, and an embarrassed Ba Su bowed his head. Hardly anyone ever heard the father and son speak directly to each other. Mostly, the father signaled his disapproval or reprimands via a series of throat-clearings in varying tones, each "frequency" having its own meaning: "Don't touch that antique vase or other valuable item," or "Why didn't you fold your arms and greet your elders?" In this instance, the throat-clearing apparently meant, "Grown-ups are talking; you shouldn't butt in."

That morning, during a family photo session, Ba Su had also earned a sharper, more annoyed version of the same throat-clearing, prompted by an offhand comment. Standing behind the photographer, he overheard instructions on how everyone should stand and where they should look. Suddenly, Ba Su shouted, "Dad! He told you not to raise your 'snout' like that!", instead of politely telling his father to lower his head for the picture.

Ba Su was less fortunate, born and raised without sufficient learning opportunities, yet he was naturally very bright. Later, when he began training as a mechanic, it took him just over a year of working on car engines before a friend of Officer Tư noticed his talent and referred him to work as a mechanic's assistant at the Volkswagen dealership on Nguyễn Huệ Street. While studying both academics and the trade, he was sent to Germany for further training, and upon returning, he became the head mechanic.

At the dealership's garage, German engineers held Ba Su's ingenuity in high regard. Whenever they encountered tricky issues, such as delays in shipments of spare parts from Europe that left the German specialists stumped, Ba Su remained undeterred. He often crafted a temporary replacement part, allowing the vehicle to stay operational until the proper parts arrived.

As the evening unfolded, the conversation naturally turned to the "Quartet of Colette." Any major gathering at Thanh's house would be incomplete without them. Thanh hadn't seen her three closest friends in ages, and the occasion of Ông's ceremony provided the perfect chance for the once-inseparable group to reunite. Once they were all together again, nobody wanted the moment to end. Before anyone could even consider leaving, Loan enthusiastically suggested:

"Hey, why don't we hit the Thị Nghè Fair this weekend, ladies?"

Amid this rare period of peace, both government and business leaders had eagerly organized the biggest fair yet, a celebration that mirrored the country's newfound optimism.

Thanh demurred. "I'm busy taking care of Thảo right now. Poor girl, she's been hitting the books hard this year, getting ready for the Gia Long's high school entrance exam."

"That's strange," Loan teased. "She's the one taking the test, not you."

Dung, who lived near Thanh and visited often, gave her a sympathetic look.

"If Thanh could take it herself, she probably would. She's been so attentive to Thảo. The poor kid's had asthma since she was little. Even Grall Hospital couldn't manage it. Thanh's tried everything from Western medicine to traditional remedies, anything people suggest, she'll give it a shot. For the past month, she's been stewing chicken with pomelo rind every week for her to eat."

Loan furrowed her brow and asked,

"What kind of weird dish is that?"

"It's a traditional herbal remedy, that's what," Dung replied. "Not sure you'd be able to stomach it. It's basically a whole silkie chicken stuffed into a hollowed-out pomelo and steamed all day. It's so bitter that Thảo's practically afraid of it now."

"I had no idea it was that extreme," Mỹ Lệ commented.

Loan then suggested,

"Well, bring Thảo along so she can have some fun. Getting out in the fresh air is better than being cooped up indoors studying all day… I'm taking my two kids, too."

Thanh hesitated:

"That place gets really crowded and chaotic, and I'm worried I won't be able to keep track of her. If I lose sight of her in the crowd… you know how strict my dad is. I'd never be able to go home."

"You're always overthinking things," Loan teased. "We hardly ever get a chance to go out. Don't worry! I'll bring my housekeeper to watch the three kids. How about that, my dear 'Big Sister'?"

She emphasized the words "Big Sister" and winked at Mỹ Lệ. Thanh blushed, realizing Loan was jokingly pairing her up with Loan's older brother. Picking up on Loan's suggestion, Mỹ Lệ added encouragement:

"What's there to be shy about? It's been ages since we've gone anywhere together. Honestly, even though we're older now, I still get excited thinking about us wandering around like we used to."

Loan cut her off:

"Who are you calling old? Don't include me in that!"

Mỹ Lệ suddenly widened her eyes and raised her voice:

"I just remembered - you really have to come, so someone can try out their brand-new camera, right?"

Loan quickly agreed:

"Oh, that's right! We can take pictures while we're there."

She turned to Thanh and pleaded,

"You love taking photos more than anyone. Stop pretending otherwise."

Just then, Sáu arrived, placing drinks on the table.

"Please have a drink, Miss Thanh. Please, everyone…"

Thanh interrupted:

"Sáu, do you want to go to the fair? I can take you along to help me keep an eye on Thảo."

"Thank you, Miss," Sáu replied eagerly.

Mỹ Lệ clapped her hands in delight:

"That means you're going after all!"

Loan hesitated.

"Whose daughter is she?"

"She's from our hamlet. Whenever we need an extra hand for odd jobs, we call her," Thanh replied.

Noticing Loan's contemplative look, as though she still had questions about Sáu, Thanh added to put her at ease:

"She's very careful and trustworthy in everything she does. I treat her like a younger sister."

"Does she own a formal long dress?" Loan asked.

"I doubt it. She works odd jobs all day long. Who would she wear a long dress for?"

"That won't do," Loan objected. "Goodness, if she goes out with us in just a 'bà ba' blouse, how's that going to look?"

Had anyone else spoken that way, Thanh might have been offended. However, since she and Loan had grown up together from childhood, she was more tolerant of her closest friend. Whenever such moments arose, Thanh recalled Loan's mother, the wife of a provincial governor, who taught Loan the traditional 'tam tòng tứ đức' (the Confucian virtues for women). As the family's only daughter, Loan was expected to uphold the wealthy and refined heritage her mother had inherited from Loan's grandmother, even with the inevitable imperfections in those "precious gems."

Thanh looked at Loan and spoke softly,

"In this day and age, you're still too old-fashioned. She's only coming along to help look after the kids. Let her wear a 'bà ba' for convenience."

"My mom would scold me to no end if she found out," Loan replied.

Thanh nodded sympathetically, pitying her friend who still couldn't break free from the rigid, sometimes unreasonable rules that hinder social progress. By the weekend, though she was extremely busy, Thanh still made time to alter one of her own long dresses for Sáu to wear.

In the days and months following the commemoration of "Ông," Officer Tư experienced a rare stretch of relative peace. Though political unrest still simmered, he remained grounded and informed, staying attuned to the nation's developments through his cherished radio.

He had grown especially fond of the "radio cabinet," which he had purchased at a bargain from a French soldier married to a Vietnamese woman. The couple, along with their young son, had left Vietnam following the signing of the Indochina Armistice Agreement in Geneva on July 21, 1954. Officer Tư called it the "radio cabinet" because the radio was placed on a yellow-varnished cabinet about a meter high, which also stored a record player and records below. For more than ten years, it had proudly sat in the living room, under the pendulum clock, keeping him company.

His wife often complained, "All day long, he just sits there hugging that radio." And he really did embrace it. Whenever there were rumors of a coup, Officer Tư would pull up a chair and sit for hours in front of the radio cabinet to catch the news. Sometimes he looked anxious and restless, unable to sit still; other times, he seemed sad. Occasionally, he would suddenly get up and start dancing with the radio cabinet, perhaps partly under the influence of alcohol. Once, during one of those moments, Mrs. Tư happened to be sweeping the house and walked by. He grabbed her and made her his dance partner. Embarrassed, Mrs. Tư quickly pulled away from his embrace, scolding, "What's gotten into you today?" before shyly retreating to the back of the house.

Thanh was worried that her father might be suspected of involvement in underground political activities and arrested by the secret police. Although he had previously served as a police officer under two regimes - first under the French colonial authorities and later under the Republic of Vietnam - she feared that the recent frequent changes in power made the situation unpredictable.

Just recently, Teacher Hai's daughter from the neighborhood, following her mother's instructions, went around informing her father's drinking buddies, including Officer Tư, that her father had been arrested by the authorities. Upon hearing this, Officer Tư hastily gathered all the books and newspapers he had stored in the ancestral altar cabinet and threw them into a barrel near the chicken coop behind the house to burn them. Some of the materials may have contained politically sensitive content that Teacher Hai had once asked him to keep. However, so much time had passed that Officer Tư could no longer distinguish one book from another.

Among the burned items were treasured collections of books and magazines belonging to Ngon, Officer Tư's adopted son. Ngon was the son of a friend who had herded buffaloes with Officer Tư back in Cai Lậy. Officer Tư had taken Ngon in after his father was killed during the resistance against the French.

When Ngon learned what had happened to his collections, he sat crying, his face buried in his hands, distraught over the loss of the precious books and magazines he had carefully collected over a number of years. Even now, every time he remembers the incident, he still laments the loss of his beloved 'Skull Party' series. What he liked most was the way this organization communicated, with lines of text projected onto the Saigon sky above Bến Thành Market using laser beams. During those moments, traffic would stop, and people would stare up at the sky, anxiously following the announcements about the 'Skull Party's' upcoming actions to eliminate evil!

In recent years, Officer Tư would eagerly tune in to the weekly lottery broadcast just to listen to the song '*Reconstruction of the Nation through Lotto*' by the 'bizarre' Trần Văn Trạch on his radio. Whenever he was delighted, he would turn up the volume, and the more he liked it, the louder he would turn it up to share his joy with the neighbors.

"*Reconstructing Lotto*

Uplifting our people

Building for all

So everyone can have a place to call home

...

Millionaires we'll become

For just a few bucks

Get yourself a car and a house

Wealth will soon be yours..."

Officer Tư was even more captivated by the comedic talent of Mr. Trần Văn Trạch, especially when he heard the performance of the piece '*Chuyến Xe Lửa Mùng 5*' ('*The Train Ride on the Fifth*'). In this piece, Mr. Trạch, playing the role of a passenger on a long train journey, passes the time by counting the lamp posts whizzing by outside the train window. By chance, he is seated next to another passenger who persistently asks him question after question. Mr. Trạch hilariously juggles responding to his fellow traveler while trying to keep track of the lamp posts, leading to mixed-up words and confusing statements. Fully engaged with Mr. Trạch's comical responses, Officer Tư stroked his beard in amusement. Additionally, Mr. Trạch delighted the audience by vividly recreating the lively atmosphere at the train station, mimicking the sounds of the train engine sputtering as it started, the whistle blowing, and the clatter of the train as it picked up speed on the tracks. Officer Tư sat alone in front of his radio, grinning from ear to ear.

Officer Tư was also a passionate soccer fan and never missed an opportunity to listen to sports commentator Huyền Vũ narrate matches from the Cộng Hòa or Tao Đàn stadiums. His commentary style was incredibly lively and captivating. Officer Tư often turned up the radio's volume, letting the entire neighborhood listen along. "It's not as enjoyable to listen alone," he'd say. The neighbors were enthralled by Huyền Vũ's commentary, hanging on to every description of the ball passes, whether fast or slow, vividly brought to life through his words. Huyền Vũ heightened the suspense with vivid commentary: *"The ball penetrates deep into the forbidden zone,"* sometimes from the right wing, sometimes from the left. He thrilled listeners with *"lightning-fast shots"* that would occasionally *"shatter the goal frame,"* though more often the ball would *"just soar over the crossbar,"* prompting collective sighs of disappointment. When the match dragged on without any goals, Huyền Vũ reassured his audience with the memorable phrase: *"The nets on both sides remain virgins."*

Another talent of Huyền Vũ that fans often mentioned is his remarkable ability to remember the names of foreign players, whether they were from Indonesia, Malaysia, or Thailand, despite the names being long and unfamiliar. He would recount them fluently and without hesitation.

Officer Tư was advanced in age, and typically, the older one gets, the less they look forward to Tết (the Vietnamese Lunar New Year). The allure of Tết was not what it once was for him. However, in recent years, Officer Tư had fortunately rediscovered the excitement of anticipating Tết. He noticed the apricot blossoms on the altar seemed fresher, and the sounds of the lion dance drums and firecrackers more cheerful. This renewed joy was largely due to the emergence of the *'comical band'* AVT[1], as his son enthusiastically called it. One of Officer

Tư's greatest pleasures during Tết in these later years was turning on the radio to listen to the AVT band, known for their satirical songs with witty, sharp, and humorous lyrics delivered in three regional accents - Northern, Central, and Southern Vietnamese. Their lively banter and clever exchanges made even the most serious listeners crack a smile, and many became so hooked that they found themselves listening over and over, finding joy every time…

"Quietly listen to how they (um-uh) bless each other,

Wishing each other to be strong and healthy like a buffalo,

Wishing for wealth and money to be as abundant as water (uh-uh),

Wishing that right after giving birth... they get... they get pregnant again..."

The whole family enjoyed listening to the AVT band, not just Officer Tư, but his daughter would sometimes feel embarrassed and shy at the lyrics, which might hit too close to home for young women of marrying age or poke fun at the physical abilities of older men. As for Mrs.Tư, there was no modern music program she liked, except for the AVT band's show. However, she had her own observation: "The Northern guy and the Vietnamese guy sound funny, but the Central guy - I really don't understand what he's saying." Hearing his wife refer to the Southern singer as "Vietnamese," Officer Tư would grumble, "I keep telling you, whether they're from the North, the Central, or the South, they're all Vietnamese. We live in the South, so we're Southerners."

Besides that, Officer Tư didn't care for anything else on his beloved radio. He scoffed at modern music, joking that the singers' names reminded him of racehorses, though the comparison made no sense. Mrs. Năm would often chide him, "You're so old-fashioned." He also dismissed 'cải lương' and 'vọng cổ' (traditional Vietnamese theatrical plays and music) as overly sentimental.

Only their daughter Thanh enjoyed the poetry recitations on The Poetry and Literature Tao Đàn Radio Program by Đinh Hùng, which featured Nguyễn Đình Nghĩa's enchanting "Magic Flute". Every week, she eagerly waited for Saturday evening to listen, but Officer Tư would always wonder, "What are they saying? I can't understand a thing." It was a familiar refrain! So Thanh got herself a small Japanese transistor radio, small enough to fit in her palm, so she could enjoy listening to singer Hoàng Oanh's poetry recitals undisturbed.

Mrs. Tư, on the other hand, was deeply passionate about 'cải lương' (Vietnamese theatrical plays). Each day, she eagerly waited for the advertising cart to pass by her house so she could find out which play would be performed that evening at the nearby theater.

The advertising cart was actually a fish cart, resembling a horse-drawn carriage without a roof. In the morning, it would transport fish to the market. By afternoon, it carried a lion dance drum in the middle, with someone beating it loudly as they went through the neighborhood, announcing the new play with large, colorful posters on the sides of the cart, depicting the actors and actresses in grand costumes, almost larger than life. These days, Mrs. Tư seems to be very fond of Hương Lan, constantly praising her: "That little daughter of Hửu Phước is only 5 years old, but she's so talented!"

As for young Ngon, he preferred modern music, but his taste was often ridiculed by his friends as being "old-fashioned." One particularly sharp-tongued friend even added a jab, calling it "ridiculously old-fashioned." This was because, in his moments of enthusiasm, Ngon would loudly sing those marching songs he had learned in the schoolyard of Lý Thái Tổ Elementary School from their gym teacher. The teacher would stand in the middle of the yard with a whistle hanging around his neck, counting, "One, two, three, four… One, two, three… One, two… One, two." The students would run around the field, singing loudly:

"This is the mighty Bạch Đằng River

Of the lineage of the Fairy and Dragon,

The Lạc Hồng race, the heroic race, North, Central, South…

… The white waters under the clear sky.

From ancient times, it has upheld the heroic example,

Even in the face of thunder, storms, rain, and sun,

Bạch Đằng River remains bright, a guiding light for the lineage to follow."

Whenever one sings, it gives them goosebumps. That's the song 'Bạch Đằng Giang'[2] ('Bạch Đằng River'.)

Another song is 'Khỏe Vì Nước'[3] ('Strong for Your Country'):

"Strong for the country, building the nation.

Our youth contributes their talents.

Creating a new, powerful livelihood for all.

Uniting our strength to build a prosperous Vietnam.

Strong for the country, with firm and resilient spirit.

The Lạc Hồng race, with boundless heroism.

In adversity, we bravely face life and death.

Vietnamese youth, heroic forever."

How could Ngon not be teased? Society is now at the dawn of peace, a time when 'a hundred flowers bloom', welcoming new opportunities. People are embracing the time of *'The sky is rosy, and the morning is clear,'*[4] of *'Every summer brings a wistful melancholy,*[5] of '*On spring days, we raise our glasses in a toast everywhere,*'[6] or of '*Today is bright and clear, the wind gently brushes the flowing robes...*'[7] with many songs that have become essentially ceremonial music at year-end parties, student reunions at the beginning of the year, or weddings in the community.

Unfortunately, the days of relative peace celebrated in music and cherished in the hearts of the people quickly faded. The war escalated further once American troops first landed in Đà Nẵng in the mid-1960s, and the conflict grew increasingly intense. Though the fighting initially occurred in distant locations with unfamiliar names, even in the heart of the city, people could see and hear its impact - whether through the sight of a hearse during the day or the mournful sound of a bamboo tocsin echoing through the night. Gradually, the sound of the tocsin was no longer just a monotonous noise leading listeners to a specific home in the neighborhood to grieve for the fate of someone they knew, perhaps an elderly mother or a young wife with small children. Now, the sound of many tocsins rang out simultaneously from various places, growing more intense, from the upper end of the neighborhood to the lower.

Through the night, the haunting sound of bamboo tocsins from someone's funeral urged wandering souls to find their final peace, while in the daylight, the music enticed people into a realm of gambling, where the stakes were nothing less than the fate of a lifetime or even one's own life.

As the battlefield raged everywhere, the Saigon home front resonated day and night with the sound of music, drowning out the noise of gunfire and bombs. The romantic music that had come from the North with the 1954 migration, viewing the war through rose-colored lenses, gentle and dreamlike, as walking on clouds, was no longer suitable. From then on, the music became more gritty, more worldly, with lyrics like "*The one who died twice, flesh and bones shattered,*"[8] or "*He returns, sometimes in a flower-adorned coffin, He returns on a stretcher... He returns, he returns as a defeated soldier with amputated legs."*[9]

In impoverished neighborhoods, people sought solace in forgetfulness through the melancholic tunes. Radios had become a common possession, broadcasting melodies throughout the day, resonating from the beginning to the end of the alley. Even children had memorized the poignant verses:

'Tomorrow is someone else's wedding,

Why is the mountain girl Phà Ca still sad.'[10]

The emotions conveyed ranged from the sorrow of a mountain girl to the despair of a sedge mat seller:

'This mat I won't sell, if I can't find you...

Oh... if I can't find you, I will use it to lay my head on every night.

...The Cà Mau mat boat has anchored on the banks of Ngã Bảy,

why doesn't the girl from the past come out to greet.'[11]

The voices of singers Thanh Nga, Út Bạch Lan, and Út Trà Ôn sometimes soared to touch the heavens, and at other times descended low to the thick earth.

Outside, on the street, immersed in the sparkling lights illuminating the universe, the resounding voice of Thái Thanh filled the air, echoing the soul of rivers and mountains, resonating with joyous melodies following each step of the pioneer's marching procession on the main road to the South - Con Đường Cái Quan[12]. The singing brought to life the steps of exploration, expanding horizons, and arousing belief through the radiance of a bygone era.

If that is the call of the sunflowers, silently blaming the endless night, then the whisper in the corner of the dance hall is the voice of a rose drifting in the mist, embracing dreams of a dawn that exists only in nostalgia.

The enchanting voice of Thanh Thúy filled countless glasses with wine, toasting to pilots after night flights[13], soldiers just separated from fallen comrades on the battlefield, or a wanderer trying to forget in the haze of alcohol and smoke. It is the intimate murmur of a lonely heart, gently carrying a subdued sadness, encapsulating the fate of Vietnamese women - who, through generations, have never complained or blamed but have always offered deep empathy as an eternal companion to the men of their era.

Chapter 11: A Soldier Husband

As the war intensified, many young men found themselves drafted into service. For the "Quartet of Colette," the conflict hit close to home with Teacher Án, Dung's husband. A year earlier, Án had graduated from the Thủ Đức Military Academy, widely recognized as South Vietnam's top reserve officer training school, and was assigned to Quảng Trị Province in Military Region 1 to help guard the border with Laos. Recently, he had been granted leave to come home for Tết, the Vietnamese New Year, so he could reunite with his family.

His uncle, Uncle Tư, believed that Án's assignment to a distant outpost was a punishment imposed by the southern government on those with brothers serving in northern forces. In reality, there were rumors that the government sought to avoid situations where siblings might end up fighting each other on the battlefield, by deliberately assigning recruits to regions far from their hometowns.

Án's father frequently lamented Án's unfortunate circumstances to relatives. Despite being the family's most academically accomplished child, Án seemed to be consistently beset by misfortune. After successfully passing the French scholarship exams, which promised him the opportunity to study agricultural engineering in France, Án had eagerly prepared for his departure. However, the National Department of Education unexpectedly announced that two France-bound scholarships would be redirected to the United States. The shifting dynamics of Vietnam's political landscape, with the growing dominance of the United States and the waning influence of France, prompted this change, even as the French government at the Élysée Palace sought ways to retain its former colony.

A major question surfaced within Án's family: should he accept the scholarship to study in the United States? The family held discussions, with some relatives expressing support. In the end, Án turned down the offer, citing concerns about racial discrimination in America. However, a deeper, unspoken reason, likely tied to the political leanings of certain family members sympathetic to the North, seemed to weigh heavily on the decision. To maintain harmony and avoid conflict, the family ultimately chose not to discuss the matter further.

In the end Án remained at home and took the entrance exam for the National Teacher's College in Saigon. Upon graduation, he secured a position as a French literature teacher at Thoại Ngọc Hầu High School, situated near the Hoàng Diệu Bridge, connecting the two banks of the River of Long Xuyên, in the Mekong Delta region.

As fate would have it, by this time Dung had also left Saigon with her family and settled in Long Xuyên, her maternal ancestral hometown. Since childhood, her life had been entangled in the seemingly unending turmoil of a war-torn country.

On Dung's paternal side, she was recognized as the granddaughter of a prominent landowner in Cái Bè. However, Dung's grandfather faced elimination by anti-French forces in a land dispute, compelling Dung's father to sell off hundreds of hectares of valuable land. The proceeds were used to move the family to Saigon to escape imminent danger. Struggling with the unfamiliar world of trade, Dung's father encountered losses and mounting debts, culminating in his tragic decision to end his life by jumping into the river under Bình Lợi Bridge.

The downfall of Dung's father in the business world mirrored the fate of many affluent families during the transition to post-feudal society. They fell victim to outdated social prejudices that deemed trade a dishonorable profession, adhering to the hierarchical classification of the Four Classes: First Scholar, Second Farmer, Third Worker, and Fourth Trader.

Subsequently, Dung's mother faced the daunting task of raising her three children alone. At the age of fifteen, Dung had to leave school to contribute to household responsibilities, assisting her mother at the family-run food stall that specialized in serving broken rice - a popular breakfast dish also consumed as a quick lunch. A year later, leveraging her proficiency in French, Dung secured a tutoring position to generate additional income for the family. Despite these efforts, life in Saigon became increasingly difficult for them. As the result, Dung's mother made the decision to relocate the family back to the countryside to live with relatives. There, they established a small eatery at the foot of the Hoàng Diệu Bridge in Long Xuyên City.

Professor Án, like any high school instructor respectfully addressed in the country, was a bachelor and a devoted patron of "Miss Dung's" eatery, visiting every afternoon. Upon completing his lunch, he was courteously accompanied by the gracious owner for a brief stroll on the bridge fondly named in their shared memory as "*Ô Thước*" - The bridge evoked the echoes of a legendary love story where a pair of lovers on opposite sides of the Ngâu river were fated by heaven to meet only once a year, traversing a makeshift bridge formed by gathering crows.

Like any heartwarming love story, they had tied the knot and were blessed with a son. By then, Án had returned to Saigon, and they resided with his parents, until he was drafted.

The family decided to turn Án's welcome party into an extended family reunion. Án's two uncles, aunts, and a few cousins all gathered to greet him. Relatives encircled the dining table, eager to hear Án's stories from his time away. Among them was Án's fifteen-year-old youngest brother, affectionately nicknamed 'Tiny Út,' who had patiently waited for his turn to inquire:

"Brother, how was it flying on the plane?"

Swiftly, the older sibling scolded Tiny Út, "You ask that? Well, the plane just flies you up into the sky, what else?"

Án felt a pang of nostalgia for his siblings, their innocence reminiscent of his own past. He hugged the youngest sibling and shared, "Yeah, after the plane ascends, looking down, all you see is rooftops, like a bunch of matchboxes laid flat below."

Curious, Tiny Út asked, "Can you see cars and people on the street, Brother?"

"When it's a little higher, you can't see people anymore, but you can still see vehicles, like ants crawling," Án replied.

The inquisitive older sibling chimed in, "Does the plane go up to the clouds, Brother?"

"Of course. It even goes beyond the clouds and flies even higher," Án affirmed.

Tiny Út, still curious, asked, "What about the clouds, how do they look, Brother?"

"From above, you see clusters of clouds like cotton balls," Án began, but before he could finish, his father intervened, scolding the two young sons, "Why are you asking so much? Let your brother eat and talk to your uncles and cousins."

From the kitchen, Dung brought up a large bowl of chicken curry to the party table. She briefly noticed that the men were laughing joyfully, but their merriment suddenly fell silent. However, two words caught Dung's attention, 'Ngủ đò' (Boat sleeping), sparking her curiosity. Though unfamiliar with the term, Dung's instincts told her there was something mysterious afoot.

After the party when most guests departed, Dung approached her husband:

"Earlier, I overheard those men talking about 'Boat sleeping.' What does that mean?"

Án, startled, sobered up from the beer:

"Um... it's a refined pastime on the Perfume River for scholars and literati in the past. At night, they would take a boat to the middle of the river, under the clear moonlight and cool breeze, to compose extempore poetry or listen to classic songs amidst the vast river scenery. Something like that."

Án's explanation initially made sense to Dung, but she couldn't shake the feeling that there was more to the story, given the secrecy surrounding it. She wondered if such pastimes still occurred in the present.

Seizing an opportunity when Án's Uncle Hai, growing impatient, went to the kitchen urging his wife to go home, Dung asked:

"Uncle Hai, what is 'Boat sleeping'?"

Slightly intoxicated, Uncle Hai scolded her:

"Women and kids... why bother asking about that... It's the rendezvous between 'heroes' and 'boat girls' at the Imperial City."

Dung finally understood. That evening, as the couple lay in bed, a bolster pillow symbolically marked the boundary between them: *"You have your side, I have mine; that's all there is to our relationship."* (Humorously borrowing from the poem 'Giây phút chạnh lòng' by Thế Lữ: *"Anh đi đường anh, tôi đường tôi, Tình nghĩa đôi ta có thế thôi."*)

Late at night, reflecting on her husband's situation amid the thorns of war, Dung dared not think further. Recalling the past year, every time she encountered a military Jeep driving into the neighborhood, her palms would sweat profusely, and her feet would drag her back home, praying the vehicle wasn't coming to her house to deliver bad news.

"Now my husband, after rare days of leave to visit family, and I'm still grumbling about him all night," Dung thought, feeling guilty. She decided to heed the advice from the verses of the infamous poem, Kiều[14], '*Close her eyes and take a step. Let's see where the whirlwind of fate takes her.*'

Thanks to her compassion, fortune smiled upon them, and a year later they welcomed another child - this time a girl - bringing balance to the family since their firstborn was a boy. Still, it was hard not to feel sorry for Lieutenant Án. During that leave near his post in the Citadel city, he did nothing that would disappoint his wife's expectations. Even so, he dreaded the teasing from cousins and uncles if he admitted that he had refrained from indulging in the romantic delights the Perfume River was known for. To save face, he parried their prying questions with carefully crafted responses, though deep down he longed for the simple joys of family life.

The next morning, filled with cheerful anticipation, Án eagerly sifted through his backpack, revealing several trays of Huế specialty sesame candy. He delicately placed a portion on the ancestral altar as an offering while reserving some to share the joy with his parents. With a sense of nostalgia, he explored the drawers of the old bureau desk, uncovering two large firecrackers, remnants from his military academy days. Having safeguarded them until then, Án seized the opportunity to set them off by the pond behind the house, unleashing thunderous bangs that reverberated through the heavens and the earth. He celebrated Tết, shared joy with the neighbors, and, last but not least, commemorated personal victory! Pity befell the innocent fish and shrimp below the pond surface, forced to float belly up in the water.

Chapter 12: Twelve Harbours

As the Vietnamese saying goes, *"A woman's fate lies in twelve harbours; clear waters if fortunate, muddy if not."* ('*Phận gái mười hai bến nước, trong nhờ đục chịu*') This implies that a woman's life - starting as a girl, growing up, marrying, and depending on her spouse's character - may lead her to a happy union with a loving husband or a tumultuous one with an abusive partner. Her in-laws, too, could be supportive and kind or hostile and vindictive. However, Thanh seemed to have charted her own course, choosing to remain single and devoting her life to raising her late sister's daughter as her own.

After two years of leaving her nursing career behind, family circumstances unexpectedly propelled Thanh into a new venture she had never previously considered: running a taxi service and a school transport business. One might say it was a career she built almost singlehandedly, though she certainly couldn't overlook the support of Officer Tư and his "troops."

Officer Tư, who had worked for the French and lived in Saigon, rarely returned to his hometown in the countryside. He felt uneasy because most of his relatives lived in areas controlled by the anti-French resistance forces. Nevertheless, when he did visit, he would often bring one or two nephews back to Saigon, to provide them an opportunity to learn a trade, as he often cited his favorite saying: *"Nhứt nghệ tinh, nhứt thân vinh"* (*Master one trade, ensure a prosperous life*). He always expressed concern for the youngsters in the countryside, lamenting, "Those poor kids have nothing to do except weeding and herding buffalo," just as he had done in his own youth.

After bringing his nephews to Saigon, he would ask a foreman at the local distillery to arrange for them to learn a trade.

Whether it was turning, welding, electrical work, blacksmithing, or anything else, he'd be delighted to see them learning a skill, proudly announcing to everyone, "Look at my 'troops' I brought up. Now they all have hands-on experience." Unfortunately, the distillery could not always employ Officer Tư's 'troops.' Sometimes they worked only a short time before being laid off. He constantly wondered how to find a practical way to secure long-term employment for his 'troops.'

"Everything seems destined by Heaven," Officer Tư would often remark about his post-retirement days. His granddaughter, Thảo, whom he had named himself back when they lived at the police residence, had just completed primary school and been accepted into Gia Long, a prestigious girls' secondary school in Saigon. While the entire family celebrated the news, Thanh, who had taken on the role of Thảo's mother, was burdened by a pressing worry she couldn't yet resolve. The school was nearly ten kilometers from home, and Thảo's delicate health, having been deprived of breast milk as a baby and suffering year-round from asthma, made it unthinkable for her to ride a bicycle to school like the other local girls.

As they pondered how to get Thảo to school each day, Thanh told Officer Tư, "Even if I have to carry her on my back, I'll do it." Luckily, fate seemed to intervene. Near the end of summer, Officer Tư's former boss passed away, and his widow decided to sell the old Deux Chevaux car he had left behind. A solution Thanh had never imagined suddenly appeared: she suggested buying the car to take Thảo to school.

Officer Tư was delighted and eagerly volunteered to be his granddaughter's chauffeur, shuttling her to and from school each day. Although the car was old and prone to frequent breakdowns, he saw it as a perfect chance to fulfill a long-held dream: "training his unemployed troops" in car maintenance. All he needed, he thought, was to find a master mechanic to train them, and he already had someone in mind: one of his best army buddies. Officer Tư had formed a close friendship with Mr. Năm Tiết back when they were conscripted by the French. They had met on the ship bound for France, where they were sent to fight in what history would later call the First World War, defending "Motherland" France.

During his time in the French army, Mr. Năm Tiết had been fortunate to learn the mechanic's trade. Officer Tư always admired his friend's skill, often praising him for his ability to "disassemble a car engine piece by piece and put it back together like new." Now that the family had a car, Officer Tư saw a perfect opportunity to ask Mr. Năm Tiết to teach his "unemployed troops" how to fix it. However, one pressing matter still needed to be addressed.

Two years earlier, a devastating fire engulfed the Khánh Hội area, completely consuming Mr. Năm Tiết's stilt house. As the flames approached, he and his wife scrambled to toss all their belongings into the pond below before fleeing for safety. After the fire was extinguished, Mr. Năm Tiết spent an entire day diving into the pond, desperately trying to recover what he could. Tragically, this effort left him with a severe nervous system illness, causing his hands to tremble uncontrollably.

Officer Tư made every effort to help his friend find effective treatment, but despite their attempts, the illness persisted. He believed the polluted pond water, tainted by waste from nearby brothels, was a major factor in Mr. Năm Tiết's condition. Some criticized Mr. Năm Tiết's decision to risk his health for mere possessions. Officer Tư, however, expressed deep sympathy: "Poor Năm. That house held everything he owned. What choice did he have but to wade into that filthy water to save his life's work?"

Every month when Officer Tư went to the Treasury Bureau to collect his pension, he often rode his bicycle directly to visit his friend. They would sit together over tea and reminisce about their shared past, be it cutting open date sacks in the ship's hold on the way to France, or narrowly avoiding a meal of poisonous mushrooms gathered by homesick Vietnamese soldiers in southern France. Before leaving Mr. Năm Tiết, Officer Tư never failed to quietly slip some money into his friend's pocket. As he pedaled home, he felt a growing weight of concern, always wishing he could do more to help.

When he purchased the car, Officer Tư had already formed a plan for Mr. Năm Tiết. Every week, he invited Mr. and Mrs. Năm Tiết to his home. After a hearty meal, he would take his friend to the garage to train his "troops" in car repairs. Watching her husband at work, Mrs. Năm Tiết couldn't hold back her tears. "Ever since he fell ill, this is the only time I've seen him truly happy," she said.

Before long, Officer Tư's household boasted its own team of mechanics. As for Thanh, after a week of observing Officer Tư drive his granddaughter to school every day, she had a sudden inspiration: "Why not start a student shuttle service?" Thus began Thanh's entrepreneurial journey. Starting with a modest French two-horsepower car that could carry three student passengers, she soon expanded her operation. By the following year, she added a German Volkswagen van. After modifying the vehicle with two rear benches, it was capable of transporting nearly ten students.

The business thrived and grew steadily over time, thanks not only to Thanh's tireless efforts but also to her exceptional leadership. As a woman managing a team of male drivers and mechanics in a traditionally male-dominated field, she demonstrated an extraordinary ability to inspire and lead.

As for the other members of the Quartet of Colette, they had each settled into life's "Twelve Harbours," married and raising children. Yet, much like Thanh, they were like cactus flowers that flourish even in harsh conditions. Under colonial hardships and the ravages of a prolonged war, each managed to carve out a bright spot, not only for themselves, but for their loved ones and the community. Their quiet strength and enduring love helped sustain a spirit of hope and resilience, preserving the duty and determination that allowed their nation to endure and thrive as it had for generations before them.

This is further illustrated by the experience of another member of the "Quartet of Colette." After enduring a deeply distressing event at Thanh's mother's gravesite, Mỹ Lệ was able to transform the course of her life. She later married Paul, a development that became possible when Năm Chảng voluntarily withdrew his earlier proposal.

In the laborers' neighborhood near the infamous Cầu Muối bridge, the tale of "Brother Năm's" noble gesture spread quickly. Known locally as "Brother Năm" with a mix of respect and affection, Năm Chảng's reputation continued to grow. The struggling community, which often benefited from his acts of generosity, believed he had magnanimously stepped aside upon learning about Mỹ Lệ's new suitor. In reality, however, Năm Chảng, despite his image as a benevolent benefactor, was deeply entrenched in the underworld. He was motivated by personal ambition and the pursuit of prestige as he worked his way up the criminal hierarchy.

When Paul expressed his intention to marry Mỹ Lệ, Năm Chảng saw an opportunity to secure a lucrative business arrangement. The French colonial authorities often turned a blind eye, allowing gangs to protect entertainment venues. This gave the authorities an opportunity to exploit a tax goldmine from casinos, brothels, and numerous auxiliary services catering to revelers, such as nightclubs and bars.

Năm Chảng's condition for permitting Mỹ Lệ's marriage to Paul was straightforward: Paul had to secure permission from the French authorities to let Năm Chảng extend his influence beyond the Saigon Market. Specifically, Năm Chảng aimed to gain control over the renowned Kim Chung casino, second only to the prestigious Đại Thế Giới casino in the neighboring district of Cholon.

Boss Gauthier, recognizing Paul's value as a government asset, agreed to Năm Chảng's terms. From the French authorities' perspective, the exact identity of the gang holding sway over these venues was unimportant - what mattered was that someone maintained order in the city. In the end, the colonial powers benefited from all the political and underworld maneuvering, regardless of which faction came out on top.

Soon after the clandestine wedding ceremony, meticulously conducted within the renowned Saigon Notre Dame Cathedral, Paul found himself compelled to relocate his entire family to Đà Lạt, situated some 300 kilometers north of Saigon, owing to pressing personal security concerns arising from the exposure of his identity. They settled into a villa atop a pine-covered hill, overlooking a small stream that meandered around large and small rocks along its banks.

Regrettably, the cool climate of the highland region, prized by French expatriates and earning Đà Lạt its nickname "Paris of the East", exacerbated Aunt Sáu's arthritis, despite its charms. Within just six months, Paul arranged for the family to relocate to Bảo Lộc. This move not only provided a warmer, more comfortable environment for Mỹ Lệ's mother but also reduced the travel distance to Saigon by about a third, making it easier for Paul to carry out his frequent covert operations.

Paul's work extended beyond his responsibilities with the infamous "Second Bureau," where he oversaw internal surveillance of the Cao Đài and Hòa Hảo religious sects. He also operated as an agent for MI5, the French intelligence network, gathering intelligence on the activities of France's allies in Indochina and reporting directly to the headquarters for Indochina affairs located in Kunming, southern China.

After World War II, France clung to its aspirations of maintaining colonial rule in Vietnam, but mistrusted its allies, including England, the United States, and Russia. France, keenly aware that each nation pursued its own national interests, remained alert, continually watching for signs that its allies might take advantage of its domestic challenges to gain control of its colonial holdings.

After relocating to Bảo Lộc, Paul acquired a tea farm and a coffee plantation near the Đạ Huoai River, both managed by Mỹ Lệ. The tea was sold exclusively in domestic markets, while the coffee was exported internationally, primarily through France. Historically, import-export licenses were granted only to the French or those with French citizenship, but after Vietnam gained independence, Mỹ Lệ became a trailblazer as the first Vietnamese woman in this field.

At first, Mỹ Lệ depended greatly on Paul's guidance in managing the family's business ventures. Tragically, Paul's life was cut short during a dispute with the boss of the Đại Thế Giới casino. After his death, Mỹ Lệ took on the full responsibility of running the enterprise herself. She quickly proved her remarkable ability to care for her children, tend to her aging mother, oversee a large farm, and manage the import-export business, all with exceptional dedication and skill.

In what seemed like no time, Sáng, Mỹ Lệ's eldest son studying in France, turned 21. Living in Bảo Lộc with her second son, Mỹ Lệ called Loan to announce her upcoming return to Saigon to renew her coffee company's import-export license. Despite the heavy demands of both family and business, Mỹ Lệ never missed an opportunity to see her old friends whenever she came to Saigon to handle administrative matters or meet with her bank.

Loan promptly contacted Thanh, suggesting that the four "sisters" get together again. Since she and Dung were living with their in-laws, hosting a gathering at home wasn't a practical option.

Thanh, the only single "sister" among them, often welcomed impromptu gatherings at her home. But this time, with her business rapidly growing - she had just purchased a fifth Volkswagen van to convert into a school bus - and the ongoing garage expansion at her house, Thanh regretfully declined.

Reluctantly yet with a trace of excitement, Loan assumed the responsibility of organizing a welcome party for Mỹ Lệ. She had her sights set on using her mother-in-law's vacation house in Thủ Đức, a charming retreat perched on a gentle hill between two lush garden plots. The property was dotted with enticing fruit trees that had always made Loan think longingly of her closest friends. Each time she visited with her mother-in-law, she would silently wish: "If only they were here so I could treat them to these delights."

Normally, the house was inhabited solely by Uncle Chín, her husband's uncle, and his family, who took care of the home and maintained the gardens. Though only 20 kilometers from the city, that distance was enough to dissuade her mother-in-law from visiting often. However, on those rare occasions when her lady friends fancied the garden's sweet, fragrant custard apples and playfully urged her to host a Four-color card game (Trò chơi bài Tứ sắc) at the retreat, she was more than happy to oblige.

Loan's mother-in-law could lack anything, but not a Four-color card game every week. Understanding her mother-in-law's weakness, Loan began whispering cleverly to the 'tricksters' that the fruit garden in Thủ Đức was ripe and waiting for them. Loan's scheme bore fruit as expected, providing the sisters of the Quartet of Colette with a wonderful place for a festive gathering and her mother-in-law with the Four-color card game she loves dearly.

The family's vacation home sat elegantly atop a gentle hill, surrounded by lush greenery and overlooking the Biên Hòa Highway. Across the road, the bright white villas of Thủ Đức University Village offered a picturesque view. The party's car traveled smoothly along the newly constructed highway, then turned onto a dirt road shaded by two rows of mangrove trees. At the intersection marked by a dense tamarind tree, it turned right, heading toward the front gate.

Crafted from ironwood columns with a gleaming dark brown finish, the two-story wooden house bore a distinctive hexagonal-shaped upper floor. Its windows opened in five directions, inviting the refreshing breeze. It was on this floor that Loan's mother-in-law and her companions gathered, seated around a sturdy wooden plank engaged in their favorite card game.

While the ladies enjoyed their time upstairs, Loan eagerly led her friends and two children to the fruit garden behind the house. Ripe red rambutans delighted everyone, but Loan's enthusiasm directed them to a towering mangosteen tree she had been eager to share.

The mangosteens, full and round, hung from the branches, each fruit bursting with sweet juice. A cool breeze carried the sweet and nostalgic scent of fruit blossoms, creating a rare sense of peace and comfort for Mỹ Lệ - a woman seemingly destined to overcome fate. Dreamily looking into the distance, she embraced old memories flooding back - a time when the group gathered for photos by ancient trees in Bờ-rô's shaded garden, sat in a circle on the grass carpet in front of Bách Thảo's botanical garden, next to clusters of golden daisies glowing in the sun.

There were moments captured with abundant longan trees in Long Thành's garden, or the durian and mangosteen orchards in Lái Thiêu, followed by the plum orchard in Mỹ Tho and the star apple fruit orchard in Cai Lậy.

Suddenly, Loan's voice broke through, pulling Mỹ Lệ back to reality,

"Let me check with Auntie Chín, the gardener's wife, to see if she can pack a few mangosteens for the kids to enjoy at home."

Loan turned to Mỹ Lệ, guiding her toward the garden near the Hibiscus hedge fence. There, she proudly pointed out a bushy guava tree adorned with ripe, glossy green fruits, some tinged with a hint of light yellow. Retrieving a small package from her handbag, Loan handed it to Mỹ Lệ, playfully asking, "Does this suit your taste?" Recalling from their childhood that Mỹ Lệ favored spicy food, Loan had prepared a package in her purse that morning to ensure she didn't forget. Mỹ Lệ had a habit of dipping most fruits, whether sour like tamarind and mango, bitter like pomelo, or sweet like plums, in chili salt before indulging.

The sisters gathered around, picking and savoring the guavas, but Loan was eager to guide them back to the rambutan trees. Observing this scene, Dung felt compelled to remind everyone, "Indulge in whatever you desire, but make sure to leave some space for later. I've brought an abundance of cakes, fruit jams, and confectionery." The unanimous decision was made to gather at the picnic table beneath the sprawling jackfruit tree. The diligent gardener had already added two plastic chairs for the two children alongside the four existing stone seats. However, the two youngsters remained entranced by the fruits in the garden and were reluctant to join the group.

Loan, noting the time, suspected that her mother-in-law's card game might conclude soon. She subtly hinted, "It might be time to kick off our celebration." Thanh and Dung hurriedly unpacked the food from the baskets, while Loan called upon the gardener's wife to bring plates and dishes to set up the complete table. Thanh meticulously arranged the powder cakes on a plate. Ordinarily, she would have ordered them from Dung, but this time, with Dung occupied creating confectionery for her customers, Thanh purchased the powder cakes from the daughter of Mrs. Sửu, her former home economics teacher.

Mrs. Sửu played a significant role in their school memories, especially her memorable scolding that they still reminisced about: "The four of you are like four demons, not like four virtues as other girls are." Whenever the four friends had the chance to meet her, she would recount the same story of Loan's ambitious attempt to achieve a higher score in her class. The "student" Loan once added ink to dye her pickled cucumber to a perfect green.

Dung carefully took out a box of "Choux" pastries from her handbag and placed it on top of the jar of soursop candies. All of it had been made by her own hands. Mỹ Lệ also rummaged through her bag and brought out a bundle of tea shoots and fresh tea leaves, which she had asked a worker to pick yesterday. She handed it to Loan, asking Aunt Chín to brew a pot of tea for everyone.

Philippe, Mỹ Lệ's twelve-year-old second son, who had accompanied her on this trip to Saigon, was standing outside in the garden chatting with Thảo. When he saw the table laden with food, he immediately ran over and stood next to Mỹ Lệ, eyes hungry and fixed on the plates of pastries and candies. Seeing this, Dung beckoned Philippe over and handed him a choux pastry. Philippe, curious, asked,

"Why don't I see any mooncakes, Auntie?"

Mỹ Lệ chimed in, explaining to her son,

"That's your Aunt Thanh's idea; she wanted to encourage using homemade cakes."

Loan added,

"Your Aunt Thanh wanted to start a little revolution. She wanted Mid-Autumn Festival treats to have a more traditional, local feel. So, instead of mooncakes, she replaced them with Aunt Dung's bánh in (powder cakes)."

Dung, looking thoughtful, said,

"Poor Aunt Thanh, at first, she just wanted to help me have some work to do. Her business is big, so every year during special occasions, they'd buy gifts to give to clients and workers at the factory. In recent years, instead of buying mooncakes for Mid-Autumn Festival, Aunt Út would come to me and order powder cakes to give as presents. Thanks to that, I finally have a bit of extra income to get by."

Dung seemed to quietly express her gratitude toward Thanh. Since the day her mother-in-law fell gravely ill, the growing cost of medicine had forced Dung to make and sell cakes and sweets to supplement the family's income. During the time when her husband Án was away serving in the military, Thanh had gone above and beyond to help Dung's family. She had taken Dung's mother-in-law to the renowned French-run Grall Hospital for treatment on several occasions, always assisting with medical expenses when needed.

For this reason, when Dung's husband, Lieutenant Án, was sent to Malaya for anti-guerrilla training with the British forces, he stopped by Singapore to buy a new Philips reel-to-reel tape recorder as a gift for Thanh. It was his way of expressing his family's heartfelt gratitude.

Mỹ Lệ sat watching her "old friends" bustling around to host her and felt a light, nostalgic joy reminiscent of her ponytail days. She playfully blamed fate, saying,

"Celebrating the Mid-Autumn Festival without the moon isn't very poetic."

Loan sneered,

"Sáng is almost ready to get married, you know. And here you are still dreaming."

Dung raised her voice to scold Mỹ Lệ:

"Whose fault is it but yours? If you could stay a few more days, we could wait until later tonight to celebrate properly."

Loan scoffed and teased Dung:

"Oh, please. Do you think Mỹ Lệ actually misses the legendary Cuội character on the moon? And it wasn't her beau Sứ?"

Thanh shot Loan a disapproving look, silently reproaching her for reopening an old wound of Mỹ Lệ's. But Mỹ Lệ waved it off,

"Never mind, it's all in the past. By the way, how is he these days?"

Loan teased her again, "You're saying it's nothing, but here you are asking about him."

After the fateful graveyard encounter where Paul assaulted her, Mỹ Lệ had distanced herself from Sứ, her first and, she believed, deep down, her only true love. Yet if for men, a first unfulfilled love might become a cherished memory, for women it often remains a sorrow they strive to forget. Forgetting is necessary to uphold the duties of a wife, to fulfill the responsibilities of a mother.

"I heard he joined the Gendarmerie," Thanh answered. Dung, with intent, added, "And he's still single, if you must know."

All eyes turned to Mỹ Lệ, brimming with curiosity.

"Give me a break," Mỹ Lệ dismissed them in her characteristic offhand tone. "Do you all think I haven't suffered enough already?"

Hoping to shift the conversation and rescue Mỹ Lệ, Loan suddenly turned the topic to Thanh.

"So, we've been talking about Miss Thanh for a while now, but we forgot to ask how things are going with her engineer."

Dung chimed in, "She's got all the luck. It's nothing but engineers and doctors chasing after her."

Aside from Engineer Trương, Dung was referring to Doctor Phước, an instructor in the female nursing training program who had been sweet on his student Thanh, for over a year.

It had been a long time since Thanh last heard mention of Doctor Phước. The first image that rushed into her mind was of a rainy noon when she arrived late to class, soaking wet from the downpour. As soon as she entered, she was called upon to recite her lesson. Stepping up to the teacher's podium, Thanh slipped and fell into the arms of teacher Phước, who had recently returned to the country after completing his studies in France.

To the female students, he was especially noteworthy: still single and of the ideal type: "handsome, accomplished, and from a wealthy family." The days that followed were filled with whispered gossip and teasing comments from her classmates. Some joked that Thanh had done it on purpose, while others jealously speculated that the teacher had staged the incident because he was smitten with her.

Loan suddenly seemed to remember something. She fixed her mischievous gaze on Thanh and asked, "Hey, now that you mention it, how's Doctor Phước doing these days?"

Mỹ Lệ shrugged. "His mom pressured him so much that he finally settled down and got married."

Loan unwrapped a piece of mangosteen candy, popped it into her mouth, and chewed it with the same casual ease as she used to in her childhood. The familiar sweet-and-sour taste brought a wave of nostalgia over her. She declared, "Now that you all brought up Doctor Phước, I feel like telling you a story…"

Thanh interrupted, "What's she up to now?"

"Hey, I'm just telling it like it is," Loan replied.

Mỹ Lệ urged, "Come on, spill the beans. Stop being so cryptic."

Loan sipped her tea, letting the moment linger before she finally said, "Alright, I'll tell you this story. It's a secret though."

Thanh snapped, "What are you up to now? Be careful. Let's see who has more secrets."

Loan replied casually, "I've got nothing to be afraid of." Her words, a mix of jest and seriousness, carried the ironic tone of a wife estranged from her husband for several years. Loan squinted mischievously, glancing towards Mỹ Lệ and Dung, and continued, "Did you guys know that the couple had been to Long Hải beach one time?"

"What? Why wouldn't I know that?" Mỹ Lệ looked at Thanh accusingly. "I thought there were no secrets among us."

Dung, usually calm, consoled Mỹ Lệ, "Do you remember where you were at that time? A lot was happening, and even if we spoke, you might not have been in the mood to listen." Mỹ Lệ suddenly realized that during that period, when Thanh was taking nursing courses, she was in Bảo Lộc, just starting her import-export career. Shortly after Paul's tragic death, she had to handle everything inside and outside. Understanding what Dung meant by keeping her in the dark about Thanh's newfound love, Mỹ Lệ turned to Loan and playfully scorned, "So, you're pretty good at keeping secrets from me, aren't you?"

Loan defended herself, saying, "Just teasing you guys a bit, no real secrets here." She deliberately savored another piece of mangosteen jam, which Dung had made slightly sour, knowing her friends liked it that way. Raising her head to the sky, Loan relished the sweet and sour flavor not only from the mangosteen in her mouth but also from the tamarind at the entrance of the alley leading to her old house, the guava in the backyard, the plum sold at the fruit stall at the Trung Lương intersection - a popular gateway to the heart of the Mekong Delta, the pomelo in Biên Hòa, the sapodilla in Lái Thiêu, and even from the fruit orchards in one friend's hometown to another's that they had the chance to visit and disturb, taking photos. Loan immersed herself in the frame of memories, cherishing the sweet and deep sisterly feelings. The images of that day when she and Thanh struggled to choose the right swimsuits for Thanh came back, dancing before her eyes. Loan recounted,

"At that time, Doctor Phước organized a leisure trip to Long Hải beach for the whole class," Loan explained, pausing before pointing at Thanh and continuing, "Our girl here refused because she didn't have a swimsuit and concocted an excuse that she could not obtain permission from Uncle Tư (her father). Well, that may be true if she did actually ask Uncle Tư. You guys know how strict he is; he'd never let his children wear those 'revealing' outfits."

Loan took her time sipping her tea before continuing, "What I want to say is, why, with the absence of just one student like Thanh from the class, did Professor Phước have to drive all the way to her house to meet Uncle Tư, seeking permission for Thanh? 'Monsieur' even promised to personally pick Thanh up to go on the trip with the whole class and return her to the house at the end of the day, so Uncle Tư could be reassured."

Mỹ Lệ interjected, "Oh, seems intriguing, huh?"

Loan teased, "Listen to this. She had to secretly go to my house to try on my swimsuits. And you guys knew how skinny she was back then, while I... wasn't quite as slender..."

Mỹ Lệ retorted sharply, "Stop it, dear! Whoever said you were chubby then that you'd find the need to protect yourself like that."

"Just reminding you guys that once upon a time, I also had curves, okay."

"Fine, your waist is like a frog's. Satisfied? Now tell us, what did those two do besides going to the beach?"

"Well, think about it: someone as disciplined as Thanh, what could she really do? I just recall the time the two of us were picking out swimsuits at my place. I was sitting there watching her choosing colors, picking styles, and helping her try one on, then another. Helping her adjust the bust darts on this side, then on that side, to make them even. Seeing her fumble awkwardly while trying on a swimsuit for the first time, honestly, I felt like a mother helping her daughter choose a wedding dress."

Dung chimed in, "Come on, your eldest daughter at most was only eight at that time."

"You know what I meant. At that time, we were all married, with one or two kids, and my 'sister' here... she was still in her girlish days."

Suddenly remembering something, Loan asked, "Who wants to see Thanh's pictures in a swimsuit? I have those photos hidden at my house until now."

"I forbid you, okay?" Thanh ordered, her tone sounding almost pleading. Mỹ Lệ acquiesced to her friend, "If she doesn't want us to see the pictures, then let it be. And how's the doctor doing?"

Loan took a sip of tea and shared with a tone of regret:

"He pursued her so persistently, but she kept refusing. After a year of trying, he had to listen to his mother and get married. I feel bad for Thanh; she kept making excuses about having to care for her family and turned him down. He comes from a wealthy family and is a doctor. He could have easily supported her and any number of households. Yet, she was firm in declining him. I kept urging her, but she never listened."

As Thanh gazed out at the garden, her eyes caught sight of Thảo standing amidst the plum trees, meticulously counting the fruits. Admiring Thảo's graceful presence in her white schoolgirl dress, Thanh couldn't help but be filled with warmth and confidence in her decision to postpone marriage. She comforted herself with the realization that Thảo, unlike many in Thanh's generation, had the opportunity to complete high school and was now pursuing her dream of becoming a doctor at medical school.

With a faint smile, Thanh sought to conceal a modest pride brimming with a sense of accomplishment. In her reflections, Thảo's success rested on her own efforts and abilities, yet as a 'mother', Thanh had exerted every effort within her grasp to aid her daughter in realizing her dreams. Thanh felt a deep sense of satisfaction whenever friends or neighbors in Plum Tree Hamlet lauded Thảo. They praised her by acknowledging the nurturing care of her aunt, saying things like, "Little Thảo comes from Aunt Thanh's training school," to highlight the girl's grace, not just in her speech but also in the way she treated others. A clear sign of Thanh's teaching was seen in how Thảo addressed "Rat, the daughter of Mrs. Betel," a nickname everyone in Plum Tree Hamlet, young and old, commonly used. Thanh on the other hand had taught Bé Thảo that this was a disrespectful and disparaging term. As a result, Bé Thảo always referred to her respectfully as "Sister Sáu, the daughter of Mrs. Bảy."

Even at important family gatherings, Thanh never missed a chance to impart a moral lesson to Thảo, a habit her friends often teased her about. On these occasions, Thanh would direct the household helpers to bring food to needy families in the area. She would always remind Thảo, "Remember, we must set aside food for the less fortunate before we serve our guests, so it doesn't seem like we're giving them leftovers."

Thanh's heightened concern for instilling ethics in Thảo seemed to stem from a variety of motivations, many of which appeared tied to family influence, particularly from her father. Although he served as a police officer under the oppressive French colonial regime, he stood out as a moral exception, guided by a strong conscience in his daily conduct. After witnessing injustices, he would return home and share these experiences over family dinners, using them as teaching moments to emphasize the importance of treating the underprivileged and marginalized with fairness and compassion.

The story about the prison meals was one he often recounted with a tone of sadness. He would frequently lament about Officer Hai, a colleague in the department, saying, "He receives the money from the office allotted for prison meals, but then pockets it and gives the inmates only leftovers from his own household." Officer Tư would also criticize another colleague for abusing his position by forcing rickshaw pullers to shuttle his children to and from school each day. As a result, Officer Tư strictly prohibited his own children from using rickshaws, even if they paid for them.

To him, "How could you just sit there while someone else breaks their back pulling you? That's unacceptable." This lesson left a lasting impression, and Thanh continued to avoid even using cyclo (or pedicab) well into adulthood. On one rare occasion when it was absolutely necessary, she found herself with no choice but to hail a cyclo to get home. But to avoid upsetting Officer Tư, she got off two blocks away and walked the remaining distance.

Beyond the familial influence, where ethical lessons were regularly echoed by her father, a more profound societal factor seemed to permeate Thanh's subconscious, leading her to be seemingly obsessed with the responsibility of cultivating ethics in her "daughter." Thanh came of age during a prolonged period of historical turmoil, marked by seemingly endless chaos and suffering. She bore witness to death, brutality, and the pervasive ascent of evil. It raises the question: Did her heightened sense of moral duty stem from an instinct to preserve the lineage, recognizing that a nation couldn't endure without its moral compass?

While Thanh was lost in her own thoughts, Philippe stood silently near the picnic table, savoring Aunt Dung's delicious pastries and enjoying the rare peaceful moment. After finishing the last two pieces of mango candy, he decided to question Thanh's choice of celebrating the Mid-Autumn Festival with traditional "homegrown" treats. He addressed all his "Aunties":

"Aunties, Choux pastries aren't Vietnamese."

Philippe's unexpected query left the ladies perplexed, but Loan stepped in to defend, saying, "Well, since Aunt Dung made them, they must be Vietnamese, no doubt."

Teacher Dung smiled, attempting to clarify for Philippe and prevent any misunderstandings, "You're correct, but the ingredients and preparation methods may differ somewhat from those used in France or elsewhere, for that matter."

Adding a touch of humor, Loan interjected, "You know, even the names of the pastries have been Vietnamized for a long time. If you don't believe me, just ask your grandmother. She calls them 'Nipple cakes.'"

Loan's eyes sparkled mischievously, concealing a playful smile as she continued, "But everyone agrees that Vietnamese 'Nipple cakes' are much better than the French Nipple …!"

Thanh gave Loan's sleeve a sharp tug, casting her a reproachful look as if to say, "How can you speak so carelessly in front of the child?" Dung, aware of Thanh's seriousness when it came to educating children, tried to lighten the mood, jokingly interjecting:

"This lady is about to become a grandma, yet she still talks so recklessly."

Loan defended herself:

"Honestly, you guys don't have any sense of national pride."

Mỹ Lệ clapped her hands, laughing heartily, before stepping in to rescue Loan by recalling an old story.

"You guys know how she is. Remember back in our final year of Cours Moyen (equivalent to fifth grade)? We were all pretty grown up by then, but after gym class, as we returned to the classroom to change clothes, she stood on a desk and yelled, 'Get out of the way, everyone! If you stand too close, it's on you - I'm shaking off my soiled pants!'"

The four sisters burst into laughter, tears streaming down their faces. These tears held the essence of deep emotions, sparkling in the moments of shared joy that would forever reside in their hearts.

Mỹ Lệ's recounted story unintentionally transported Loan back to the carefree days of a girl growing up in luxury, like a rare flower accustomed to receiving admiring glances from friends and family. Little did anyone know that even such a flower couldn't escape the fate of Vietnamese women, drifting along with the nation's fortunes through infrequent peaceful days with calm waves and gentle winds, while facing more frequent tumultuous storms and strong winds. The smile always bloomed on her lips, and elegance radiated outward, but it was a reflexive shield originating from an inexhaustible inner strength to control the pain within, rather than a superficial gesture born to attract life's applause.

This was Loan's state of mind. Though nominally still Nhân's wife, she had been living in the shadows for the past four years. From morning till night, she cared for her mother-in-law and looked after the children.

Nhân, Loan's husband, returned to Vietnam disappointed after graduating from France, as his ideals for serving his homeland did not materialize as expected. According to his father, he was born at the wrong time. Returning to the country after studying in France at a time when the influence of the United States was prevalent, Nhân served in the education sector and witnessed a sea change in the academic approach. Previously, the system leaned towards training intellectual elites with a theoretical emphasis on lofty philosophies, differing from the American tendency to train practical human resources to meet economic and societal development needs. Additionally, internal conflicts, disputes, and infighting emerged. As an outsider, Nhân found it challenging to adapt.

Nhân felt lost in his own homeland and decided to return to France. His plan was to stabilize his life overseas and then bring his family over. However, after two years of work and cohabitation with a French woman, his plans changed. Both Loan and her mother-in-law were disappointed, and the dream of a family reunion seemed to fade away. Nhân's letters became less frequent, and apart from the occasional packages sent to the family, the connection grew thin.

As time passed without a husband, *'the market remained busy,'* as the saying goes. The daughter-in-law immersed herself in daily chores - caring for and educating the children, attending to her mother-in-law, and managing the household. Unlike many women, she was fortunate not to face the harsh struggles of poverty; her husband's family had been well-off for generations. Servants and helpers were always on hand. Loan's primary duty was simply to ensure her mother-in-law's betel tray was always stocked with leaves from Bà Điểm and Hóc Môn, neither too young nor too mature, just as the elder preferred. When an extra hand was needed for the Four-colour card game, Loan was readily available. And so, the days flowed into months, with mother-in-law and daughter-in-law living together in quiet harmony.

Suddenly, three semi-naked Japanese men appeared out of nowhere, squatting by the well behind the house. The unexpected sight caught all the guests off guard, except for Loan. She recognized them as Japanese engineers who had come to Vietnam to supervise the renovation of the bridge on the Biên Hòa Highway, which had been in operation for several years. They had rented the three ground-floor rooms at Loan's mother-in-law's vacation home for their stay during their mission in Vietnam. Each evening upon returning home, their first task was to draw water from the well for bathing.

Their presence served as a reminder to Loan that it was time for her party to head back to Saigon before nightfall. She quickly asked her friends to clear the dining table, preparing for the return trip.

Rumors circulated that the Americans built the Biên Hòa Highway for their military planes to land in emergencies when Tân Sơn Nhất Airport was under attack. However, those in the know believed it was part of a long-term infrastructure development plan. Nevertheless, the Japanese government, as part of the Second World War's reparations program, had completed a portion of this project.

On the journey back, as the car turned left onto the highway, Dung shifted her gaze towards Long Thành, overwhelmed by a pang of longing for her husband. It had been just a little over two years since the tragic incident. Following his military service, Án, her husband, had sought employment as a trainer at the Rural Construction Training Center in Vũng Tàu. However, fate took an unfortunate turn when, on his way home one day, the bus he was on struck a landmine and erupted in an explosion.

Dung personally went to the Long Thành intersection to retrieve her husband's remains, cherishing memories of her kind and exemplary partner. Án had been devoted to his wife, attentive to his children, and showed utmost respect to his parents. The loss left a void that lingered, and Dung couldn't help but reflect on the warmth and love that defined her late husband's character.

She made a solemn commitment to herself, vowing to care for her mother-in-law in Án's stead. Several years prior, Án had reclaimed the tape recorder he had once gifted to Thanh. However, this wasn't for recording the latest Vietnamese or French music as per the prevailing trend. Due to the government's implementation of the Law on the Protection of Morality, which banned activities such as gambling, prostitution, and dancing, many individuals discreetly organized home parties. Faced with such restrictions, people had to substitute live bands with tape recorders.

Meanwhile, Án utilized the recording device to capture the voices and messages of his parents. His commitment went further, extending to Rạch Kiến, where he visited various relatives' households, recording the words of his grandparents, aunts, uncles, and great aunts. He sought to preserve the cherished voices that had shaped his identity. Unfortunately, Án departed suddenly, leaving behind no farewell for his wife and children. War, with its cruel dynamics, could transform a pure soul into a killer or erase its existence in the blink of an eye.

As Thanh approached her home at the far end of town, approximately two kilometers away, the road became increasingly congested. Vehicles were lined up along the historic An Thông Hạ canal, patiently awaiting their turn to cross the U-shaped bridge. In the distance, two American military bulldozers maneuvered on the opposite side of the waterway - one advancing, the other retreating - raising and lowering their massive buckets in front of each vehicle. A cloud of dust enveloped the scene as they demolished two rice warehouses that had stood abandoned for several years on the canal's bank.

In the place of the demolished warehouses, rumors circulated that the Americans planned to construct a military supply depot and a military compound. Each afternoon, after a day of seemingly moving mountains, young American soldiers, neatly dressed in civilian clothes - jeans and short-sleeved shirts of various colors - wandered through the streets. Some confidently engaged with the locals, expressing a zest for life and seeking conversations with hospitable families. They were particularly interested in households whose children knew some English, eager to learn more about Vietnamese culture.

Meanwhile, other young conscripts were drawn to the lively sounds of music emanating from bars and pubs, scattered both nearby and in the distance.

The presence of American soldiers on the streets of Saigon and other cities, both large and small, along with the influx of U.S. aid and the dominance of the dollar, profoundly reshaped Vietnamese society at every level. Thanh, having witnessed firsthand the disruptions caused by foreign interference - years of French colonial rule, the brief but consequential Japanese occupation, and the escalating American involvement in the nation's bitter war - still found herself deeply saddened by what she observed, especially its impact on the younger generation and on the lives of those who followed her and her friends from the Quartet of Colette.

In Plum Tree Hamlet lived Phong, who, after two years of improving his English at classes offered by the Vietnamese American Association, spent a few years working as an interpreter. By then, he had built a new house and purchased a scooter. Yesterday, just as he rode his Vespa out of the gate, he spotted Rat heading to the market with a basket in hand, buying food for Thanh. He waved Rat over and started a conversation.

Phong told her that he knew a bar owner looking for someone to help with washing and ironing clothes - steady work that would save her from wandering around the hamlet doing odd jobs. Although Rat had never set foot in a bar, she'd heard enough to imagine what they were like. Knowing her mother would never approve of her working in such a place, she gave Phong a noncommittal reply and left it at that.

Still, Phong's suggestion stayed on Rat's mind, stirring daydreams of earning money to support her mother and maybe even buying her the nice things she had seen in wealthier homes.

It crossed her mind to seek Thanh's advice. Thanh's opinion carried weight with her mother, and if Thanh thought it was a good idea, her mother might be convinced to allow it.

Sitting under the Jamaican cherry tree in the front yard, Thanh listened carefully as Rat recounted Phong's suggestion that she consider a job at a bar. Thanh's brows furrowed. The phrase "bar job" echoed in her mind with a note of caution, sparking an almost instinctive protective concern, like that of an older sister looking out for her younger sibling.

"Normally, I'd have told you straight away that this isn't a good idea," Thanh admitted. "But knowing Phong comes from a respectable family, I'm not quite sure how to advise you."

"Yes, I've heard all sorts of rumors about bars," Rat replied, "but I've known Brother Phong since we were kids. I honestly don't think he'd mislead me."

"I don't think he'd trick you," Thanh said. "It's just that in those wild places, a girl like you might have trouble keeping yourself safe."

"If I ask my mom, she probably won't agree either," Rat said. "But if I stay here, how am I supposed to earn enough money to buy medicine for her? For almost a year now, we've been relying on the medicine you gave us to get by. I can't keep coming to you every time we run out. Mom already feels so bad about it."

Thanh nodded in understanding. "I know it's not easy, but it's not always just about money. I've had chances to get involved in big business dealings with the Americans, like renting cars to them or taking on contracts to do their laundry, but I turned them down. I've seen too many people jump at opportunities like that, only to end up worse off. We've lived through the French era, the Japanese era, and we've watched others, drawn to quick gains, get burned like moths to a flame. I'm not blaming anyone;

everyone's situation is different. But if we can avoid it, we probably should."

"I understand," Rat said. "So what should I do now?"

"If it's really as Phong says, a steady job, that's good. Maybe you can save up after some time and then look for another opportunity."

"All right. I'll talk to my mom, and I'll let her know I spoke with you first."

"Just take care of yourself, okay?" Thanh said, her tone serious. "Don't get caught up in what others are doing. You're there to do your work, nothing else. Let the world go its own way - everyone has their own path."

"I understand," Rat replied.

Still concerned, Thanh added, "We may be poor, but we must hold on to our dignity. Think about how your mother would feel if people started whispering things…"

"I understand what you mean. I'll remember your advice."

Thanh personally altered one of her own bà ba blouses so Rat could wear it to meet the bar owner with Phong.

The following day, Phong introduced Rat to Thúy, the bar owner. Addressing her as "Sis Ba," he said:

"Sis Ba, this is Rat from my hamlet, the one I mentioned earlier."

"Perfect timing!" Thúy replied. "You must have known I was short-staffed today."

As she spoke, Thúy gave Rat a thorough once-over, surprised by her natural beauty and well-proportioned figure, even without makeup.

"Are you someone's mistress?" Thúy asked abruptly.

Rat frowned, confused, and hesitated before lowering her gaze and softly answering,

"No... why would you ask that?"

Thúy tugged lightly on the front of Rat's blouse.

"Do you have any idea how much a yard of this silk costs? If someone wasn't footing the bill for you to wear something this nice, you wouldn't be out here looking for work, would you?"

Catching on to Thúy's implication, Rat quickly clarified,

"This shirt belongs to Ms. Thanh in my hamlet. She lent it to me."

Turning to Phong, Thúy scolded him:

"With looks like hers, you call her 'Rat'? You're ruining the girl's charm."

She raised her eyebrows, giving Rat another quick once-over.

"All right, tell me, what's your birth order in your family?"

"I'm the fifth child, ma'am."

"Then I'll call you Sáu. It's simpler that way..."

Before Thúy could finish, a waitress rushed in to inform her that she was needed in the front lobby. In a hurry, Thúy quickly agreed to hire Rat as a daily helper and sent her to the back to assist Mrs. Tư with the laundry.

Until one afternoon, a group of American soldiers on leave arrived unexpectedly, quickly filling the bar to capacity. Unfortunately, the bar was short on hostesses that day, leaving Thúy scrambling to keep the soldiers entertained and worried about losing such a lucrative opportunity. "What should I do?" she thought, frustrated that two of her staff had called in sick.

Troubled, Thúy retreated to the back, grabbed a stool by the dining table, and picked up her half-finished iced coffee. She sat there, thinking hard about how to salvage the situation. As her eyes wandered to the rear courtyard, she noticed Rat by the bathhouse, doing laundry on a cement slab. Her pant legs were rolled up to her knees, revealing slim, fair calves.

Though she came from a poor family and had been working odd jobs since childhood, life's hardships hadn't obscured Rat's natural beauty. A spark of an idea flashed through Thúy's mind, one that wasn't entirely new - it had first flickered when she noticed the occasional hints of femininity that Rat unconsciously revealed.

Thúy called out, using Rat's new name:

"Sáu, what are you doing? Come here, I need to talk to you."

"I'm doing the laundry," Rat answered.

She rose, brushed the soapy water off her arms into the washbasin, then hastily wiped her hands down her pants. Flipping her palms up and down to shake off the excess moisture, she slipped into her wooden clogs and hurried over.

Standing in front of Thúy, she asked,

"You called me, Sis?"

"Yes, I need to discuss something," Thúy said. "First Hồng asked for time off, and now Thủy's at home sick. The timing couldn't be worse - business has been picking up these past few days. So I was thinking... would you mind helping me out for a bit?"

Rat didn't understand what Thúy meant, so she gave her a puzzled look and asked,

"What would I be helping with, Sis?"

"I mean, you could step in for Thúy," Thúy explained.

Startled, Rat shook her head quickly and stammered,

"No way! I can't do that. If my mom finds out, she'll scold me to death."

Thúy, expecting this reaction, smiled calmly and said,

"You're not doing anything wrong, so what's there to worry about? You'd just be sitting in the lobby, chatting with the guests like the others. Nothing more."

Seeing Rat lower her head and fidget with her shirt, Thúy softened her tone:

"I wouldn't ask if it weren't important. We're just really short-handed today. You know how tough things are for small businesses."

Thúy gestured toward the colorful clothes hanging out to dry and explained:

"Not long ago, the girls had to take all their clothes home to wash. But recently, with the bar getting busier, they've been saying they don't have time to do it themselves anymore. So I asked Mr. Phong to find someone reliable to help out…"

She stopped briefly, noticing Rat's discomfort. After taking a sip of coffee, Thúy continued:

"Mr. Phong mentioned that things are a bit tough at home for you, and that your mom's not well. I thought this might be a good chance for you. And if everything goes smoothly, I'm thinking of keeping you on regularly. I'd pay you a monthly salary - give you an advance mid-month to help out, then pay the rest at the end of the month."

Rat's heart started racing. Nothing could compare to this surge of emotion and joy. The phrase "monthly salary," though it was the first time Rat had heard it, held a meaning that she instinctively understood. It was like something out of reach, beyond her wildest dreams. Up until recently, Rat had only been paid piecemeal for odd jobs, or wages that felt more like charity from the households that hired her family. The largest amount Rat had ever earned was no more than five piasters, the pay for an entire day of backbreaking work from dawn until dusk.

Even then, the day's pay wasn't fixed, depending entirely on the householder's generosity. Sometimes Rat only received three or four piasters. Nevertheless, she would always bow respectfully, thank her employer with a warm smile, and quietly head home. On rare occasions when the homeowner asked how much her labor was worth, she would unfailingly reply with the words her mother had taught her: "Whatever the mistress wishes to give." Her mother had often said, "You have to say that so they'll feel sympathetic. That way, the next time they need help, they'll think of you and call you back."

Rat remembered the first time she held a five-piaster bill in her hand. Her very first thought was that she could now afford five slices of baguette drizzled with tomato sauce. Right in front of her thatched hut was an overgrown patch of grass where, every morning, Aunt Tư the bread seller would set up a low wooden table by the roadside. She offered two popular breakfast options: meat-filled baguettes and fish baguettes.

Many times, Rat stood by, watching as Aunt Tư prepared the meat-filled baguettes. Aunt Tư would slice thin, glistening pieces of cooked pork belly and tuck them into each baguette for her customers. Rat's mouth watered as she longed for a taste. Aunt Tư's fish baguettes were made with canned Moroccan sardines mixed in a tangy tomato-based sauce. Knowing her customers loved the sauce, she would add a bit of sweet vinegar to stretch it, ensuring every order received a generous drizzle.

Occasionally, Rat had the chance to enjoy one of Aunt Tư's baguettes. This usually happened after she had recovered from an illness, when her mother would give her a piaster to help her regain strength. However, since each fish baguette cost two piasters, Rat could only afford a plain slice of bread drizzled with tomato-based sauce, without any actual fish.

Every morning, her mother would prepare a pot of rice for herself and her two children to last through both breakfast and lunch. They usually paired it with a small clay pot of braised fish, often reheated leftovers from previous meals. While fish from the river was abundant and free for those willing to catch it, Rat's family still struggled to afford the rice and firewood needed to cook three daily meals. Elderly and unable to perform strenuous labor, Rat's mother stayed home each day gathering firewood to cook their rice. But as more people moved into the area, the supply of wood began to dwindle. In response, the family relied heavily on vegetables to stretch their meals and keep hunger at bay.

Fortunately, vegetables were never scarce. If they wanted water celery or pennywort, they could simply pull some from behind Mrs. Tư's garden at the end of the road, provided they asked her permission first. And if they fancied banana blossom, they would climb over the wall into the yard of an abandoned rice warehouse nearby, pick a tender blossom, slice it thin, and use it as greens to dip into their pepper-braised fish sauce.

Lost in thoughts about her family's situation and her sick mother waiting for her to bring back money for medicine, Rat found it hard to resist the life-changing promise in Thúy's offer. Moreover, despite her youth, Rat's early exposure to life's hardships made her recognize the underlying reminder in Thúy's words: her current job might not last if she refused her offer. Still, Rat hesitated and tried to find an excuse to back out.

"It feels weird, Sis. I don't even have a formal long dress (áo dài) to wear to go out there. And even if I do, I wouldn't know what to say to the customers. I've never been good at talking to people, let alone foreigners. I don't know their language."

Thúy was secretly delighted. She knew the fish was already hooked and quickly reassured Rat:

"It's no problem. You just sit out there, drink some water, and keep the guests company, like the others do. You don't have to say much at all. Everyone feels awkward the first time. I'll tell Đông to keep an eye on you while he's selling drinks, and he can guide you if you need help. Don't worry."

Thúy got up, warmly holding Rat's hand. "Okay, here's what we'll do. You go hang up the laundry, then come to my room. I'll find you a long dress (áo dài). In this house, we might be short on a lot of things, but clothes? Never. No need to worry."

Rat reluctantly nodded and murmured, "Yes," before heading out to the backyard to hang the clothes. Thúy returned to her room and picked up the phone to call Hồng, who had been off work for two days caring for her three-year-old son, who had been severely feverish and had to be taken to the hospital. After a few words of concern and hearing that Hồng's son was improving, Thúy asked her to take a taxi over to get Rat properly dressed "before sending her into battle." Thúy chuckled at her own joke before laughing aloud.

As soon as she hung up, Thúy picked up the phone again and called Aunt Tư, the resident manicurist, to come over and take care of Rat's nails.

After finishing the laundry, Rat hesitantly shuffled toward the inner room. Her steps felt heavy as she approached Thúy's bedroom, a place she usually entered without a second thought to pick up dirty laundry, but today it filled her with an inexplicable anxiety, as if she were about to do something she might regret. Thúy spotted her and called out excitedly, "Come over here and take a look…"

Thúy gestured toward four vibrant 'áo dài' (Vietnamese long dress) laid out on the edge of the bed, arranged by size to see which one might fit Rat. Pointing to a purple one, Thúy said,

"This one's Hồng's. I think her size should be close to yours. Try it on and see if it fits. If it feels tight, try Thủy's green áo dài, which is a bit roomier. The length should work since they're both about your height. Also, remember to try on Hồng's white muslin pants so we can see if we need to adjust the hem. After that, just sit here and wait for Hồng. She'll take care of everything for you. Poor girl, her son is sick at home, but she's still making the effort to come and help. I need to head out front and tend to the guests for a bit. If they don't see me, they won't be happy."

Sitting alone in the room filled with luxurious silks, a space that seemed to Rat to cocoon the fortunate few born into a serene, golden-threaded existence, thick with the scent of expensive perfume, she let her thoughts wander as her eyes drifted around the room. Before her, near a carved mother-of-pearl inlaid settee, stood an old metal safe with patches of green paint peeling off. Atop it was a small incense holder and a few thick, slowly smoldering incense sticks set in offering to the god of wealth. Beside that was a cluttered vanity table strewn with various lipstick shades, makeup powders, perfume bottles, and colored eyebrow pencils. At one corner of the table sat a hairdryer, something from an American PX, alongside several curling rods, a few combs of varying sizes, and a hairbrush. In front of the mirror were two imported cookie tins now filled with an assortment of jewelry: strings of pearls, earrings, necklaces, and all manner of bracelets and rings.

After surveying the room, Rat wearily looked down at the four 'áo dài' lying sprawled across the bed, each one like a careless, indifferent woman languishing after a reckless spree. Sighing, Rat stood up sluggishly, hesitating before following Thúy's instructions, and awkwardly began to change into Hồng's outfit.

Rat caught a glimpse of herself in the mirror, feeling awkward and embarrassed. She quickly returned to sit at the edge of the bed, as if retreating from the strange, unfamiliar world of "Sáu" and seeking refuge in the familiar, safe world of "Rat" - her true self. In that world, beauty and indulgence weren't things Rat ever imagined for herself. They were instead what she carefully prepared and offered to "Miss Phượng."

From a young age, Rat had worked as a maid in the district chief's household. She was often assigned small tasks like dusting furniture, cleaning the betel trays and preparing lime paste. But her main duty was washing and ironing the clothes of Phượng, the district chief's beloved granddaughter, whom Rat called "Miss Phượng." Every afternoon, Rat would peel oranges or rinse fruit, setting it aside in the kitchen so that when Phượng awoke from her nap, Rat could carry the tray upstairs and present it to "Miss Phượng." Occasionally, fearing that eating too many oranges might cause breakouts, as the district chief's wife believed, Rat was sent to the market to buy jicama, which she would peel and serve to Phượng as a cooling snack.

Over years of serving the district chief's wife and attending to Phượng's every need, Rat became more than just a loyal maid. She came to feel like a small part of the household, helping to uphold a legacy and a tradition passed down from the older generation of the district chief's wife to the younger generation of "Miss Phượng."

Until now, Rat had been content to contribute to building a paradise in which she herself had no place, simply because she had no better option. Today, for the first time in her life, she had the opportunity to choose her own destiny, and this newfound freedom left her feeling unsettled. She worried about the risks ahead and the ingrained prejudices that had bound individuals for generations. Yet, at the same time, she felt exhilarated by the prospect of an open future, one that would allow her true self to soar and explore new horizons. Ultimately, the allure of embarking on a journey of self-discovery proved powerful enough for her to embrace whatever consequences might arise from this pivotal choice.

She had no idea where this road might lead or how long it would take, but she resolved to leave that to fate. What she didn't know was that fate hinged on decisions being made halfway around the world in Washington, D.C. There, politicians were scrambling to implement a so-called Vietnamization plan - a face-saving way of saying they were preparing to wash their hands of Vietnam. If they succeeded, the patrons who kept her bar and other clubs alive might disappear overnight.

Meanwhile, in Plum Tree Hamlet, rumors about the Americans abandoning Vietnam left Sergeant Cừ deeply worried. Early in the morning, he was already seated at the Xít Tê café, eager to catch any valuable street news. Impatiently, he kept an eye out for Officer Tư and especially Teacher Hai. As soon as he spotted them strolling leisurely from the marketplace, he called out.

"Where are your bikes? Why are you walking today?"

"Teacher Hai's bike chain broke, so he left it at Năm's place for repairs. I figured I'd walk with him to keep him company," Officer Tư replied.

"I've been waiting for you two forever," Sergeant Cừ anxiously remarked.

The café owner, familiar with his regulars' preferences, brought out a glass of milk coffee for the teacher and a black coffee for the officer. Sergeant Cừ, eager for news, asked about the Paris Peace Accords. Would the Americans walk away, or would they stay in Vietnam? What would become of the country?

Reflecting on it, Sergeant Cừ realized these worries weren't new - history had a way of repeating itself. First, it was the French, then the Japanese, and now the Americans. The same anxieties persisted. Who would the country ultimately fall to? Sergeant

Cừ couldn't help but recall something Teacher Hai had said nearly twenty years earlier, which still rang true:

"Our Vietnam is just like a chess piece on a board controlled by those celestial beings in the sky. We're just pawns. They move us wherever they please. Sometimes, if they're bored, they'll sacrifice us, and we have no choice but to go along. Those celestial beings aren't really in the heavens, but their advancement in science and technology are so far ahead of ours that the gap might as well be from the earth to the sky. So, whatever storms they want to stir up, they stir."

After everyone had taken a few sips of coffee to clear their throats, Sergeant Cừ began the conversation.

"Teacher, do you have any updates on the Paris Peace Talks?"

"Not much. The newspapers probably know as little as we do, so all they publish is fluff."

"What kind of fluff?"

"Well, they've been digging up sensational details about the U.S. National Security Advisor's secret meetings with China. The most ridiculous part is how they've been analyzing the guy's name."

"Dr. Kis... what's-his-name?"

"That's right - Kissinger. The papers claim that since his name contains the words 'Kiss' and 'singer,' it proves he won't accomplish much. After all, how can anyone kiss and sing at the same time?"

Sergeant Cừ laughed heartily, his previous worries temporarily set aside. Unbeknownst to him, the Vietnamese newspapers' seemingly absurd speculation turned out to be remarkably accurate. The U.S. had, in fact, been negotiating a way to exit Vietnam "with honor," and before long, they secured the agreement they sought in Paris.

Months later, Thúy's bar stood empty. Rat, who had long dreaded this moment, now faced it head-on. Outside, a light drizzle misted the street. She shrugged into a Hong Kong raincoat she'd bought from one of Thúy's friends the month before, mounted her Honda dame scooter, and departed for the last time from the place that had offered fleeting joys, shadowed by persistent shame and regret. Braving the rain, she hastened back to Plum Tree Hamlet, seeking guidance and grounding from Thanh, who had become a trusted confidante in her early journeys of self-discovery.

"What's got you in such a rush?" Thanh asked.

Rat cautiously glanced around before leaning in and whispering in Thanh's ear, "Tomorrow's my last day at work."

Thanh had known this day would eventually come, but she still felt the weight of Rat's apprehension. "What will you do next?" she asked.

"Thanks to you, I've saved a little over the past two years. Whatever comes my way, I'll just manage," Rat replied. "What else can I do?"

Thanh offered her comfort. "You used to have nothing, and you and your mom still got by."

After a pause, Thanh added, "Honestly, I'm kind of glad for you. Maybe it's for the best. You've saved over ten thousand dollars by now - that's enough to start a small business. Your mom will be happy too. If she knew what you've been doing these past few months, she might never forgive you."

Thanh reached for the bunch of keys on her desk, went into the bedroom, and unlocked the safe to retrieve the money Rat had been entrusting to her all this time. The two of them sat on the edge of the bed as Thanh handed Rat a biscuit tin filled with stacks of green U.S. dollars, along with a few red notes - special currency issued for U.S. military personnel that Rat hadn't had a chance to exchange. Altogether, the sum came to nearly twelve thousand five hundred. Thanh had Rat count each bill carefully. Watching Rat handle such a large amount, Thanh grew concerned and repeated the advice she'd given before:

"Remember how I always told you to save up until you had enough to start a business?"

"Yes, that's why I hardly spent anything. I only bought little things now and then to make my mom happy. I remember you saying that when I had enough money, you'd help me find a business opportunity. Have you found one yet?"

"I know someone who wants to rent out the ground floor of a townhouse by the canal. What do you think?"

"I wouldn't know, Sis. You'll have to figure it out for me."

"The spot is right in the middle of a busy market area, near several schools. I was thinking: what if we opened a 'bazaar' shop for school supplies? Schools seem to be popping up everywhere these days, and you can't walk a block without seeing students, teachers, and professors."

Rat's heart raced at the thought of becoming a shop owner, but then reality set in. She shook her head quickly and said:

"I can't do that, Sis. I don't know anything about running a business. I can't even read properly. How am I supposed to sell anything? Sure, I can count money, maybe. But when it comes to figuring out profit and loss? I have no clue."

"Don't worry. I'll take care of things at first. You'll get used to it soon enough."

After a moment of quiet thought, Thanh added:

"Remember not to be wasteful, okay? If you just sit around spending money, even a mountain of it won't last. And, we'll plan for opening a shop, sure, but who knows how it'll turn out?"

Rat left Thanh's place with mixed emotions. She felt sad, knowing her current job, often with the nightly stacks of cash each night, was now behind her. At the same time she felt uncertain about what the coming months would bring. Yet there was also a sense of relief, as though a heavy burden had been lifted. Every day she had worked under the weight of fear, dreading the moment her mother might find out what she had done at the bar. Nearing home, Rat hoped her mother would be cooking in the backyard so she could quietly hide the money under her bed.

When she stepped inside the house and didn't see her mother, Rat assumed Mrs. Bảy was indeed cooking outside. She carefully tucked the stacks of cash under the foam mattress on her side of the bed and smoothed the bedsheet back into place. After thoroughly checking the bed, making sure nothing looked suspicious or out of the ordinary, she stepped outside to find Mrs. Bảy, still unsure if she should tell her mother about losing the job just yet.

Eventually, she would have to tell her mother, but saying it now might only make her sad. Rat suddenly noticed her mother lying on the old bamboo bed out back, and the cooking area is cold and lifeless, with no firewood in sight. Startled, she asked,

"Mom, are you sick?"

Mrs. Bảy lay curled on her side, facing the wall, offering no response. Growing more concerned, Rat gently shook her and pressed,

"Mom, are you okay? Should I take you to the hospital?"

Mrs. Bảy shoved Rat's hand away and snapped,

"Oh, you want me dead, don't you? Fine, let me die so you can be happy."

Rat was taken aback.

"Mom, why would you say something like that?"

Mrs. Bảy remained silent, and Rat began to feel a deeper unease. This wasn't like the usual scoldings that quickly passed. Something was truly wrong. She tried again,

"What's going on, Mom? Why would you say that?"

"Why don't you go ask the neighbors?" Mrs. Bảy shot back.

Reaching for the patterned scarf hanging at the bed's headboard, she wiped her eyes and choked out,

"The whole neighborhood is saying you've taken up with a GI."

The world felt like it was collapsing. Her legs gave out, and Rat collapsed onto the edge of the bed, burying her face in her hands and sobbing.

Earlier that afternoon, Mrs. Tám from the neighborhood, who was preparing her son's wedding, had come by the house intending to ask Rat to help with some chores over the weekend. Stepping inside and seeing the neatly made pink-draped mattress beside the gleaming glass-fronted buffet cabinet, Mrs. Tám grew envious and remarked to Mrs. Bảy:

"Well, it looks like your Rat's done well for herself with an American husband, hasn't she, Mrs. Bảy? No wonder she's been scarce lately. I thought about asking her to help me for a few days, but at this rate, I suppose not."

With that, Mrs. Tám turned on her heel and left, leaving a sharp sting in Mrs. Bảy's heart. Overwhelmed with shame, she retreated to her corner of the bed and cried. She felt both love and resentment for her daughter. Love, because deep down she knew, "Rat did it all for me." Resentment, because she believed it was a foolish choice. Mrs. Bảy would rather die with a clear conscience and meet her late husband in peace than live on while enduring the sting of public scorn.

Rat wiped her tears and apologized to Mrs. Bảy, trying to explain that everything had been beyond her control. She recounted how she had been asked to fill in for a sick employee and couldn't refuse. She carefully avoided mentioning that her motive had been to scrape together money for Mrs. Bảy's medicine when her mother was gravely ill, fearful that revealing this would only upset her further.

Mrs. Bảy refused to get out of her makeshift bed. She skipped dinner, retreating under the covers to sleep. Rat went inside the house, lay down on her empty bed, feeling adrift in a barren oasis. Restless and unable to close her eyes, she felt all her efforts had been wasted. Everything now seemed like an illusion, gone in an instant, like a rainbow disappearing as a bubble bursts. The fleeting sense of freedom she'd felt when riding her Honda on empty roads, the moments of soaring confidence in herself after receiving praise from her boss, and the solid, reassuring heft of wads of cash handed to her by Thúy, all of it had crumbled. She had long resigned herself to living in a dreamlike world enclosed by walls of judgment. But those walls had only tightened around her, crushing her small bubble of fantasy.

The stifling night stretched on endlessly, lit by the dim, flickering glow of an oil lamp running low. Out of habit, Rat reached for the bottle of oil on her bedside table to add more, but then she realized it was a futile act. She no longer wanted a light to illuminate the details of her life. She longed instead for peace in the darkness. She set the bottle back down on the table. The half-empty antibiotic vial next to it caught her eye. Staring at it for a long moment, motionless, she seemed to find a kind of resolution. She emptied the remaining pills into her hand and swallowed them all. Then she collapsed back onto the bed, surrendering to the privacy of her own world.

By midday, when Mrs. Bảy heard no sound from within, she went in to check. It was too late. She cradled her daughter's lifeless body, weeping inconsolably.

The following day, as Teacher Hai rode his bike home from the Xít Tê café, his mind wandered to what might happen to the country once the Americans left Vietnam. Lately, he had been intentionally avoiding Sergeant Cừ's questions about what might happen, but deep down, he knew the answer. In a conflict that had once required half a million American troops without a decisive outcome, the future seemed all too clear if that level of support could no longer be sustained. Teacher Hai felt a deep unease about what lay ahead. In his short time on this earth, he had already lived through the French, Japanese, and American eras in his country. Now, what era would come next? Where was the country heading? He didn't want to think about it any further.

As he turned onto the main road cutting through Plum Tree Hamlet. marked "LVC" on American military maps, Teacher Hai saw in the distance a hearse slowly rolling by, carrying Rat to her final resting place. When he arrived, he stopped his bicycle at the roadside, removed his hat in solemn farewell to the departed and to express his condolences to those left behind. To Teacher Hai, this was a "civilized Western custom" he had learned, yet this time he felt it carried a deeper significance. It reminded him that in this world, there are deaths that preserve the meaning of life, not just departures dictated by the natural order. Reflecting on Rat's passing, her mother's life devoted to raising her daughter, and the countless Vietnamese women who had borne the burdens of home and country through centuries of continuous conflict and upheaval, Teacher Hai found himself murmuring in quiet solidarity:

"Thuở trời đất nổi cơn gió bụi,
Khách má hồng nhiều nỗi truân chuyên.
Xanh kia thăm thẳm từng trên,

Vì ai gây dựng cho nên nỗi này?"[15]

(When heaven and earth stirred the stormy wind,
Life's rosy cheeks faced many trials;
Toward that vast, deep blue sky above I ask:
For whom was this fate decreed)

- End -

Notes

1. Band: AVT; Artists (from 1966): Lữ Liên (replacing Anh Linh), Vân Sơn and Tuấn Đăng.
2. Song: 'Bạch Đằng Giang' by Lưu Hữu Phước (Lyric by Nguyễn Thành Nguyên.)
3. Song: 'Khỏe Vì Nước' by Hùng Lân.
4. Song: 'Hè Về' by Hùng Lân.
5. Song: 'Nỗi Buồn Hoa Phượng' by Thanh Sơn.
6. Song: 'Ly Rượu Mừng' by Phạm Đình Chương.
7. Song: 'Ngày Hạnh Phúc' by Lam Phương.
8. Song: 'Ngụ Ngôn Mùa Đông'; by Trịnh Công Sơn.
9. Song: 'Kỷ Vật Cho Em' by Phạm Duy.
10. Play: 'Người Vợ Không Bao Giờ Cưới' by Kiên Giang.
11. Play: 'Tình Anh Bán Chiếu' by Viễn Châu.
12. Song: 'Trường Ca Con Đường Cái Quan' by Phạm Duy.
13. Song: 'Một Chuyến Bay Đêm' by Song Ngọc & Hoài Linh.
14. Poem: 'Đoạn Trường Tân Thanh' (The Tale of Kiều) by Nguyễn Du.
15. Poem: 'Chinh Phụ Ngâm' by Madame Đoàn Thị Điểm.

Author

Vinh Quyen Tang, Ph.D., P.Eng..
(Tăng Quyền Vinh)
Ottawa, Canada.

Books published:

1. Bên Kia Bến Đỗ, 2021.
2. Đứa Con An Giang, 2022.
3. Lu nước ngọt, 2023.
4. Nails Tình Thương, 2023.
5. The Boy From An Giang: A Journey Through AI-Assisted Translation, 2023 (Under revision).
6. Tứ Quý (Truyện trích từ Bên Kia Bến Đỗ), 2023.
7. The Precious Quartet (Translated from the Vietnamese title 'Tứ Quý'), 2024.
8. Compassionate Nails: A Journey of Love and Resilience (Translated from the Vietnamese title 'Nails Tình Thương'), 2024.
9. Đôi Dòng Sông Nước, 2024.

10. Tales of the River: Journey from the Mekong Delta, (Translated from the Vietnamese title 'Đôi Dòng Sông Nước'), 2024.

11. Freshwater Jar (Translated from the Vietnamese title 'Lu Nước Ngọt'), 2024.

12. Twelve Habours (Translated from the Vietnamese title 'Bên Kia Bến Đỗ'), 2025.

ISBN 978-1-0691950-1-2

www.ingramcontent.com/pod-product-compliance
Lightning Source LLC
Chambersburg PA
CBHW070456120726
47910CB00003B/1056